Night Air Descending
A Novel by T. P. Graf

Book II
From the Trilogy - The Life and Stories of Jaime Cruz

This is a work of fiction. While some of the public places and
institutions exist and events in relation to time may be real, the
characters and context involved are wholly imaginary.
The opinions expressed are those of the characters
and should not be confused with those of the author.

This trilogy is dedicated to
the generous hearts and beautiful creatures
living under the vast West Texas skies.

T.P. Graf's Writings & Awards

As the Daisies Bloom - A Novel

PenCraft Awards - 2020 First Place, Cultural Fiction
Book Excellence Awards - 2021 Finalist, Friendship
Chanticleer IBA, 2020 First Place, Somerset Book Awards

A beautiful telling of life's trials and tribulations, always overcome by the love of family and of something greater than oneself. - Reader's Favorite

Enchanting as it is charming ... intimately and poetically told ... like a well-written symphony - Literary Titan

A powerfully written character-led novel; stark and unsettling but often funny too. Highly recommended! - A 'Wishing Shelf' Book Review

August Kibler's Stories for Tyler
Voices of Context from Eden to Patmos
(Companion to As the Daisies Bloom)

Firebird Award - 2021 Winner, Christian Poetry
American Book Awards - 2021 Finalist, Religious Poetry
Royal Dragonfly, 2021 Honorable Mention, Religion/Spirituality

A compelling and thought-provoking study of the bible and Christian history. The writing style is almost angelic! It's the sort of book you want to discuss; that stays with you for a long, long time.
- A 'Wishing Shelf' Book Review

Graf has crafted a masterful work of modern literature that takes on some very complex topics...in a format that any reader can engage with and glean wisdom from ... entertaining ... highly recommend.
- Reader's Favorite

The book offers fresh ideas ... absorbing ... thought-provoking and evokes a positive emotional connotation. - Literary Titan

Roots, Branches and Buzz Saws
More Stories of August Kibler

"Celebrate who you are, even if it is quietly...". That is what this book is, a celebration of August's life and a reminder to the reader to celebrate their life, who they are. - Literary Titan

Looking Out onto Our World
Explorations of Power, Dogma and
a World Deserving of Contemplation

The Life and Stories of Jaime Cruz (Trilogy)

Tumbleweed and Dreams (Book One)
From the Series - The Life and Stories of Jaime Cruz

Graf manages to keep readers enthralled with Jaime's day-to-day experiences chapter after chapter ... a beautifully penned tale of self-discovery and a strong main character who stands out in a crowd.
- Literary Titan

A gripping story filled with colorful and often captivating characters.
- A 'Wishing Shelf' Book Review

An immersive journey of self-discovery and a sense of home ... you find yourself invested in the lives of the people and the friendships that are made. - Readers' Favorite

Night Air Descending (Book Two)
From the Series - The Life and Stories of Jaime Cruz

A cleverly-crafted, character-led family drama set in Texas. I got so immersed in it, I started to feel like one of the family too!
- A 'Wishing Shelf' Book Review

Whether you're in the mood for a slice-of-life drama or a study of eclectic characters, Night Air Descending by T.P. Graf is a memorable read.
- Readers' Favorite

This is a beautifully written book that has a grounded and authentic feel so much that it feels like we are reading someone's diary ... heartwarming ... [with a] distinct literary aesthetic. - Literary Titan

Seeds in the Desert Wind (Book Three)
From the Series - The Life and Stories of Jaime Cruz

Every quirk, every nuance, and each daily challenge make this story relatable and enjoyable...a book that wraps around you like your favorite blanket and touches your heart in a unique way. - Literary Titan

Graf again delivers interesting, full-bodied characters that we can relate to and want to follow through to their conclusions... a story that will entertain and move you. - Readers' Favorite

A powerful, often thought-provoking end to this excellent trilogy. Highly recommended. - A 'Wishing Shelf' Book Review

A Cowgirl's Stories
Companion to The Life and Stories of Jaime Cruz Trilogy

Part I

Chapter One

It had now been almost a year since we did our house swap with Sallie. It also marked my first birthday as a gen-u-ine cowboy, as she always referred to me, and since my birthday and arrival in Fort Davis coincided, it was also my anniversary in this new adopted home.

How odd it seems to call it my adopted home when I never truly had a home before coming here. I resided in my mother's house and my father's house and my own various apartments over my thirty years in California, but none of those rose even close to being a home.

The fact that six years had passed since leaving all that behind seems surreal in that I increasingly found it hard to feel as though I had not been here and rooted all along. I had been so wholly included in the lives of the Cardonas and Schlatters I had largely forgotten—by the grace of all that is holy—what it was to be a Cruz in the context of my California life. It would always be with me as the surname that defines me legally, but it would never define my being anymore.

In celebration of both my birthday and the anniversary of my arrival, Billy organized my second-ever birthday party. I suppose that gives him more credit than is actually due. His idea of organizing was to tell his mom and Sallie what he wanted and who his mom was to invite. His great feat for the day would be to keep me working until 6:00, and then we'd show up, still in work clothes, to drop something off for his dad.

It mostly worked. I was highly suspicious of showing up at dinnertime on my birthday, and I knew it was more than a convenient drop-off when I saw Ernesto's crew-cab pickup as we drove up.

Billy asked, "Now what do you think Dad's wanting Ernesto to do now? I know he wants to get his solar panel project going, but unless Ernesto has expanded his service offerings, I can't think what else he'd be doing out here, can you?"

I answered, "One thing comes to mind, and if it's what I think it is, I suspect Ernesto probably arrived with three other passengers."

"Who would that be?" Billy so innocently asked.

I felt no need to respond as we both jumped out of the pickup and headed in. I did ask, "And we couldn't work in a quick shower before showing up? Your mom may send us straight back home."

Big surprise—I walked in to find Ernesto queued up to break into song, leading "Cumpleaños Feliz" with the "other usual suspects" Rosalinda, Chuy, Lupe and even Lupe's now near ninety-year-old mother, Elma, plus of course, Bill, Betsy and Sallie. I hoped Billy hadn't insisted on Elma going to the trouble of making a beautiful cake as she'd done for that first birthday party at Chuy and Lupe's, though I wouldn't have protested any suggestion of Lupe and Elma bringing their perfected deviled eggs.

This time around I didn't cry at my second-ever birthday party. All I could do was laugh—along with everyone else. There were no eggs and no cake.

Billy announced, "Since Ernesto's brothers and sisters years ago ate his birthday cake before he got home from six-man football, he and I agreed we should be sure you didn't get any cake after working cattle all day. But Mom did make supper for us."

Then on cue, Betsy carried in a tray of triangular-cut peanut butter and sweet pickle sandwiches with one whole, square sandwich in the middle with six candles aglow.

Billy said, "We can't celebrate your arrival here without peanut butter!"

I smiled brightly, saying, "I must confess, there is no more fitting symbol of those early days. I hate to give Billy too much credit, but this is *the perfect* birthday meal to mark six years among the living."

I picked up my sandwich to blow out the candles rather than blowing across everyone else's sandwiches, made my wish and blew them out.

Bill joked, "I'm just glad you survived on peanut butter and not canned tuna."

We didn't sit down at the dining room table but instead moved our feast out onto the north porch overlooking the ridge. I had my whole sandwich plus two more halves, and except for Elma—who is tiny and had only half a sandwich—everyone else had about the same.

As we were feasting, Bill asked, "What do y'all hear from Father Chuy? Is he still down in El Salvador?"

Rosalinda answered first regarding their youngest son, "We have lots of news on Chuy. It looks like he plans to stay there for a long time. He very much wants to continue his work in the village where he lives and the even smaller mountain communities around him."

Ernesto popped in to say, "He may be dashing Chuy the Elder's hope for Pope Chuy the First. He is in the process of joining the Franciscans. He may have to be Pope Francis the First instead."

Rosalinda said, "I don't think a Franciscan friar living in a remote village in El Salvador will ever make it to Rome, and I'm pretty sure he'd never want to, other than to visit perhaps."

Betsy added, "The boy's natural humility is well suited to be with the Franciscans."

"Is the new clinic working out?" Bill asked.

"He says it is literally saving lives and has brought the community closer together in ways where the church was not doing very well," Rosalinda said.

Ernesto expanded on that saying, "Chuy said the last few priests who served the churches lived in larger cities and only drove out to do the Mass, hear confessions, baptize and bury. To hear him tell it, their idea of absolution was to instill guilt without ever getting to know their parishioners. As he put it, 'They might just as well have sold indulgences.'"

I sat there quietly watching my birthday party unfold into a discussion of Chuy's mission work in El Salvador. Rosalinda explained the problem the small coffee farmers were facing with control of the market from large corporations turning a blind eye to child labor, and how Father Chuy hoped they could become part of the fair trade movement.

Ernesto pointed out how the men leave for a time to work in the sugarcane, but that only means coming back and spending the little they make to get by until the next harvest. Father Chuy had heard where the Mennonites had helped mountain villages like theirs build a series of aquaculture tanks using the water from the mountain springs and streams. They had even built one tank to "test the waters." Now they hoped to build more as they could though without help from the church or assistance from some other source it would be slow going.

Chuy suggested that Ernesto and Rosalinda's daughter, the "professional student," take her international business degrees and bilingual skills and work to set up the fair trade coffee connections between the farmers and roasters in Texas.

I had the notion Bill would be holding another family vote for another check to go to El Salvador. Elma, who had been quiet as a mouse, said, "I've been praying the Rosary everyday for someone to come along to help those poor people."

As the Cardonas and the Rodriquez matriarch prepared to head back to town while Billy and I headed across to the old ranch house, I was struck that Billy's playful idea of the peanut butter-and-pickle supper—the absolute simplicity of it—couldn't have better framed the context for talking about Chuy's work.

I said to Billy, "I think your peanut butter supper opened the door to talk about Chuy way more than just a casual, 'How's he doin?' could have ever done. Can you imagine the conversation going where it did if we were all sitting down to a big fancy dinner, stuffing ourselves?"

Billy replied, "It was all we talked about once we got on the subject. All in my plan."

"I'm sure it was." Then I asked, "Do you think if there is another family vote on sending some money down there to kick-start the fish ponds that your dad will include Brett this time?"

"That's a good question," Billy said. "You already know your vote counts. It might be an indication of their view as to how well Brett is coming along."

I added, "By all indications there's some improvement in that Pamela hasn't divorced him yet, but otherwise he still seems dull as dust to me."

Billy laughed, "Sallie likes to repeat her response to things obvious. In that spirit I'll just say, 'Too true—too true.'"

When we settled in for the evening back home, I said to Billy. "We've never really talked about you and Sallie when you were growing up. She never married. You never married. She's about as live-and-let-live as anybody on the planet, and so are you. Was she that influential, or is it one of those cases of genetic wizardry—just like you looking exactly like your grandpa Geermann?"

Billy joked, "As pertains to marriage, I'm not sure who she was holding out for. I was, of course, saving myself for you."

"You're a mess."

"But I'm your mess."

Then I added, "I think you were going to say more about Sallie before your mind went on to our 'love life.'"

"I've always wondered if Sallie spent most of her years as lonely as I was up there in Van Horn. I hope not. I know she at least had her mom and dad for a long time, and Dad has always been as close to her as any brother could have been. I never heard even an iota of irritation from Dad regarding any of his in-laws, and they certainly worshiped the ground he walked on."

I responded, "As I look at these ranches, it is holy ground as best I can tell, and it has been blessed with the stewardship it deserves."

Billy continued, "I certainly spent a lot of time with Dad and Sallie—usually together—when I was growing up. Much more than Brett—or at least, so far as I know. Maybe he went to the ranch more after I left. I've never thought to ask anyone that. Before I left, he rarely went along and probably wasn't on a horse half a dozen times in his life. Dad and Sallie worked so well together, I always wondered if he shouldn't have just gone for the 'older woman.' He could have lived on the ranch instead of in town all those years."

"I assume you haven't shared this notion with your mother."

"I came close that day I finally told her off, but no I didn't and now, never would," Billy reassured me.

"Good," was all I said.

"Mom says I got Grandpa's looks, Dad's heart and Sallie's independence. I asked her what I got from her since she didn't claim anything for herself. You know what she said?" he asked.

"I have no idea. Maybe her level head and sensitivity. You both have a certain measure of each."

"Maybe," he replied, "you need to remember she lost her level head for twenty years. She's got a lot of catching up to do, which is why she looks so levelheaded now. She says I got two things from her."

Before he could enlighten me I said, "I hope you're not going to say one of them is your ass."

Billy replied, "No, we don't know where that came from. We can't even blame the mailman since we don't have one, clear out here."

I laughed, "Sallie says it must be a recessive gene. So, what two things did you get from her?"

"Sense enough to see a good man when he comes along and sense enough to hang on."

"I can't quite hear her saying that," I replied.

He said, "She might have phrased it more along the line of taking good care of a friendship once you have one."

"Now that I do believe," Then after a bit, I added, "I sure can't see any hint that Sallie is lonely now, but I do think the years you were gone left a hollow spot she never could fill even with your dad's friendship."

"I'm the son she never had," Billy stated quite matter-of-factly.

"I believe that is true in a sense, but even a mother can't assume a real kinship of spirit the way you and Sallie share a certain spot somewhere deep inside."

We'd gotten about as deep as Billy ever wants to get in one sitting. He excused himself to "grab something from the kitchen." I figured he'd come back with two beers and a bag of potato chips—not that we needed either the beer or the chips. I just laid my head back on the couch and closed my eyes just to rest them and my mind for a moment.

He quietly came in the room without me even hearing him, and while standing in front of me on the couch, he said, "You can open your eyes."

When I did, he was there with a small, but beautifully decorated cake. I exclaimed, "That has to be an Elma cake!"

"It is. She just couldn't stand you not getting a cake. She called Mom saying she wanted to bring a cake. 'He's such a nice boy,' she said. And then she told Mom, 'I would have made Ernesto a cake all those years ago if I'd known those brothers of his ate all his cake.' She is something—and I only know her at all because of you."

Well, that was all it took. I cried on my birthday after all.

Chapter Two

After pantry distribution the next Saturday following my birthday, we, of course, went with Ernesto and Rosalinda to the Slo Poke Cafe. The two guys from Dallas who had now retired and were living in the former Schlatter home in Fort Davis were also there. They had sold their Jag before moving to Fort Davis full-time and got something that Billy described as "easy to work on and boring as hell." He was quite disappointed to see the black Jag go.

He went right up to them, but didn't immediately bring up the car as he'd planned. "Howdy, gents. In case you don't remember, I'm Billy Schlatter and this guy behind me, who I introduced the first time we met as my sometimes live-in, is now permanently shacked up with me."

I interjected, "Of a kind."

Then James, of John and James, suggested, "If you have time, why don't you stop by the house after you're done with lunch? We can show you what we've done to the place."

I was going to say John might want more advanced warning than that, but Billy jumped at the chance. "We'd love to. What's the address?"

"Yes, he's crazy," I noted. "I guess we'll see you in about an hour then."

To which John confirmed, "That sounds good."

Ernesto saw us talking to the two men and, of course, Billy had to give his report. "We're going to the gay guys from Dallas' place after we leave here."

I reiterated, "I remind everyone again, we don't know that they are gay."

"Right," Billy said in the somewhat dismissive tone he always used towards my notion they might not be gay.

"Yeah, sure," Ernesto stated just as dismissively.

Rosalinda joked, "You know what I say about you two compared to them."

I smiled, "But you'll be nice enough today not to say it."

"As you wish," she replied.

Then Sara approached our booth to take our orders but first had some news for us. "John and James said they were thinking of opening a restaurant in Alpine. They wondered if I'd leave here. I didn't tell them no, but I'd have to know it was going to actually make it before I'd even think about it. And I'm pretty well settled here. I'm not looking for any new restaurant drama."

Billy got all excited. "*Jaime*, that's probably why they want us to come over. They want two hot cowboy bartenders for their new place!"

"Your folks and Sallie might not take too kindly to you and me moving into Alpine. And you'd last working late at night instead of gettin' up at the crack o' dawn about two days. Then you'd be leaning on me saying, 'Take me home—take me home! I'm too tired.'"

Billy conceded, "We'll have to disappoint them, I guess."

"Yeah, I guess we will." I replied.

"I wonder what they have in mind?" Rosalinda asked.

I answered, "If we find out and don't have to take another vow of silence, we will let you know."

Ernesto had his opinion on the subject. "A good barbecue place would be nice. I don't know why that is so hard to find around here. Think how many Masses I miss because I have to watch that smoker."

Rosalinda jabbed her husband, saying, "I'm sure with a barbecue place in Alpine, you'd never miss Mass again."

Ernesto was feeling a bit frisky. He put both arms around his wife next to him in the booth and squeezed her saying, "Oh, my little *Chaquita*, you adore me, so much!"

Rosalinda pushed him off and said, "I may need to adopt *Jaime's* line. You're a mess."

"But I'm your mess," he said.

"Hey find your own line!" Billy protested.

I just shook my head, replying, "Good grief."

Once done with lunch, Billy and I headed over to the old family home on Front Street—now the home of John and James. Billy asked, "Should I see if my key still fits?"

"I'd just as soon you not try, but if you actually have one, you might give it to them."

He replied, "The one detail I didn't think to tell you about the day I left after my choice words with Mom, was I walked by her—still in the kitchen in some state of dismay as she stared out the window. Then, with my clothes in a garbage bag in one hand and my house keys in the other, I rather dramatically held the keys over the trash can and dropped them in. She never turned to look, though I'm sure she heard them as they hit the empty bottom of the can I'd emptied just an hour earlier."

As we were escorted into the old family home, the "ranch foreman" decided he needed to remember his duties, stating, "We can only stay a few minutes. I gotta get Cowboy Jaime back to roping steers yet this afternoon. He can finally get the rope on their neck instead of his own."

James said, "Cowboys we are not. We've ridden a horse one time in our life and that was at a dude ranch. We always thought saddles looked pretty comfortable but not after a few hours of being stuck on one."

Billy joked, "You just gotta let your hind end know who's boss. It gets better."

"We'll take your word for it," John said.

We looked around the place. They'd had a year or so of trips back and forth from Dallas to work on it and had brought in some help as well. I hadn't been in it to see the "before" but Billy deemed it as "purdied up real good." It certainly leaned towards the more modern minimalistic—not quite Marfa-esque but veering in that direction.

I said, "This is my first time in the house. It looks very nice."

Billy's curiosity was gnawing at him. "Sara says you are thinking of opening a restaurant in Alpine. She thought probably you wanted two hot cowboys like Jaime and me to run the bar."

"I can assure you that is *not* what Sara said," I countered, given Sara's inability to defend herself in that moment. Then I added, "And don't take the boy seriously. He is fully committed to a ranch that he left once in his life and will never do again—even when he kicks the bucket, as he and I will both be put up on a far ridge where his grandparents now rest."

John replied, "We haven't decided one way or the other regarding the restaurant. We've always wanted to try, but realize we haven't given retirement much of a chance yet."

James added, "We did want to ask you about Jean and Mary-Alice. Our realtor, Annie, said they are accountants, and she thought maybe they had some experience with restaurant accounts."

"I think they have a couple accounts like that," I noted.

Billy offered, "I don't know if you are Christian, heathen or somethin' in between, but the first Saturday of every month our mom hosts a Quiet Day at our ranch. It starts with a short service at 7:30 and wraps up at 2:30. The girls are always there. You could stay for a little while afterwards to talk to them."

James raised his eyebrows and replied, "We are rather long-lapsed Baptists."

"As for the day, it's rather special," I said. "You don't have to be anything in particular to find the setting, the quiet and the few readings a contemplative experience. If you love excitement, nonstop noise, long prayers and any of that, let's just say Quiet Day would not be your cup of tea."

They looked at each other to render a decision on the spot. John confirming, "We'd like to come."

Billy said, "Grab me some paper and a pen, and I'll give you the directions to the ranch. You'll get to see the house my live-in designed and built with that guy we are always with in the Slo Poke Cafe."

"We've heard you can't live in this town long without getting to know Ernesto," James responded. "We've not met him yet."

I laughed, "Well, you won't meet him at Quiet Day, but a good way to meet him and Rosalinda would be to volunteer at the food pantry. Rosalinda runs it now. We can give you the schedule if you want it."

"Sure," John said. "Write it there with the directions to the ranch if you don't mind, Billy."

"Okey-dokey."

We had one more stop in town to make before heading to the ranch. We stopped to get the week's collection of mail. As per our routine, I drove home as Billy started sorting "ranch east" from "ranch west." It had been a year since I'd mailed my "love poems" to my parents, sister and brother. None had responded. As Billy was sorting he came to a card addressed to me.

"Jaime, do you know a Zoey Mendoza?"

I answered, "Well, I knew a Zoey Cruz who became a Zoey Cartwright, but that doesn't preclude her from being a Mendoza by now. That would be my sister."

Billy then asked, "Do you want me to open it now or do you want to read it in private?"

I laughed, "Private—exactly when have you and I instituted any policy remotely resembling privacy?"

That was all the encouragement he needed. I heard the envelope ripped open and waited to see what was in store inside.

Billy held the card in my direction, so I could see it. It was an ocean scene—nothing written on the front. "It's one of those blank cards. No verse or poem in it." Then he proceeded with reading it to me.

Dear Jaime,

It has been many months since I received your letter, and I don't mind confessing I had no idea what to make of it at first. I was going through divorce number two at the time and was in a general state of disgust. I almost threw it away, but I didn't. Since then, I have read it dozens of times. Could this be from my brother—really? I thought you must have copied it from somewhere or had someone else write it. However, the more times I read it, I realized there was something deep down inside the words that was in me as well. That is when I knew it was genuinely from you. And if those weren't your words, they were at least chosen for me.

I can see from the letter that you have learned to stop transmitting onto others the pain of our childhood and our many failed relationships since. My new husband, Mark Mendoza, came along as I was healing—in no small part as a result of your letter. I'm sure you are curious. I still have nothing to do with our brother or parents. Perhaps you've heard from them. For me, the last time I heard anything from them was late 1999.

With you in Texas and me still here in California, I don't expect us to be much more to each other than wrecks who have been rescued by fates bigger than ourselves. But I hope we can write each other from time to time. It would mean a lot to me. I can say with certainty, your well-chosen words were most healing even if the patient took months to grasp the depth of their power.

Your sister,

Zoey

Billy stared at it a few more seconds and put it back into the envelope.

I drove for about five minutes without saying anything. Then I sighed, "Four seeds. One sprout. That's one more than I expected when I scattered those seeds to the wind."

Chapter Three

The following month, Jean and Mary-Alice arrived for their Friday night routine to stay in the bunkhouse for Quiet Day the next morning. We all met at the house for dinner. The girls offered to give Betsy the night off, and she accepted. They made a Tex-Mex dinner of beef and shrimp fajitas, guacamole and margaritas. Even the Geermann sisters both decided one margarita wouldn't kill them. Of course, that sent Billy scrambling to grab the biggest mugs he could find.

Betsy, Sallie and Bill were out on the north porch watching the sun begin its slow descent. Betsy took one look at the drink and exclaimed, "Heavens! I'll never be able to drink all that."

Billy offered her a big thumbs up and saying, "Go for it, Mom."

Bill offered, "What she don't, I will."

Sallie chuckled, "Bill, you aren't getting any of mine." Then she said to Billy, who had settled with his own in the chair between me and Sallie, "I would have thought you could have found a little bigger mug in there somewhere. I guess you could have just handed us each a pitcher full."

"I thought about it," he noted.

I was going through my first one fast. I leaned over to Billy and whispered, "There is one major problem with Mary-Alice's margaritas—they are too good!"

We were both ready for another. Billy went to "fill up," and I just hoped dinner would be ready soon, since I was already feeling the effects of tequila on an empty stomach.

Sallie took one look at her drink and one at her sister's. "Well, Sis, you're doing all right on that drink. You're ahead of me."

Betsy smiled, "I've never had a margarita before. Quite good."

Bill noted quite matter-of-factly, "We'll see how you feel about them in the morning."

Mary-Alice came on the porch to announce, "Dinner is served."

We'd no sooner made up plates and sat down to eat when Billy said, "Jaime has big news."

Looking at Billy, I asked, "I do?"

"The letter."

"Oh, right. That is pretty big news as news in my life goes. I got a letter from my sister, Zoey. You may recall I wrote those four letters to my family a year ago at Quiet Day. Well, she finally wrote to say that she didn't know what to make of it at first, and she wasn't even sure it was something I could have written."

Billy interjected, "She thought he must have copied it from someone else."

I continued, "She was going through divorce number two at the time, and it sounds like that marriage was as toxic as all our other familial happenings. She kept the letter, and once through the divorce, read it a number of times."

Billy interjected again, "She did more than just read it, she credits the letter for healing her a lot and opening her up to finding a new husband and a marriage that has more than a fair chance of making it."

I said, "Yes, she seems to be on a good trajectory with her new husband, Mark, and she wants to keep in touch."

Betsy asked, "Did she say anything about your parents or brother?"

"Only that she's not seen or talked to any of them in six years—which is about as long as it's been for me, though I have a year or more on her in that regard. It's just as well if she wants to keep Mark away from that toxic mess."

Sallie asked, "Do you think she and Mark will come here for a visit?"

"I don't know about that," I answered. "For now, she's just said she would like to keep in touch. I plan to write her back tomorrow at Quiet Day."

Billy rightly noted, "Writing at Quiet Day seemed to work last time. You get inspiration from the day."

"Yes, I do," I said.

Bill surprised us a bit when he added, "Two out of three. It seems to be the odds as they run in the Cruz family and the Schlatter bunch. Though I can't lump our odd duck in the toxic category—just more the clueless category."

Betsy said to Bill, "Maybe you should write a letter tomorrow as well. Could be since Brett's never gotten a letter from either one of us, it would wake the boy up."

Sallie gave her little head-bobbing chuckle, joking, "I'd love to know the first thoughts that would go through his mind when he sees that handwritten return address on the envelope."

Jean said, "He'll think he's been cut out of the will." Then noticing her mother's empty glass, she asked, "Mom, you want another margarita? I see you finished that one off after all."

She answered, "Bill says I may not like them in the morning as much as I do right now. I think I'll stick with water from here on."

"Good decision," Sallie added.

"I was looking forward to the entertainment if she had another," Billy joked.

Bill agreed, "No doubt, it might have been quite entertaining."

Seeing everyone had packed in all they were going to, I said, "Mary-Alice and Jean, the Slo Poke Cafe has nothing on your Tex-Mex skills, and that's a pretty high standard in my book."

Bill added, "They can match the food, but they don't provide the level of entertainment for Betsy's old church bunch that you and Billy do."

"We still get the stares from them, all the same," Jean noted.

Betsy sighed, "Yes, I'm sure you do. All that seems like a lifetime ago."

I said, "I hate to eat and run, but Quiet Day starts early which means the few chores we need to attend to come even earlier. I'd best take the foreman home to get him rested up."

"It would seem we're ready to go," Billy added.

Back home, we sank into our respective ends of the couch and didn't say anything for a time. Then Billy asked, "Brotherly love—where does that notion come from? I barely know my brother and you certainly are as estranged from yours as one can be. Cain killed his brother, so it's not like it was a thing from the very start. As you pointed out to Mom a while back, Joseph and his brothers weren't exemplars of brotherly love."

I replied, "I noticed when the new checker at the Thriftway asked if we were brothers, you borrowed my line, 'of a kind.'"

Billy gave a little chuckle. "I thought that was the perfect answer and left her wondering what it meant."

"As it often does," I said. "Exemplars—that's a dollar-word for us nickel-cowboys."

Billy laughed, "I didn't even know I knew that word. Being a high school dropout, it's a wonder I can even read."

"Well, you can give yourself a little credit in the learning department. You did get your GED."

Billy conceded, "The truth is I never studied for that. I just decided to take it and see how bad it was going to be, so I could decide if I was going to worry about it or not. It surprised the hell out of me when I passed."

"You ain't no dumb cowboy," I said.

Billy asked, "You ever met a dumb cowboy?"

"None I can think of offhand, but we do seem to have veered off course from your topic of brotherly love."

Billy replied, "Oh, yeah. I was thinking about the brothers and relatives in the Bible that never got along and then the real friendships who do get called out."

"Such as?" I asked.

"Well, David and Jonathan, Ruth and Naomi, Jesus and John—you and I are a lot more like them."

I responded, "I learned the story of Ruth and Naomi from Sallie, and they were, of course, relatives of a kind, but I get your point. The only thing that bothered me about Jesus and John is we only get John's opinion on the subject. At least we mostly tell the same story about ourselves—your version offering the usual Billy embellishments."

"Part of my charm," Billy interjected.

"Yes, it is," I said. "I don't know chapter and verse, but about the only time I can recall Jesus saying something to John was him overhearing John and his brother James arguing about who was going to be on the right and left of Jesus when he was 'crowned in glory.' More 'brotherly love,' as you rightly point out—each trying to be superior over the other—never mind all the other disciples."

Billy interjected, "It does say Jesus said to his mother from the cross, 'Woman behold your son,' and then he says, 'Son, behold your mother.'"

"Yeah—according to John that's what happened. It's not in the other Gospels, which is kinda my point."

"Oh, that's true," Billy acknowledged.

I added, "Come to think of it, even Jesus seemed to ignore his brothers. Remember when they wanted him to come out of the synagogue and he says, 'Who is my mother, and who are my brothers and sisters?' As far as we know, he left them all standing outside.

"As you know, after listening to the story of David and Goliath on that CD of Bible stories Lupe gave me, like I did for Joseph being sold into slavery, I dug into the story in the Old Testament. Digging into David turned out to be a lot more time-consuming than I'd realized it was going to be, but what a screwed-up family he had!

"It does seem like the closest example to our 'brotherly love' is David and Jonathan. I'm not too sure I like lumping either one of us in with David, but he definitely loved Jonathan. It could be he'd have been a better man and better king had he stuck with his true love instead of exploiting the women in his life."

Billy said, "I think we're both persuaded of two things."

When he didn't continue right away, I asked, "What might those be?"

"That brotherly love is bullshit and that you and I are exemplars of friendship."

I said matter-of-factly, "When you're right, you're right."

Chapter Four

At Quiet Day that Saturday, Bill and I wrote our letters. I know Bill shared his with Betsy before sealing it in the envelope, and I did the same with Billy, as I'd done with my first letter.

When the regular attendees and James and John had left and it was just family, Bill asked everyone to sit down for a chat about Chuy's work in El Salvador. He first filled in Jean and Mary-Alice about Chuy deciding to stay there and joining the Franciscans. Then he laid out the two projects Chuy was trying to get started — the fish tanks and fair trade coffee.

He explained, "As I see it, an infusion of cash up front will help one of those projects a lot more than the other. They have the labor. They just need the materials to get those tanks built. The coffee trade is all logistical, and throwing some money at it at this point isn't going to help much.

"Jean and Mary-Alice, I'm hoping you might be able to commit some of your time to look into the fair trade movement and see how we could connect things here with the farmers in Chuy's area."

Betsy added, "The Cardonas are hoping they can get Father Chuy's sister, Conchita, on board for helping set things up here in the Big Bend and in San Angelo. You should definitely talk to Rosalinda about that."

Mary-Alice, looking for any pushback from Jean and seeing none, replied, "We will certainly see what we can find out."

"As to the fish project," Bill continued, "I'd like to send the same or more than we did as a family last time. We certainly saw the good that money accomplished. It's amazing how far they make a little bit go."

Sallie said, "Whatever you send as a family, I'll add my own ten thousand."

Betsy added, "We can always find out from Ernesto and Rosalinda how far they were able to stretch it and could add to it later on."

Billy suggested, "I believe I hear a motion to send $35,000 between the Schlatter funds and the Geermann funds."

"I don't think we need a second to that motion," Bill responded. "All in favor?"

"Aye!" we all said in unison.

On Monday, Bill contacted the bishop in El Paso again and laid out what the family had in mind. The bishop said he would talk to his counterpart in El Salvador and get back to him. He wanted to be able to reassure Bill that designating funds specifically for the fish tanks was going to be well-received. Two days later, Bill received an enthusiastic approval, and the two checks were sent.

A couple weeks later it was food distribution Saturday, and Billy and I drove into town to help. Ernesto was working elsewhere that morning but told Rosalinda that he planned to join us for lunch at the Slo Poke Cafe. When we pulled into the parking lot, he was there waiting in his truck—window down, radio on.

We made our way to our usual booth, and Sara, seeing us come in, was already there with our iced teas. Soon John and James came in as well, and Billy and I gave them a little wave.

I noticed that they always sat in the booth where Claude had always sat—who I didn't know for the longest time was Emma's brother. Seeing them in that booth always made me remember the unique relationship that brother and sister had. It was especially acute on this Saturday because of the conversation Billy and I recently had about brotherly love. It should have occurred to me that night to remember them, and I had not. It felt a bit like a betrayal I would have to rectify on the drive back to the ranch.

I didn't have an opportunity to think anything more about it at that moment as Rosalinda exclaimed, "We have big news! Elma praying that Rosary of hers seems to have done the trick."

Ernesto added, "Chuy called us last night and said that his bishop had received funds to build the fish tanks. According to the bishop, it was from the same people who donated the money for the clinic. Chuy said, '*Papá*, be sure to let Mr. Schlatter know. He was so interested in our work here, I want him to know about the fish project.' We told him we'd told y'all about them when we were out for *Jaime's* birthday."

As best I could tell, the family's secret gift remained so. Only Chuy and the two bishops knew who the benefactors truly were.

Billy said, "I know if I need an answer to prayer, I'm going to call Elma from now on."

Ernesto added, "She's ninety—we'd all better pray she keeps living a while longer yet."

Rosalinda looked at her *esposo*. "I wish I could think you said that as something towards her good health and not because you want her prayers for you."

I said in Ernesto's defense, "For Elma, those two things are indistinguishable. Her well-being and her prayers for others are who she is."

"*Es verdad!*" Ernesto exclaimed.

"Yes, you are right," Rosalinda added.

Billy asked, "Do you have a trip to El Salvador planned anytime soon?"

Rosalinda answered, "We know Chuy doesn't want to take any time away for quite a while, so we think we may go down over Christmas. We'll have to decide pretty soon and let him know."

Billy surprised me when he added, "One of these years we ought to go down there. Mom, Dad, *Jaime* and me."

I said, "That would be an adventure for all of us. The farthest any of us have been outside the country is to go to *Ojinaga* for lunch. For the two of us that's been once. I'm not sure how many times your mom or dad have been there."

"Not much more than that," Billy replied. "I think they went a few times when they were dating. Once, when we all went to Big Bend, we did take the boat over into *Boquillas*."

Rosalinda noted, "You could do that before 9/11."

I asked, "Is *Boquillas* bigger than *Ojinaga*?"

They all laughed.

Ernesto answered, "Population about a hundred. Twenty-percent bigger than *Dancer*."

"So the boat is just across the Rio Grande?" I asked.

"A row boat—the livelihood for the man doing the rowing," Billy replied.

Rosalinda offered the novice travelers some clearly needed guidance, "The post office in Marfa can actually take your passport picture and send in the paperwork. The one in Fort Davis doesn't handle that. I don't know about the one in Alpine. It probably does as well."

Ernesto added, "Once you have one, they are good for ten years."

I smiled, "We seem to be planning it all out. We might want to talk to Bill and Betsy—could be, they're in no hurry to leave home."

Ernesto noted, "Don't expect a five-star hotel on the other end, but you can expect to find people who can teach us a thing or two about what it takes to be happy."

"Boy, isn't that the truth?" Rosalinda affirmed.

On the drive home, I said to Billy, "Seeing John and James sitting in that booth where Claude always sat, I thought about our conversation on brotherly love."

Billy replied, "I did too, though only because of their names and not because they were in Claude's booth."

I continued, "I was thinking how I should have mentioned Emma and Claude when we were talking about siblings being friends. They really were exemplars of that, even with Claude's rather aloof personality compared to Emma's down-to-earth, nuts-and-bolts approach to every problem. And your mom and Sallie too."

Billy added, "As we know all too well, those last two had a mighty-long rough patch. In that regard, I'll exclude them from the exemplar category, but you are right that Emma and Claude belong among the ranks of such. They had a lifetime of 'brotherly love'— uninterrupted right up to the end."

I said, "It's nice to honor them by remembering both as we look to their example of what can be and rarely is. Not with my brother, and not with yours."

Billy added, "And, not with Dad and his only brother in San Angelo. I don't know of any hostility they've ever had towards each other, but as best I can tell, both like the other one far away— same way Dad says he likes kale, which according to him everyone seems to want to eat all of a sudden."

I laughed, "Yeah, when I heard him say that I thought, 'Note to self—no kale salads to potluck family gatherings.'"

Billy laughed as well, adding, "With Dad, when in doubt, bring tamales or Twinkies. You can't go wrong with either one."

I observed, "I've noticed he's cut way down on both his King Edwards and the Twinkies."

Billy replied, "Could be since Mom has come to her senses, living longer has more appeal than it did for a while there."

I laughed again. "It's so funny you say that. When Chuy and Lupe first told me about your mom and dad, that was exactly what Chuy said about your dad—not wanting to live too long in his present situation. But I don't think their or your own analysis of the situation is something you need to share with them."

"You don't have to worry about that. For some things I do keep my mouth shut at the appropriate time," Billy said.

I reassured him, "Having observed your well-timed gift for entertaining, I can't think of a single instance where you've said something you'd later regret."

Billy recalled, "I remember when I went riding with Sallie on my fourteenth birthday, she said, 'Boy, live your life so you have nothing to regret.' I told her I'd try. I've wondered over the years about why she thought, as a fourteen year old, I might be ready for such advice—though I never forgot it, and we've never talked about it again. I've wondered if it came out of some teenage choice she'd made that she did regret—maybe some forsaken love she might have had.

"I took my saying 'I'd try' as a kind of pledge to her. For twenty years, I wondered if I had betrayed that pledge. But when it all came back together, I realized I didn't have any regret about leaving that day, even though I did have a lot of years of loneliness."

I said, "I have plenty to regret from my past, but the fact that it brought me here to be a part of this family has taught me the difference between regret and overcoming a dark past. No matter what grief or pain may come into my life now, I know that it will never be loveless like those first thirty years of my life. For you, it was years of separation, but you still knew how to love, and you knew you were loved—if not by your mom, you had Aunt Sallie and your dad's love with you."

In Sallie fashion, he replied, "Yes, I did. Yes, I did." Then he exclaimed, "Oh, shit! We forgot to stop and get the mail."

"That's what happens when you jump in the driver's seat after lunch on a Saturday. Turn around, boy."

On the drive back into town, Billy asked. "Do you think you'll have a letter from Zoey yet?"

"I don't know. It's only been a couple weeks since I mailed mine."

Billy said, "Your letter was a lot longer this time, but I thought you were right to get into some detail on your life with the Cardonas and how you came to live with us on the ranch. I'm not sure she will have clued in on how much you are actually part of our family. I figured you were trying to ease into that so as not to rub it in if she doesn't feel part of Mark's family."

"Then, I succeeded in my intent. I am concerned about rubbing in my good life. I'd like to think she and I are on the same trajectory of hope, but I can't assume that."

When we pulled into the post office, I slid over to do the drive home as is our normal routine so Billy can sort the mail. I could probably do the mail sorting by now, but why mess with what works.

Back in the truck, he did a quick shuffle through the bin of mail. "No letter from California just yet," was all he said.

"Just yet"—we'd both gone from never expecting to hear from any of my family to the assumption that a letter would be in the mail any day now. And I found myself looking forward to when that day might come.

Chapter Five

A few days later, when Billy and I got back from moving cattle from one section of the ranch to another to turn them onto some fresh grass, there was a call on the answering machine from Ernesto. "*Jaime*, give me a call. I want to see about you drawing a house and talk to you about Chuy's retirement—my brother—not Pope Chuy."

I dialed his cell. "Hey, Ernesto. It's *Jaime*. *Qué pasa?*"

"Hey, *muchacha*, there is a couple who bought a lot here in town and talked to me about building them a house. They are renting the little rock house by the Baptist church right now. I forget where they said they moved from. They both just retired. Anyway, I wanted to see if you could come meet them on Saturday at their lot and see what inspiration comes to you."

"Sure, I can do that. What time?" I asked.

"Let's say you come by here about ten-till-ten unless you hear otherwise."

"Okey-dokey," I replied.

Then he asked, "Did Chuy tell you he's retiring from the tomato farm?"

"No, I didn't know that, though I was pretty sure it wasn't far off."

Ernesto continued, "We're going to have a big Cardona fiesta and want the Geermann-Schlatters to all join us. I think I can guarantee dozens of deviled eggs and probably the biggest cake Elma's ever made. We're thinking a month or so from now."

Billy, overhearing the entire conversation, grabbed the phone from me. "Hey, Ernesto. I'm not sure we got enough cattle on the ranch to feed all the Cardonas and their extended families who may show up to such a fiesta, but let us donate some good Geermann-Schlatter beef. I'd offer to cook it, but I know you're the barbecue king."

He didn't wait for a reply and just handed the phone back to me. "Ernesto, it's *Jaime* again. You'll note the fact that since you weren't given time to reply, it's a Billy 'take-it-or-leave-it' offer."

Ernesto chuckled, "We'll take it. Though if we schedule it for a Sunday, I might have to miss Mass watching the barbecue."

"That goes without saying!" I noted. "You can tell Rosalinda, 'Blame Billy. He insisted on barbecue.'" Then I asked, "Seriously, how many people do you think would be coming to this, so we have some idea of how much meat to get to you?"

"I'd say pretty near sixty counting all of you. Maybe seventy if you invite Brett and his various family branches."

"You want us to invite Brett?" I asked with obvious surprise in my tone.

He said, "Sure, what the hell. We invite our misfits. You might as well invite yours, too."

"Okay, I will let Bill and Betsy make that particular call."

Billy grabbed the phone again. "Hey, Ernesto, if Brett and his wife and kids fit in, we might leave them with you. Let me ask you. Having you ever slow smoked whole ribeyes?"

Ernesto answered, "Only once or twice. But if that's what you have in mind, that's generous to say the least. Hell, if that's what you want, that's what you'll get."

"All right then!" Billy ended his conversation for the second time and handed the phone back to me.

"It's *Jaime* again. Was there anything else, or shall I just see you Saturday morning?"

Ernesto answered, "We're done. Bring Billy along on Saturday and we'll have lunch afterwards."

"Okey-dokey," I replied, though I'm not sure Ernesto heard it. He ends phone calls as abruptly as Billy.

After hanging up, I asked, "Where are we going to get that much ribeye? And your dad and Sallie might think you got a little carried away offering that much Geermann-Schlatter prime rib."

Billy answered, "You know how once a year, Dad sends steers off to get meat for the food pantry—having the butcher sell off the best steaks in exchange for the processing, and he has the rest ground into hamburger. I figure if we get moving now on that, we can get the ribeyes from the steers, and they'll have just the right time to dry-age before Ernesto smokes them."

I just shook my head. "Your mind can put together a scenario with no apparent pitfalls on shorter notice than anyone I've ever seen. I'm not sure where you get that from. It appears to me, the only thing to work out is being sure the butcher can schedule you in."

Billy noted, "I don't think we have to worry about that. Dad's gift is getting people to want to please him."

"He is master of that," I confirmed. "I think you might want to call him and let him know what you've committed to sooner rather than later."

Billy said, "I think we need to drive over there now and get the ball rolling."

I didn't see it was quite that urgent, noting, "We haven't even had supper yet."

"Also in my plan. Maybe Mom will offer to feed us."

I just shook my head at the boy. "And she probably will."

We no sooner cracked the door open to Billy's now customary "Anybody home?" when his mom asked, "Well, to what do we owe a midweek visit from the two of you this late in the evening? It's not a mail-delivery day."

Billy said, "I've got cattle business to talk over with Dad and Sallie. Jaime came along to see what he could do to help you in the kitchen to get some supper on the table."

Betsy looked at me and I at her. We both just shook our heads. "Come on, Jaime. It looks like we've been given our marching orders from the foreman." Then she said to Billy, "You could have at least brought your harmonica and Jaime's guitar, so you two could sing for your supper. You're getting off cheap tonight."

To which I said, "Believe me, y'all aren't getting off cheap with what he has in mind."

Betsy feigned a serious tone, "That doesn't sound good. Billy, you'll find the two you're looking for back in Sallie's office."

With Billy off on his mission, and Betsy beginning to pull things out of the refrigerator, she asked, "What's he up to now?"

I told her all about the call with Ernesto.

"The boy is all heart," she said. "And you're right about his ability to piece together anything in an instant. I think he gets that from that same man whose appearance he takes after. Daddy could add any string of numbers in his head and map out just how to go about anything he put his mind to with no seeming effort whatsoever. Sallie and Bill are more the pondering kind, and I don't know what I am. I guess I take after my mother who was just grateful to have the life she had."

I replied, "I don't know about your mother, of course, but if there is anyone more gifted in hospitality than you, I'm hard-pressed to imagine it. Even the most simple meal is a gift, and you've made Quiet Day very special from the first time out of the gate. You have the true gift of making people feel welcomed."

"You're right to call it a gift," she said. "Like you drawing this house and others since, it's hard to take any credit when it just seems to come up from somewhere inside."

"Yes, it is."

Betsy gave consideration to supper possibilities. "I think on this short notice the best I can do is get some chili burgers with cheese going. I don't have any buns, but I don't guess we need them with chili anyway. Does that sound okay?"

"Bill will probably want a kale salad to go with that, don't you think?" I asked.

She laughed, "And I'll want two or three margaritas, so I can have tequila nightmares all night! I never had such crazy dreams in all my life. Bill says it was the tequila."

I suggested, "Perhaps just some tortilla chips to go with the chili burgers."

"We might have some room for Blue Bell Dutch Chocolate after that, don't you think?" she asked.

"I wouldn't turn it down."

When the three emerged from the back, Bill updated Betsy. "He talked us out of eighty pounds of prime rib, and I see he talked you into making his supper as part of the deal. Somehow he managed to work things out real good for himself, and I'm still trying to see what we got out of it." He put his arm around my shoulder, asking, "Jaime, are you a bad influence on the boy? Was this all your idea?"

I answered, "It sounds like something I'd come up with, doesn't it?"

Billy adding flatly, "You get the pleasure of our company on a weeknight."

Sallie asked, "Don't you boys usually have to play some music for your supper?"

I noted, "That's what your sister said."

Sallie chuckled, "In lieu of that I guess I'll just have to quote Saint Paul, 'If I speak in the tongues of men and of angels, but have not love, I am a noisy gong or a clanging cymbal.' Billy, you're neither gong nor cymbal—you've got love, that's for sure."

Chapter Six

Everything aligned to Chuy's retirement fiesta as predicted. The meat got processed and aged; Ernesto missed Mass, getting all prepared for the Sunday-after-church get-together at their home; Elma, with the help of her daughters, made dozens of deviled eggs and the biggest layer cake I'd ever seen—complete with whipped cream and fresh berries instead of frosting; and Brett was invited and showed up with his four kids and Pamela and her three kids.

Bill and Betsy had not heard from Brett since Bill mailed the letter he wrote during Quiet Day more than two months earlier. They had begun to think perhaps it hadn't helped and only made things more awkward between them. Both were glad he came, taking it as some sign it was just Brett being Brett that he'd not responded one way or the other. With nine of them all in attendance, they decided to stay in town rather than cram into the bunkhouse. Billy and I were relieved not to have to host one chunk of the group to make room. We would have, had Brett asked, but he never did. We could have offered out of courtesy, but we were both aware of the silence after the letter was mailed. We thought it best to see where Brett's connection with his mom and dad was headed before we waded into something we might wish we hadn't.

Figuring Billy wouldn't think to do it, I was sure to introduce Pamela to all the Cardonas there who I knew, which included Chuy and Ernesto's brothers, Rogelio and Mando. I hadn't seen either one of them in months. I really liked Mando's wife, Tanya. I loved her great laugh and how amused she was by much of the world as it passed her by.

She informed me of her big news. "Did you hear I won a scratch-off?"

"No," I replied. "I hadn't heard that."

"I did," she continued, "and I told Mando I know exactly what I'm going to do with the money."

I replied, "I take it, it was more than a twenty dollar win."

She laughed, "It was a hundred thousand!"

"Oh, wow!" I exclaimed.

"I told Mando, 'I'm quitting the job at the school and joining you in the hauling business.' We drove up to Midland, and I'm getting my own dump truck. I'm going to give him a run for his money—prove to him a woman truck driver can keep up with any man."

Billy joked, "I don't know about any woman versus any man, but I'd give you the short odds in this case."

Mando looked at Billy—shaking his head. "Thanks a lot, bro. I appreciate you putting me as the long shot against my own wife."

Billy asked, "Knowing the odds then, are you putting your money on yourself or on your wife?"

Mando exclaimed, "I ain't no fool! My money's on Tanya."

"It's supposed to be ready by Thursday," Tanya continued. "They are painting 'Cardona & Brister Hauling' on each door and across the front of the hood. On the driver-side door, they're adding that image of the 'We Can Do It' woman—you know, the one in the red bandana and she holds her arm just, so."

Tanya proceeded to raise her right arm, flexing her bicep which was amazingly well-formed.

"Damn!" Billy exclaimed. "I know *your* theme song—'I am Woman Hear Me Roar.'"

Tanya laughed, "I thought about having a picture painted on the passenger side, for when Mando rides along, of that guy in *9 to 5* where the ladies string up their boss in that sling—but I decided it might be bad for business."

She was most amused at her idea of such an image of Mando.

Mando said, "I guess you both know she never would take my name. She kept her maiden name."

Tanya added, "And now it sounds like a bigger business— Cardona and Brister Hauling."

Just then Ernesto came up to greet us, saying, "I guess you've heard the big lotto news. I told Mando if she gives me ten percent off his rates, she gets all my business."

I immediately picked up a flaw in Ernesto's idea. "Somehow, regarding the Cardona and Brister Hauling sales numbers, I'd expect the rate might go up and not down as they corner the hauling market in Fort Davis."

"Hey, I like that idea!" Mando exclaimed.

Ernesto looked at me and called me something he hadn't in a long time. *"Cabrón!"*

I gave him a head nod, "Only a *pendejo* wouldn't have seen the flaw in his own logic of getting Tanya to go cheap."

Mando gave his brother a sharp jab. "He got you there, *hermano!"*

I asked Ernesto, "Do you have a song planned to sing to your big brother?"

He answered, "I thought about 'Take This Job and Shove It,' but that doesn't really fit him, and I knew his old boss would be here. So, I did some changin' up to Garth Brooks's song, 'Much Too Young To Feel This Damn Old.' It should be a hit."

Billy said, "Hey, *Jaime*, if you're ready for a new theme song, you and I might adopt that one. I like the title. We can adapt the rest to fit."

"I'm pretty sure your mom will enjoy that about as much as she does 'Wall Street *Bandidos.'"*

I saw Elma look our way and wave. I said to Billy, "Let's go say hello to Elma."

When we got over to her she asked, "Are you two nice boys keeping Ernesto in line?"

I answered, "Rosalinda is the only one with that gift."

She thought that was funny and said, "You know, I was good friends with his mother. Even she didn't have the gift Rosalinda has, but she and Ernesto certainly had their own special love for each other. I wish she could have lived to see his youngest become a priest."

Billy said, "I hear your prayers were answered about getting help for his work in El Salvador."

Elma proclaimed, "Oh, *gracias al señor*—I'm so happy for him. *Jaime*, we made lots of deviled eggs. You be sure to get some."

"I will," I said. "I always look forward to your wonderful eggs, and I never got to thank you for the cake you made for my birthday. When Billy brought it out after the party, I was truly surprised. You made me cry."

"Oh, you. You two are such good boys. Don't you tell my daughters, but you are nicer than any of my grandsons."

Lupe came up just then and obviously heard the last part of that exchange. She asked, "Is *Mamá* trying to adopt you two? She always says to me, 'Oh, they are such nice boys.'"

Billy replied, "She's the only *abuela* either one of us has anymore, so I guess we've sorta adopted her."

That really tickled Elma. Lupe laughed, "You can adopt Chuy and me, too."

I put my arm around her. "You forget—you adopted me when I first arrived here. I must have looked like a pitiful shell of a man, walking around with a dark cloud over my head the same way the dust cloud follows poor Pigpen in the *Peanuts* comics."

Lupe said, "You were certainly quiet for a long time, but none of us saw the despair we came to realize was so much a part of your life before you got here."

Billy interjected, "Think how I could have cheered him up so much sooner if I'd been around."

"I don't think I was ready for the likes of you." Then to Lupe I said, "I can only attribute my lack of transmitting my despair of those days to the kindness you and Chuy showed me from day one, and the immediate seed of hope I had from that first night's sleep here in this place."

Chuy came up to us just then, and I reached out my hand to shake his. "I knew the tomato farm could survive without me as long as you were there. I'm not so sure now that we are both gone."

"They're gonna have to. My working days are done," he proclaimed.

Billy issued a directive, "Chuy, wait here a minute. *Jaime* and I have a gift for you, and I need to get it out of the truck."

Chuy saw me shake my head, and so he knew it was going to be a Billy-inspired gift. He was soon back with the gift-wrapped package with a big pink bow.

Chuy took one look, saying, "The size of that gift looks awfully familiar." He took it, and opened it to find exactly what he'd suspected from the size. It was a case of red-ripe tomato farm tomatoes. "Oh, thank you, Billy. I don't know when Lupe and I have had such fresh ripe tomatoes!"

Billy added, "I had to drive to the Marfa plant to get them so I would be sure I didn't run into you."

Lupe noted, "I guess I'll be canning a few tomatoes tomorrow before they go bad. The old man gets to retire, and I get to work."

"I was hoping we could make another CD of our music," I said, "but we seem to have things interrupting our music nights the past few months."

Chuy smiled, "We play that one you gave us more than you'd ever imagine. Lupe likes to leave the door open, and we sit out in the lawn chairs like we did those evenings when you'd sit outside the casita and play."

I asked, "Speaking of the casita, do you have a new tenant by now?"

Chuy answered, "No, *mi esposa* says until another *Jaime* comes along it's going to sit empty. I told her there won't be another *Jaime*."

Lupe clarified, "I just mean when someone needs our help in the same way you did."

I instinctively stepped close to hug Lupe, and Chuy hugged us both. Of course, that prompted Billy to hug the lot of us as he coaxed Elma into the growing huddle.

All huddled up, I added, "In case you didn't know it, there is no hugging cluster big enough for Billy."

Billy said, "Dad says we needn't make a habit of such things."

From across the way Ernesto hollered, "Break it up over there! Old man, get over here!"

Chuy made his way to his kid brother, who was then joined by all the Cardona siblings. Ernesto put his arm around his brother. "Since you're the oldest, you always got everything new and the rest of us got your hand-me-downs. I got your bike when it looked like a piece of shit. We thought it only right that it come back to its rightful owner."

Rosalinda came rolling up with the old bike.

He continued, "As you can see, I've given it a fresh coat of orange neon paint, so you can be seen as you ride around town."

Chuy exclaimed, "I thought you took that to the scrapyard years ago! I can't believe you kept it all this time."

Lupe started to applaud, and we all joined in. Ernesto shouted, "Boys get your instruments." His brothers in the Cardona mariachi band sans their trumpet player got their instruments, and they all queued up to accompany Ernesto in his rendition of "Much Too Young To Feel This Damn Old."

Billy and I stood on each side of Elma with our arms around her. She smiled while saying, "His mother would pretend she didn't approve of his carrying on like this, but she'd be just as tickled as the rest of us."

I said, "As Chuy said when he first told me about Ernesto, 'You gotta love him.'"

After Ernesto's song, Chuy hollered over the applause, "Are we ever gonna eat?"

Ernesto addressed the crowd, "Billy donated his folks' and Aunt Sallie's prime rib if I'd smoke 'em. We'll have everything set out in five minutes. Let's hear a round of applause for the generosity of the Geermann-Schlatter family—especially for Billy who offered his dad and aunt's beef before talking to them!"

Everyone laughed and applauded.

As we gathered to line up to fill our plates, Chuy waved me over to where he and Lupe were at the front of the line. He asked me quietly, "Would you say that blessing you said for us?"

"Sure," I answered.

Chuy turned to the line behind him and raised his arm to quiet the crowd. Then he gave me a single nod of the head to proceed. Chuy and Lupe made the sign of the cross and the Cardonas all followed suit.

I prayed that simple prayer.

Let us taste no food that does not strengthen us to show thy great love and mercy. Amen.

All again made the sign of the cross as the cross-conversation of the crowd quickly returned after its momentary pause.

Brett and his entourage were near the end of the line with Bill and Betsy. I noticed that Noah, Brett's youngest, was hanging onto his grandmother just as he had at the Slo Poke Cafe when I first saw him—before I even knew his name. These two had a closeness not forged through frequent connections, but seemingly more from some natural bond.

When I mentioned this to Billy, he smiled and stated matter-of-factly, "He must be Geermann."

Jean and Mary-Alice joined us to bring up the rear.

Billy asked, "Have you two been hanging out with Brett?"

Jean answered, "No, he's actually been chattin' it up with his old school mate, Caleb. We did 'hang,' as you put it, with Pamela since he seemed to be ignoring her."

Mary-Alice adding, "Away from Brett, she's actually pretty interesting. We didn't know she was so athletic. She plays tennis and golfs and was actually a competitive swimmer in high school and college."

Jean said, "And while Brett might have said all that to brag, she really didn't. We just discussed our interests, and those were hers."

Billy asked, "She didn't list Brett as one of her interests?"

Jean responded, "He never came up in the conversation."

"Then I don't guess she mentioned the letter from your dad," I said inquisitively.

"If she knows about Brett getting a letter from Dad, she didn't mention it. I didn't sense anything new to their world now from before the letter."

Billy speculated, "He probably never told her about it. What do you think Dad said in the letter?"

Jean shrugged, saying, "I'd guess some version of, 'Wake up, Son!'"

Bringing up the end of the line, I figured the deviled eggs would be long gone, and I thought the meat would be close to gone if not out altogether. Just as we approached, Lupe came out with the last plate of eggs—grinning from ear to ear. "I don't have to tell you who gave me orders to get these set out for you and Billy."

Not only did we have Elma's wonderful eggs, but Ernesto's perfectly cooked meat as well. There was plenty left for us and anyone wanting seconds. The cake was served in bowls, so you could spoon over the raspberry, blueberry and strawberry mixed fruit.

On the drive home, I said to Billy, "You and I agree that brotherly love, as is too often bandied about, is bullshit, but all you can do is look at that Cardona bunch and know that familial love does exist even as they each live their very independent lives. That said, I'm not at all sure the next generation will bear any resemblance to Chuy's generation. It looks to me like they are drifting apart as so many families do."

Billy responded, "I would say it's because there is nothing to keep people around here, but I don't think that matters much. There are plenty of families around that don't even speak to each other even though they've lived in the same town all their lives."

I added, "Certainly, scattering around the country doesn't help, but as you and I have proven, family can crop up where you least expect it. All you have to do is embrace it."

Billy smiled, "You have beautiful thoughts from time to time."

"You're my inspiration."

"I thought I was your mess," he replied.

"Well, you're that too, which is why I love you as much as I do."

Billy gave an uncharacteristically long sigh. "Aaahhh, my God, Van Horn seems like a blur to me now. I think I only kept my sanity by making those long Sunday rides—just me, my horse and God's creation—knowing that somehow love was going to heal all wounds if I'd just ride patiently through my days."

I added, "You have beautiful thoughts from time to time."

Part II

Chapter Seven

Each time Billy and I would collect the mail, he would rifle through the bin to see if there was a letter from Zoey. Each time Brett would show up at the ranch, we all waited to see if he would have a serious conversation about Bill's letter—or even acknowledge he ever received it. Both seemed to pass with an ever-growing doubt as to whether Zoey or Brett would reach out. It was now more than nine months since we mailed our letters. In a couple more weeks, I'd be another year older and celebrating my seven-year anniversary amongst the living.

Then, finally, after the last April food pantry distribution and our customary lunch at the Slo Poke Cafe with Ernesto and Rosalinda, we collected the mail and found a thick envelope from Zoey Mendoza. Billy opened it while I drove towards the ranch.

He said, "I think we'll wait to read this until we get home. It's eight pages long, handwritten and a little hard to read her swooping cursive."

"What's the first paragraph say?" I asked. Billy read aloud as requested.

Dear Jaime,

I am sorry it has taken me so long to write back to you. My marriage to Mark and our life together had quite a wrench thrown into it right after I wrote to you. I was diagnosed with cancer and have been really dealing with doctors and treatments that make one wonder if life is worth the struggle. Fortunately, Mark has been incredible throughout the ordeal. I did make him promise early on that if I didn't make it, he was to write you to let you know. As I am writing now, you can see that I have made it through—at least for the time being.

"Well, that's paragraph one," Billy noted.
"Holy shit!" was all I could say.

When we got back to the ranch on that calm April afternoon—the wind having subsided after several days of blowing like crazy—we settled in the chaise lounges on the back patio. I picked up the letter and started to read aloud to Billy.

"Well, I'll just start with paragraph two."

I hated the idea of writing to you and laying the burden of my illness on you so soon after my first letter to you. I had no inkling at the time of that letter what was in store for me and Mark. It wasn't a week later I knew something was wrong. I had all the usual surgery, radiation and chemo one comes to expect these days with a major cancer—if there is anything else but major cancer.

In some respects, the months ground by at a snail's pace—but at the same time, one week passed quickly to the next until I realized it had been nine months since I received your letter. You can't know how comforting it was during my illness to see someone from our family in a happy situation as your life clearly now finds itself. I hope it continues for you just as I'm confident my own happiness with Mark will continue.

I couldn't help but feel you were holding back on what may be the most important pieces of your new life. If that is the case, you needn't do so for fear of some kind of jealousy on my part. I can only draw inspiration at this point. Any ego I held onto as needing to be special or somehow better was radiated along with the cancer. If suffering is a sound teacher, I've had lots of sound instruction.

You never knew my second husband. What a mistake that marriage was. I still wonder how I got caught in his narcissistic net to the degree I did. Perhaps the somewhat wild and rough sex of our first date should have been clue enough for me. But having come out of failed marriage number one, I was looking for something to cling to, and he was glad to have someone so vulnerable and, it must be said, controllable. Our intimacy (if you can call it that) after marriage resembled rape far more than love, as he took what he wanted, when he wanted and how he wanted. He was sweetness and light whenever anyone else was around, but his disposition changed the instant we were alone. People would tell me how lucky I was to have someone so thoughtful and so important. Oh, I didn't mention—he was a bigwig in Silicon Valley and was practically worshipped. Of course, he loved that!

Once, when I rather bluntly let my unhappiness be made known in a gathering of some of his "important associates," he announced that we were going to go to couples therapy. That was the one hopeful sign we had in our marriage—or at least I thought it was at the time. I had no idea how effectively a perfected narcissist can manipulate even the professional therapist. She was probably a little too star-struck to actually be effective, which is no doubt why he chose her in the first place. His company "retained" her services so she, in effect, worked full-time for him and the company. The only thing that came out of our two dozen sessions together was the list of things I needed to do.

Fortunately, when I added up the list, I knew the one thing it all added up to—I needed to leave, and I didn't see any point in getting into a legal battle, though I certainly should have gotten something of his wealth. At that point, I just wanted away from him as quickly and as permanently as possible. I walked away with nothing and moved well away from Silicon Valley.

Your first letter arrived from my forwarded mail just after I had moved out. As I said before, I didn't know what to make of your letter at the time, but I'm glad I kept it and reread it all those times over the next several months. It was truly a big part of getting my life back together—or maybe as you acknowledge—together for the first time ever. Mark doesn't even know you, and he already says he loves you. As he puts it, "Jaime is the one good thing in your life. Cherish him." Of course, that's not entirely true, but humble of Mark to put it that way. Without the two of you, there is no way I could have dealt with my cancer or with my messed-up life that preceded my diagnosis. I don't know all the causes of cancer, but as you and I have rightly acknowledged the toxicity of our earlier life, I have little doubt there is a direct connection somehow between my body being invaded by such a predatory force just as my soul had been invaded by all that preceded it.

To the cheerier side of life. Mark and I have a nice condo with a pool, tennis courts and a small gym. We've both adopted a lifestyle we feel we can maintain for our overall well-being. Mark works from home mostly, and I plan to get back in the workforce when I've had a couple more months to recover all my strength. Mark assures me, that is something I can do if I want to, but not something I have to do. We live modestly but comfortably, and we are both content with what we have together. How did I finally luck into such a good man? You and I both seem to have fallen into new lives beyond anything we could have imagined—growing up as we did.

You mentioned in your second letter that your first letter was not a letter where you asked for any kind of forgiveness for your own failures or for anything that you might have ever done to hurt anyone in our family. It contained, as you put it, "quiet reflections on the abundance of life, freely given for any open to those gifts." You said you had "the realization that inside us is that place where wounds of the past reside, not to inflict their harm on us over and over—though many yield such a power to them —but as a kind solace for us to understand how far we've come on the journey."

I'm so glad you shared that. When I read it to Mark, he said, "That is a soul that has healed." Just hearing him say those words made me burst into tears as I realized how healed I was even in the midst of the early stages of my cancer. That healing is in no small way attributable to your kind words—the prayerful words of your letters.

I don't know if you have a computer and email. I have to admit, I rather hope not. I like seeing and holding your handwritten letters. I guess that's crazy in this day and age. Perhaps in addition to being penpals (of a kind—to borrow your line that Mark has now adopted for his own), we might see each other before much longer. To be blunt, Mark says I should coax you into inviting us to the ranch—perhaps over Christmas. If that is an imposition, bad timing or just too plain scary, just say "perhaps we can find a convenient time someday." If you are open to it, we'd love to see your new life. After your second letter we watched "Dancer, Texas Pop. 81" and Mark said, "I can see where someone tired of their life in one place could pick up and go as your brother did."

I think it's funny to hear him refer to you as my brother. Whoever thought we might find some bridge to the healthier notion of such a kinship? Certainly not I, and I think you feel (or felt) the same. Well, now you have a real sister, finally, and one who still barely knows you, yet holds a genuine love for you.

Much love,

Zoey

41

P.S. Mark and I have never been on a horse, but he's hoping for a real Texas experience should the welcome mat be rolled out for the likes of us.

Billy said, "You need to drop her a note right away and let her know they are welcome to come at Christmas—and no, they won't be staying in the bunkhouse. They are staying here with us."

"I think I'll keep you."

Billy added, "I think you forget who's the foreman around here."

Chapter Eight

Since we had no immediate plans for a trip to town, Billy called his folks to let them know we had a note for Zoey we wanted to get in the mail if anyone was running into Fort Davis. His mom answered, and he just told her we'd gotten a letter from Zoey—it would be easier to tell everyone next time he and I were over there.

Billy added, "Which, if convenient with your schedule this evening, we could make it work with our schedule."

Betsy responded, "I suppose we can work you in. I know Sallie has plans to run to Alpine on Monday to go to the bookstore. I told her I'd ride along. We'll drop it then."

Billy said, "Sounds good. What we having for dinner?"

Betsy informed him, "You'll eat whatever I put in front of you. If you two boys could put together a meal besides peanut butter and sweet pickles, you could feed us once in a while. I know you both can grill a steak."

Billy joked, "And I make a mean kale salad—Dad would love it."

"Yes, I'm sure he would. We'll see you about 6:00."

Billy announced, "Free dinner tonight next door—menu unknown."

"We won't leave hungry," was all I said.

I only heard Billy's half of the conversation. I asked, "Do you think I should read the letter to them or just summarize. I'm inclined to summarize since I don't think they need to hear how wonderful I am."

Billy replied, "They already know that. It wouldn't be any news to them, but I can't quite see you getting through it reading it word for word."

"Summary it is then."

The foreman got up off his backside to do the little bit of work we needed to get done before heading over for dinner. "You stay here and write your note and invitation to Christmas. It's time you introduce me proper to them, so they can look forward to meeting me."

"I do need to do that," I noted, and he was out the door.

While my earlier letter had spelled out my years at the tomato farm, my living in the Cardona casita, the design and building of the ranch house, and how that led to my employment as a very contented ranch hand, Zoey was correct and Billy was well aware that I held back everything to do with my inclusion into the Schlatter family and my life with the firstborn son. Other than dropping their names, I had not said anything really about them. In this third letter, I thought I was either going to have to make it a booklet if I laid it all out, or I was just going to have to condense a lot and assure her and Mark that all would be revealed upon their December arrival. I kept it short and to the point.

Dear Zoey,

The welcome mat is out! We hope all works out for a Christmas visit. Don't make it a rush trip. We have plenty of room at the ranch to allow you to make yourselves at home. I have much to tell you about my life here, but it's best to let you see for yourself. Assure Mark—horses will hit the trail unless some blizzard blows in to prevent a ride around the ranch. It's the desert and it gets cold. When that night air descends, you'll feel it! Pack accordingly.

I have a computer but no email out here on the ranch. The only thing we can get is satellite Internet and their reputation for service at this point is not too good. For now we live without. We remain phone dependent.

I look forward to you meeting the special people who have taken me in as their own—Bill, Betsy and their oldest son, Billy, and Betsy's sister, Sallie, who is a gen-u-ine cowgirl. We all live out in two separate houses on the ranches. And Billy? Well, you're just going to have to meet him to understand. That should leave you in some suspense.

Directions to the ranch and our phone numbers are included. Keep in touch.

Much love,

Jaime

P.S. I can tell I like Mark already, and if he needs Internet for work while he's here, they do have access at the library in town.

I showed Billy the note before sealing it up. "I'm mysterious—I can live with that."

We had plenty of time to show up early. I suggested, "I think we should sing for our supper. It's been a while since we've done that. Grab your harmonica, and I'll get my guitar." We headed over for dinner and to fill them in on Zoey's letter.

As we walked through the door, Sallie saw we came prepared to entertain. "Well, this is a nice surprise. I don't know when we've had live entertainment on a Saturday evening. It's been too long."

Betsy turned her head from the kitchen sink where she was tidying up. "Yes, it has."

Bill grabbed his mandolin to join us. The men serenaded the women for the next half hour while Betsy finished up another Billy-imposed, impromptu dinner.

When we sat down Billy said, "I was sure it was going to be a peanut butter night."

And Bill added, "I was fearing canned tuna with kale salad."

Betsy said, "What you've got is cream cheese, walnut and chipotle stuffed pork loin with an apricot sauce. I was all out of kale, so you'll have to make do with tomato parmesan gratin, asparagus and cornbread."

"It's like you knew we were coming!" Billy exclaimed.

Sallie tattled on her sister. "She was about to call you to come for supper when you called and invited yourself."

Bill asked, "See what we get, boys, when we sing for our supper?"

I was inspired to offer a blessing. "I'll be glad to offer a blessing." I knew they expected the old standby.

It would be impossible to eat this lovely meal without a heart overflowing with gratitude. Bless the hands that cooked it as it shall surely strengthen us to greater love and service. Amen.

"Well, Amen," Billy added.

Sallie smiled, "Why Jaime, that was beautiful. I don't know if you'll remember it to use it again, but I hope you do."

Betsy left the table and went into their bedroom. Bill said, "Jaime, it looks like that was all it took to send her out of the room like you did the first time we met you. Eat up everyone. She isn't going to want us fussin' after her."

Betsy soon returned with a pleasant smile on her face and no sign of a tear. She went to her firstborn and put her hand on his cheek saying, "As foreman of the ranch now, I don't want you ever running off your helper."

Billy joked, "I'm thinking he's buckin' for my job!"

Bill stated flatly, "That, I doubt."

"Tell us about Zoey, Jaime."

I laid it all out as Zoey had spelled it out in the letter, including their possible visit at Christmas time and Mark wanting to go horseback riding.

Billy added, "Dad, I thought I'd take them out to the rock outcropping where you took me for the father-son talk, and where I took Jaime to propose to him."

"Good lord," Bill replied. "It's a wonder you didn't run Jaime off instead."

Betsy said, "I think you should all go on that ride, unless you think it will be awkward for Zoey and Mark. I'll stay here and get a nice late lunch put together. You know you're not getting me on a horse."

"I guess that's where Brett gets it from—or is it, doesn't get it?" Billy replied. "Anyway, I don't recall him ever wanting to ride unless forced."

Bill noted, "That didn't change after you left. Ranch life was never an interest to him."

Sallie offered, "Well, I'd love to go along. I'll bet not only have they never met gen-u-ine cowboys, they've almost certainly never met a gen-u-ine cowgirl. I'll even take my Swisher Sweets along for the ride."

I was already creating the ride in my mind as Sallie envisioned it. "I'll bet they'll want a picture of that—you up in the saddle with your cowboy hat on, spurs and a Swisher Sweet."

"I'm getting excited just thinking about it!" Sallie exclaimed.

Betsy replied, "Sister, you aren't gettin' into town enough—to traipse around as the local eccentric cowgirl—if a ride on our own ranch gets you that excited."

Sallie gave one of her little head-bobbing, dry chuckles, "Too true, Sis. Too true."

The second Billy shoveled in his last bite, he declared, "Mom, that was delicious. Other than a piece of pecan pie, I don't think I could eat another bite."

Sallie added, "I doubt any of us need the pie, though I'm a bit like Billy, I wouldn't turn down a small slice."

"Clearly, I left the pie in too obvious a place. It didn't even make for any suspense as to whether there was dessert or not."

"Billy beat me to the draw," Bill said. "I knew you made a pecan pie earlier, and I was going to say, 'Wouldn't a piece of coconut cream pie go good with that meal.'"

Betsy mused, "You always do like to suggest whatever side dish or dessert you know I *didn't* make."

Bill replied, "That's why you love me."

She said back to her husband, "Well, I love the whole package as it comes, I'll grant that."

Billy and I looked at each other, considering the fodder that could be made from that comment, but we both had enough sense to let it be.

Sallie issued a call for action. "Boys, I think we three should get goin' on the dishes. Our hostess has earned the rest of the night off, don't you reckon?"

"Too true. Too true." Billy and I responded in unison.

Chapter Nine

That Sunday morning, after we'd had our family service in *La Capilla de la Rosa* and a light lunch, Billy and I returned to the house for a quiet afternoon. We weren't home ten minutes when he said he had an important announcement.

"Dad says I'm way overdue giving you some vacation time. I hadn't thought about it, but he's right. You've not had a week or two off since you moved out here. I know you didn't take any vacation time while you were at the tomato farm or when you worked with Ernesto."

I replied, "Well, I hadn't thought about it either. I don't really know what I would do other than watch you work."

He continued, "I have an idea for that. You should go down to Big Bend for a week or two. You've never been, which is pretty amazing since you've lived out here almost seven years."

"I thought about going down early on, but with that old Ranger pickup of mine I had at the time, there was no way I could risk it. After that—well, life happened as you know, and I just never got it done. I would like to get down there."

He said, "You should go for your birthday."

I asked, "Am I going alone or is there some cowboy you know who might go with me? I don't know that I want to go by myself, which is kinda funny, since that's the only way I would have wanted to go just a few years back."

Billy replied, "Dad said, 'Now, Billy, don't impose yourself on his time off. If he wants you to go with him somewhere you can go, and Sallie and I will attend to the ranch—but if he wants to be alone, let the boy be alone.' He made me promise to let it be your decision."

"I want you to go."

Billy exclaimed, "Now you're talkin'! I think we should go over your birthday."

I considered the short timeline proposed. "Well that's right around the corner. Are you sure we can get away that soon?"

Billy replied, "I have the assurance of the headman himself, and the head cowgirl was standing there when he gave his okay. We're good to go next weekend if you're up for it."

"I'm up for it. Is this a 'roughing it' trip? Do we sleep in the bed of the truck and hope it doesn't rain—which it rarely does in May? Do you have a tent or tents, or do we stay in a lodge?"

He answered, "We could do any one of those. I think there is an old tent around here somewhere. Sallie would know. I have no idea if it is any good anymore. I'm not sure I'd recommend just putting a bedroll out on the ground. A rattlesnake might decide we're the warmest thing around to curl up with at night."

I replied, "Memo to self—'no bedroll on the ground.' I'm fine with either the tent or just as fine with the bed of the truck, as long as we lay something in there to smooth out the bottom. I'd just as soon not stay in the lodge. I'd like to be out in the night sky."

Billy said, "I'm gonna go in the kitchen and call Dad to let him know. How long do we wanna be gone? Two full weeks?"

I thought about it a bit and added, "Ten days at the most, but you should let him know we might be back earlier, which would not be a sign we didn't enjoy the break—just that we were ready to get back home."

"Okey-dokey," and he was off to call Bill. I soon heard from the kitchen, "Jaime! Dad wants to talk to you."

I went in the kitchen and took the phone from Billy, "Yes, sir?"

I kept the phone tight to my ear knowing Billy would want to listen in. I just smiled at him. Billy couldn't hear what his dad was saying despite his efforts to do so. I responded to Bill, "I appreciate that … yes, that's right." I gave a little chuckle and said, "Yes, I'm sure … Sounds good … yup, goodbye."

Billy said, "I assume he wanted reassurance that my tagging along on your vacation was your idea and not mine."

"You assume correctly."

Billy asked, "Was he persuaded?"

"He was," I replied. "He even said, 'I suppose the boy has earned time off as well, and you might as well have some company for the trip.'"

Billy jumped out of the kitchen chair where he was seated. "Oh, I forgot to ask about the tent."

49

He was right back on the phone, and Betsy answered. "Mom, ask Dad and Sallie if we still have that old tent around here somewhere?"

"Hang on," she replied. She was soon back. "Sallie says it should be in the storeroom of the bunkhouse. She put a new one in there when Jaime and Ernesto fixed up the place. She said the old one had fallen to pieces when she tried to move it so it would be out of their way. Are you sure you want to sleep in a tent? We may call you 'boys,' but your bones and joints may not be too happy sleeping on the ground."

Billy said, "We'll figure out some kind of padding. Tell Sallie thanks for replacing the old tent. Jaime's birthday is a week from Sunday, so I think we'll head down there the Wednesday or Thursday before that. We'll probably stay a week or ten days."

Betsy added, "I'm sure we'll see you several times before then. Goodbye, son."

Billy turned to me. "I guess you heard most of that."

"Yes, I could hear her. You seem to be falling into the perfect plan, yet again."

Then the foreman said, "We'll need to check out the Coleman stove and lantern to be sure they work, and make sure we have all the parts to the tent. We should be able to get anything we need in Alpine at the hardware store the way down if we see we need something."

"There's no time like the present, is there? Now that we're talking about doing it, I'm kind of excited. Let's go over to the bunkhouse and check everything out. We can start our list of essentials as they occur to us."

"Well, let's go!" he said enthusiastically.

We were soon at the bunkhouse and pulling everything out. Among the gear was a Porta Potti which Billy deemed gave us "all the comforts of home." When we took the tent outside and set it up, I told Billy, "This is big enough we can take those 'plus-ones' along that you wanted to take to the Cardona New Year's Eve party."

Billy was having none of it. "We wouldn't want to have the stress of vacationing with girls we've never traveled with before. They might get on our nerves."

I played along, "It could be they'd even put us in a disagreeable mood, and we've never been in one of those before."

"That's right!" he said. "And on top of that they'd almost surely give us something to argue about."

"Well, we can't have that," I agreed. I guess it's just the foreman and his ranch hand all to themselves in this big tent."

"That sounds right!" Billy exclaimed.

I don't know why I looked forward to the trip as much as I did. We already lived among beautiful desert mountains. We had a couple of springs on the ranch that made for nice pools of water. Here, we could ride for miles as we saw fit while we wouldn't have the horses with us down in Big Bend, and I would be spending my days and nights with the same person I see every day. Still, I really was looking forward to it now that we'd committed to the time and place of my first real vacation.

We had dinner with the family that next Tuesday as we'd decided we'd head down on Wednesday. One thing about living in this vast part of West Texas is that there are few main roads. Usually, you have one or, at most, two options on how to get to a place—the shortest route or the roundabout way. You can't describe one as scenic and the other direct. The drive from Fort Davis to Alpine is both the most direct and very scenic. The only other way is to go to Marfa and then over to Alpine—which you'd only do if you wanted to stop in Marfa—but it's no less scenic between Marfa and Alpine than it is from Fort Davis to Alpine. I even like the wide plateau of the drive between Fort Davis and Marfa with its small mountain range of the Mano Prieto Mountains and the *Puertacitas* and Haystacks behind them. Barely visible in spots is Mitre Peak, which is so apparent on the drive from Fort Davis to Alpine.

Bill wanted to know what route Billy had in mind for our trip to Big Bend. He inquired of Billy, "You haven't been down there since you were a boy, unless you went while you lived in Van Horn. Do you remember how to get there?"

Billy answered, "I did go down there several times over the years, and I took the three main ways of getting there one time or another. Whichever way I went on each trip, I either took the river road going or coming—but never both in the same trip with one

51

exception. A few years back when I was taking the river road to get there, the wildflowers were incredible. I'd never seen them so prolific. And those Big Bend bluebonnets were over a foot tall. The whole park was full of wildflowers too, but I had to take the river road back to Van Horn just to see all the flowers one more time."

Bill noted, "You'll be past the wildflower season by now, but you should still see prickly pear and ocotillo in bloom. I love the ocotillo down there."

Sallie mused, "You keep talkin' like that, and I'm going to stow away in the back of the truck. It's been *years* since I've been down there."

"Y'all could make a day trip down for Jaime's birthday on Sunday," Billy suggested, "and we could meet in the Basin for lunch at the restaurant."

I thought I should make it clear that I would be okay with Billy's addition to the agenda. "That would be fine by me."

Betsy responded, "I'd really like that."

Bill added, "Well, Sallie, it looks like you won't have to stow away this trip at least. I don't see any reason we couldn't make a day of it on the 6th."

Billy continued, "As to the route this time, I think we'll take the river road going and come back up to Alpine instead of going the longer way through Marathon. That way Jaime can get a good look at Cathedral Mountain."

"I'll miss our chapel on Sunday morning," Betsy noted, "so we might take the opposite route. I'll see Cathedral on the drive down. It is my favorite mountain."

Sallie chuckled, "Jaime, I know you think you have seen a lot of rock and mountains living here, but you're in for a real treat. Daddy always said it looked to him like God took all the leftover rock from creation and dumped it all around the Rio Grande and Big Bend. You'll see what he meant when you go along that river road from Presidio and into the park."

Bill asked Billy, "Do you remember how to get to Cattail Falls? As I recall, they don't exactly advertise that spot the same way they do the two big canyons."

Billy answered, "You'd better jot down where I need to turn if you remember—I'm not sure I do. It's been a *long* time since I've gone up in there."

Betsy interjected, "You know, your father has a mind like a steel trap when it comes to directions and like a carrier pigeon when it comes to navigation. You could drop him anywhere and he'd find his way home."

Bill agreed, "I am pretty good at that, I have to admit."

Sallie joked, "Betsy and I can get lost in Alpine—that's how bad we are at navigating. Jaime, you won't want to ask either of us how to get from point 'A' to point 'B'. The Schlatters seem to have a built-in compass we Geermanns were denied."

I asked Billy, "As pertains to directions are you a Geermann or a Schlatter?"

Billy replied, "I've got a pretty good Schlatter compass built in, but as to remembering directions, I'm more Geermann it would seem."

As we were getting ready to leave, Bill noted, "We'll plan to be in the Basin no later than eleven. We might want to be in the restaurant well before noon in case they get busy. You don't need to be up there by eleven. We'll sit and enjoy the view down the canyon and out to the Chisos Window until you show up."

Billy jested, "We could all work off lunch hiking up Emory Peak."

Bill stated flatly, "You young'uns can hike up on our behalf. I never have taken that hike. It always looked too far up for my spindly legs to carry me."

As we were heading out the door, the ever-vigilant mother cautioned, "Now, you boys remember to always have water with you. You hear of young people dying down there who wander off on a trail and get dehydrated and disoriented."

Billy reassured her, "We will, Mother—and it's on those trails when the Schlatter compass comes in handy."

Chapter Ten

It must be said that one of the reasons Billy and I get along as well as we do is how much we both appreciate silence. I imagined the long ride down to Big Bend with Chuy or Ernesto, where the AM radio would be cranked up the whole time. I could count on one hand the number of times Billy and I had turned on the radio while we were in the truck. We even had a CD player in his latest truck, but rarely played anything except the occasional cowboy songs or my *Beethoven 7th* that I still hung onto.

I offered to drive, but Billy said I needed to be free to gawk around as we drove from Presidio to Big Bend. He also announced, "We're gonna leave real early, so we can watch the sun come up as we drive down."

We do get a lot of amazing sunrises in this part of the world with pink skies that stretch across the entire horizon. The cosmos must have gotten Billy's memo to make this particular morning special for our trip, as the pinks and purples on the drive as we got past Marfa were spectacular. Neither one of us said a word. We just stared out at the beauty of it all.

At one point he spoke long enough to say, "You see that one mountain there by itself all lit up by the sun? That's Cathedral. You get a lot closer to it on the road from Alpine."

"I can certainly see why it's called Cathedral."

When we got into Presidio, he spoke again, "We might as well have breakfast while we're here. I know a good spot to get chorizo and eggs and refried beans. Their homemade tortillas are as good as the Cardonas', and their salsa will kick your butt."

"That sounds good to me," I said.

It was as good as he'd remembered. Back in the truck, we returned to our silent-selves as he drove along the Rio Grande. We'd stop at every wide shoulder just to get out and take it all in. We even saw several aoudad sheep with their big horns up on the side of one of the mountains on the US side.

About four stops in I said to Billy, "I see what your grandpa Geermann meant about God dumping all the leftover rock down here."

He replied, "The rock will change from the browns and reds here to chalky white as we get closer to the park. Then the park has some of everything.

"By the way, I know we talk more about Grandpa Geermann just because I look like him and I'm a little crazy like he was, but I have to give Grandma Geermann all the credit for appreciating silence. She was truly a contemplative soul. What Mom and Sallie have of that comes from her."

I said, "I don't know how crazy your grandpa was, but I'm pretty sure you got more than a little from him as crazy as you are. You do have your contemplative moments though."

When we got back in the truck to head further on our journey, he spoke to say, "It's odd when you think about it. The quietest people in our lives often shape us the most, and yet we rarely think to even call them out as being important. I guess that's true for every quiet soul in the world. They go by mostly unnoticed, and yet I can't imagine being Billy Schlatter without the quiet side I know I got from Grandma Geermann."

As he said those words, I saw a tear run down his cheek. I, and he, let the silence speak all the consolation needed of the moment for this gentle and generous remembrance of his grandmother.

As we drove into Terlingua, Billy wanted to stop and show me the cemetery which, it must be said, is not like most—including beer cans on certain occupants' graves. As we wandered around, he was thinking ahead to the next stop. "Now we'll have to make a decision as we come into the park. Are we going to camp in the Chisos Basin, Rio Grande Village, or Cottonwood, or do we get a permit to camp rough out in the park?"

I replied, "I'll have to go with whatever you think. We'll be here long enough, maybe we could do a couple nights rough camping at some point. And just from what I've heard of the Basin, that sounds pretty good to me too."

Billy asked, "Since they're coming down on Sunday, why don't we start in the Basin and then work out from there where we go next?"

"Sounds like a plan," I said.

As we entered the park I added, "I remember reading that this is both the largest and the least visited national park in the system."

Billy confirmed, "That's right, and the longer people don't find it, the better for us."

We quickly went back to our silent-selves until he started to wind down the switchbacks going down into the Basin.

Then he laughed, "I bet Tanya would like to drive that new dump truck of hers down this road just to prove she can."

"I have no doubt she'd do it without dropping a tire off on the berm," I replied.

Billy jested, "She loves that truck. I can't tell if she loves Mando more or not."

I laughed, "For now, anyhow, I think it's a pretty close call. Could be as long as Mando behaves he's got the slight edge."

We picked a spot as far away from other campers as we could and set up camp. There was a burn-ban, which we expected would be the case this time of year, so there wouldn't be any campfire to sit around and enjoy at night—but as Billy rightly pointed out, "All we have to do is look up and enjoy the stars on these cloudless May nights."

And, so we did exactly that the first night. By the time we turned in, Billy exclaimed, "Damn, this ground is harder than I remembered! Mom's right, we're gettin' old."

I replied, "They say Mother Teresa slept on a little rolled-up mat wherever she went—even if she stayed in a hotel she'd sleep on the floor."

Billy said, "A lifetime of habit, I guess. Our habits are more to a Sealy Posturepedic."

"That's for sure."

Then in classic Billy fashion added, "We've never slept together before. You think you can trust me to stay in my own sleeping bag?"

I noted, "You tell John and James we're shacked up full-time. I'm sure they probably think that's true."

Billy said, "I noticed, even you add your 'of a kind' to my telling of that. You kinda like keeping them guessing as well, don't you?"

I chuckled, "I suppose I do, truth be told. I kinda like adopting your and Sallie's notion of letting people label as they see fit while confusing them at the same time."

"It is one of our charms," Billy agreed.

"Well, all I can say is if you end up in my sleeping bag, I'd better enjoy it!"

He smiled, "We'll see where the night takes us."

It took us exactly where I expected. He stayed in his sleeping bag, and I stayed in mine. By morning it was chilly, and we let the sun wake us up.

Billy muttered, "I'm in no hurry to get out of this warm sleeping bag. It's pretty chilly."

"That old *sol* will warm up the morning soon enough—quicker than it will warm up this tent. I'll make breakfast, so we can head out on whatever adventure you have planned for the day."

He said, "I thought we'd drive over to *Santa Elena* today. It could be we'll stop at Cattail Falls too while we're over on that side of the park—or we might just do that another day. We'll see how long we want to hike around the canyon."

"That sounds good to me," I reassured him.

We had packed to have one main meal a day and, of course, some peanut butter and sweet pickle sandwiches to take along with our water jugs on any hiking trips.

We weren't the only ones in the canyon, but it could hardly be described as overrun with tourists. We'd occasionally pass someone going or coming, and we took our jolly old time just sitting on rocks and staring at the tall, sheer cliffs that define the place. We'd not said a word since we arrived two hours earlier.

Finally Billy spoke, "Well, what do you think?"

"I think whatever it is about nature that feeds me, I'm being well fed on this trip. What a world for any awake enough to see it."

We sat there in silence a long time, and then I opened the little cooler we'd lugged along and handed Billy a peanut butter sandwich plus a little surprise I'd brought along. In honor of his dad, I'd packed some Twinkies.

When I handed him the Twinkie, he looked at me with a big grin, held it up and said, "Here's to ya, Dad."

By the time our Sunday visitors arrived, we'd been to *Santa Elena*, Cattail Falls and the hot springs. Plus we'd driven down some of the roads off into nowhere. We thought we'd probably hike Emery and for sure we were going to spend a day in *Boquillos* Canyon. Billy hoped we could even cross the border and have lunch in the little village. We weren't at all sure exactly what the Border Patrol was doing these days for those poor people on the Mexican side who had long depended on the US side for their provisions, and the few visitors who rowed across to support their livings. We'd heard they would have to row half way across the Rio Grande and someone on the US side would hand them their goods.

Billy fussed, "You know it's some dumb-ass bureaucrat making the decisions when they cut off a harmless place like that village for fear of terrorism when they are hours away from anywhere in their own country. It's just ridiculous."

"Surely they've eased up on that by now."

Billy said, "I guess we'll see when we get there. Last time I was down there, the 'border was closed.'"

"One little shallow ribbon of water to divide people. It doesn't take much to keep us divided, does it?" I asked.

Billy replied with the bare truth of things, "Law and order can only see the hard line unless it's the enforcers who want to cut a corner for themselves; then that line gets mighty flexible."

"You're sure right about that."

Then he added, "It's too bad some of the rank, and file who know the rules are stupid, have to enforce them or lose their jobs. It would be nice if a little common sense came along from the head of governments once in a while. Best I can tell, they're just as dumb in Austin as they are in DC."

"Best I can tell, you're right," was all I said.

Billy asked, "You know why shit-asses keep getting elected, don't you?"

I had my theory and was eager to see if mine aligned with his. "I have a theory; what's yours?"

"Because dumb-asses keep reelecting them."

"That's my theory too," I said.

Since we were already camping in the Basin, we were up at the restaurant sitting outside looking out over the canyon beneath us when our "company" arrived for their visit. Betsy came bearing cupcakes for my birthday.

I asked, "Did you have a nice drive down?"

Sallie replied, "None of us said a word. I suppose that sums it up as well as anything."

"We had the same kind of drive coming in," I noted. "I see what your dad meant about all the leftover rock getting dumped in the Big Bend."

"It's something, isn't it?" Sallie responded.

They sat on the bench next to us and just enjoyed the view before we all headed in to lunch.

Bill said as we walked in, "I hope they still got that same broasted chicken they used to have. I like the smaller pieces instead of the 'bigger-is-better' that every place else seems to sell anymore."

Then he asked, "I guess since you're here, Border Patrol didn't arrest you for swimming over to *Boquillas*."

Billy updated them on our adventures to date and that we planned to move to rough country that night and visit *Boquillas* probably on Tuesday.

Then he added, "We're thinking we'll probably drive home on Thursday. We're both missing our Sealy mattresses."

Betsy smiled, "I remember someone suggesting such might be the case. Age creeps up quickly, doesn't it boys?"

I replied, "I'll speak for both of us and say, it more like leapt on us on this trip. Billy said, 'If we do this again we'll have to sneak along air mattresses.'"

Billy picked it up for himself adding, "I'd hate for anyone to see two gen-u-ine cowboys blowing up their air mattresses. Their image of the Texas cowboy would be shattered for life."

Sallie laughed, "Your grandpa would get a real kick out of hearing you say that. He'd always say, 'You'll never catch me sleeping on the ground when I got a perfectly good bed at home.'"

Billy continued, "We figure the ground in rough camping isn't going to be any harder than it is here in the Basin, so we might as well escape all signs of civilization for a couple days before going back to the ranch."

Bill said, "We'll expect a full report upon your return."

He took one look at the menu and stated, "Well, my chicken appears to be on the menu. We'll see if some new cook has ruined it or not."

He had the waitress describe it before ordering—and when he decided it probably was the same, he ordered it, and we all did as well. Upon its arrival and his first bite, he said, "It's as good as I remember."

Then over lunch, Billy decided he needed to share with them our conversation the first night in the tent, ending it with me saying if he crawled in, I'd better enjoy it.

Bill shook his head. "Good lord. I'm sure Jaime's thrilled you shared that story with us. Jaime's right, you're a mess."

"But I'm his mess," Billy replied.

"Thank the Lord he's got more patience than Job is all I can say," Bill reflected.

Sallie chuckled, "I'll speak for Bill and say we're glad you aren't taking two full weeks. We've both gotten soft in our retirement and forgot what a day's work felt like. I go to bed about as soon as supper's over."

Betsy added, "You've never heard such moaning and groaning as these two have made just these few days you've been gone."

Billy exclaimed, "Here I was hoping we could make this an annual affair!"

Bill noted, "We'll endure a few more years if you two take off once a year. We may moan and groan, but we're not on death's door just yet."

Betsy declared, "It's time for cupcakes!"

She brought out one candle, lit it and set in front of me. Our waitress saw it and summoned the one waiter in the place. He came over, asked my name and sang, with his beautiful voice, "Happy Birthday."

I said to him, "I certainly didn't expect that. Thank you. You have quite a voice."

He replied, "It won't pay the rent, but I enjoy singing."

Sallie smiled brightly at the young man. "That's a gift, my son. That's a gift. It's nice of you to share it with strangers."

After lunch they were off for their drive home via the river road, and we were off to get registered for the rough camping spot Billy had picked out in our earlier travels. We'd broken down the campsite before heading up to the restaurant and soon had everything set up at the new site. There was complete silence. There wasn't even any grass tall enough to make any noise from the gentle breeze.

Billy observed, "We've sure lucked into good weather. I was afraid we'd have wind all week to blow us silly."

I added, "We don't need the wind to do that, but I'm glad, too, that it's been as calm as it's been."

When we got to *Boquillas* the next day, we opted not to temp fate and cross the border. It did seem they'd relaxed the border somewhat, but not to what it once was, according to Billy.

Billy looked at *Boquillas* on one side and us on the other. "Now just imagine the dumbass who tells everyone we gotta spend billions on a border wall to keep us safe."

I shook my head, "As we've already determined, dumbasses abound."

Chapter Eleven

Other than doing a quick mail drop on our way back from Big Bend, we didn't see Bill, Betsy or Sallie until the Sunday of our return. Jean and Mary-Alice were there for our Sunday chapel service, and we all agreed to make lunch a mini-potluck for something different. I decided I'd try to get creative, and I said I'd take care of dessert. I found a recipe for Crêpes Suzette in one of Grandma Geermann's old cookbooks, and I was surprised to see we had all the ingredients I needed without running to town.

Billy on hearing my plan, stated, "It sounds fancy for us ranch folk, but it does look like something you or I could master first time out the gate."

"Only time will tell for sure if that is true. I'm not sure what I'll do as a backup plan, but we're going to try to make a batch on Saturday to see how they come out."

I had an audience the entire time I was working on them. When it came time to put in the Grand Marnier, Billy said, "This much I know, if you don't get that warm enough you're gonna end up with crêpes cocktails instead of a dessert."

I smiled, "We both like Grand Marnier, so that might not be so bad."

He laughed, "Mom's eyes will water up and pop out of her head when she feels that liquor heat up her throat."

I noted, "They make a point of getting it warm in the instructions. We'll see if we can light it up without burning down the house."

Billy was in the pantry long enough to come out with a big piece of white butcher paper and then disappeared for a minute. He came back with it taped like a tube, walked over and placed it on my head.

"Here you go chef. Light her up!"

"It actually fits my head. Lucky guess," I noted.

He replied, "I just put it inside your cowboy hat and taped it up."

"Good thinking. But if it's okay, I think I'll leave it here tomorrow night. I wouldn't want to upstage your mom."

That comment put Billy to thinking. "I don't know why you still refer to them as 'your mom and your dad.' Do they have to adopt you legally for you to call them Mom and Dad?"

I answered, "Not to put too fine a point on it, but I know they are not going to adopt me—I'm a little past adoption age. They aren't legally my in-laws and your mom calls your dad the same thing I do all the time—Bill."

Billy noted, "He usually just calls her Mother."

"And she may say 'your father,' but I never hear her call him anything to his face but Bill. What works for her works for me."

"Fair enough," Billy acknowledged.

Then I picked up the pan and announced, "Stand back! I'm lighting it up!"

The Grand Marnier sent up a gentle blue flame about a foot high and slowly burned itself out.

Billy said, "I'd guess you got the bulk of the alcohol burned off. Well done, Chef Cruz. Now what comes next?"

"Now we eat 'em!"

Billy suggested, "Set the pan right here on the bar—no point in dirtying two plates. We'll just eat 'em hot out of the pan."

"Okay by me." I handed him a fork and large spoon, noting, "If it's good, we'll want to eat up all that sauce."

We both dug in. Billy barely stopped long enough to say, "Dad might give up Twinkies once-and-for-all if you make these with any regularity. These are good!"

"Not half-bad," I said. "And they're easy to make. I can do all the crêpes here and then just put it together when we're ready for dessert. It won't take me but a few minutes."

Billy speculated, "Mom will be surprised to see what came out of the kitchen on this side of the ranch."

I said, "She probably thinks it will be peanut butter cookies."

Billy asserted, "There's nothing wrong with peanut butter cookies! If you want to make a batch right now, I'll stay and watch and test them as they come out of the oven."

"I think we'll be sugared up enough with these. Maybe some other time."

We arrived the next day just as Jean and Mary-Alice were getting out of their car. Before anyone even had a chance to say hello Billy hollered, "What'd you bring me to eat?"

Jean called back, "A big kale salad."

Billy replied, "Very funny. What'd ya really bring?"

Mary-Alice, said, "She's not kidding—a big kale salad."

Jean added, "I've made my own dressing and brought Craisons and sliced almonds and Mandarin oranges to put in with it. I just want Dad to try it."

"I told her not to get her hopes up," Mary-Alice replied.

Jean asked, "What'd you bring? Jaime seems to be the only one carrying anything."

Billy answered for us, "He made crêpes for Crêpes Suzette. We tried them out last night. They're pretty good."

"Sounds fancy," Jean said. "I always wondered what they were. I guess we'll find out."

Billy laughed, "Liquor and flames are involved. It will be a whole new experience in Mom's kitchen."

As we went in the house, Billy hollered, "Anybody home? The entertainment is here as are Jaime, Jean and Mary-Alice."

Jean and I headed with our things to the kitchen and Billy and Mary-Alice joined Bill and Sallie on the porch.

Betsy took one look at the salad and the makings to go with it, "The way you cut up the kale and with all that on it, your dad might not know what it is—if you don't tell him."

"That was my plan," Jean replied. "I want to see if he actually can tell it's kale."

I suggested, "Keep the canned tuna away and you might be safe. It certainly looks like it will be good."

Jean asked, "Mom, do you know what Jaime brought for dessert?"

"I haven't a clue," she answered.

"He's made Crêpes Suzette—fancy!"

I clarified it, "Thus far I've made the crêpes. The rest comes together when we are ready for dessert. It won't take me but a few minutes when the time comes."

Betsy asked, "Have you been holding out on chef skills we didn't know about?"

I replied, "No, but you did nudge me to give some effort beyond peanut butter and sweet pickle sandwiches."

Jean interjected, "I love those!"

I added, "After living on them as long as I did, you'd think I'd be sick of them, but I still like them."

Billy was back to check on the goings on in the kitchen. "Is that a Geermann-Schlatter roast I smell, Mom?"

She responded, "Your nose is working, and Sallie peeled enough potatoes for an army."

"Mashed potatoes, roast and gravy—can't beat that!" Billy declared. "Dad can always eat those and skip the salad."

"Dad's gonna love this salad," Jean asserted. "You just hide and watch."

Betsy counseled, "You two talk about it any louder, and he'll know what's in it before he ever gets to the table."

We went to the chapel for our morning service and were back to finish preparing for lunch. Bill and Sallie were out on the porch and the rest of us went with Betsy into the kitchen.

"Billy, go tell your aunt to come and mash her potatoes. They're ready to go."

He didn't quite go and do as requested. Instead he pointed his head in Sallie's general direction and hollered, "Cowgirl, get in here and get to mashin' these taters! Your sister's orders."

We heard a faint, "I'm on my way."

With the food on the table, we all took our usual seats. Betsy said, "We always ask Jaime to say the blessing. Anyone else want to volunteer?"

Sallie piped in, "I'll give Jaime the day off."

We all bowed our heads. She continued, "I'd like us to hold hands."

We joined our hands in a circle around the table.

With the love at this table, Lord, all we need is our constant awareness of your presence in our lives and in the rich abundance of your creation. May we be mindful stewards of all you've given us. Amen.

We all repeated a soft, and certainly heartfelt, "Amen." Billy, who always sits between me and Sallie, put his arm around his aunt with a gentle squeeze and didn't say a word. His Geermann contemplation knew silence was the best thing for the moment.

We were expected to recount our vacation, which we did. Billy started by sharing with them our conversation on the river road about Grandma Geermann and the impact of the quiet souls who so often seem to go unnoticed in our noisy world. He also said how much that part of him was passed along to him by both his mother and Sallie.

It was such a gentle and serious recollection that we all sat tuned into his every word. We all tried to take a few nibbles to appear we were going on with our eating, but really we were too moved to focus on eating.

Sallie looked at her younger sister and seemed to speak for both, saying, "Billy, I'm not sure your mother could get the words out right now to say what I know is in her heart, because it's in my heart as well. I had no idea anyone understood our mother the way you just recounted the impact of her on your life. To borrow your words, she was indeed the most gentle and generous soul I've ever known."

I saw that Bill had taken the least little bit of salad when it was passed. I guess he thought we'd paid tribute enough, for the time, to Mother Geermann as he stated in his matter-of-fact tone, "Daughter, if you think you can fool me on what's in this salad, you're wrong. Everything is good but those greens. I don't know whether the cattle would eat 'em or not, but they don't have to worry about me sneaking them into their feed."

Billy and I recounted the rest of our trip to Big Bend, and he of course, had to include a retelling of the first night's sleeping bag account for Jean and Mary-Alice. Bill, of course, had to add his "Good lord" to the retelling as he had to the first.

I added, "I enjoyed every bit of our trip, but nothing more so than our nights of rough camping—away from every other human being. One day, we didn't even leave camp."

Billy interjected to say, "Mother, I know you're wondering about not leaving camp and how we might have dealt with bodily functions."

Betsy responded, "I was trying not to."

Billy carried on with his account. "Sallie's camp gear even includes a Porta Potti which we just set in the bed of the pickup and communed with nature as nature called."

She gave a little shake of her head saying, "Very reassuring."

I continued with my own recollections, "Every evening, we'd sit with Billy's harmonica and my guitar and we'd serenade ourselves and any bird or bug or critter that happened to be within earshot."

Billy added, "I swear, when we started playing, birds would come and perch on the yuccas and ocotillo just to listen."

I agreed, "It really did seem that way. I told Billy, all they probably ever hear from intruders these days are boom boxes and cranked up radios. They appreciated our quiet melodies."

Billy added, "Mom, we didn't even sing 'Wall Street *Bandidos*.' Jaime said, 'Birds aren't gonna know anything about Wall Street, so they wouldn't know what we were singing about.'"

Sallie's reflective-self offered her take. "I do believe nature joins us in the gentle rhythm of life if we can just have the gratitude it takes to get in symbiosis with her."

Billy smiled and touched Sallie's shoulder. "Aunt Sallie, you do have beautiful thoughts."

Sallie gave her customary head-shaking chuckle and said, "Billy, I'm leaving all of them in my will to you except for the ones I take with me. You be sure to take good care of them."

Besty perked up at her own recollection. "Come to think of it, Sallie and I had our own big adventure to tell you about from our trip to Alpine."

Sallie said flatly, "If this adventure is what I think it is, it wasn't an adventure and needn't be told on my account."

Betsy continued, "We were having lunch when a man, who looked like Santa Claus, came up to us—little wire-rim glasses, white beard and even a little poochybelly."

"Lord, here we go," Sallie said.

Betsy continued, "The man came up to Sallie, grinning from ear to ear. 'Why, Sallie Geermann—as I live and breathe,' the man said. I could see right away Sallie knew who it was, though I didn't have a clue. She said, 'Hello Norman. It's been a few years, but I'd know that voice anywhere. What are you doing in town?' And he said, ' just moved back here over the weekend. Must be, I was supposed to run into you first thing. How's your husband doing?'"

Sallie answered for herself, "I told him, I didn't ever have one and never went lookin' for one."

Betsy added, "Fess-up, Sister. It turns out they were high school sweethearts."

Sallie continued, "*Were* is the key word there. He went off to UT Austin and was never heard from again. And no, he didn't leave me devastated by his departure. He was amusing enough, but I can hardly call him my one great, long-lost love."

"He made it pretty clear you were his," Betsy noted. "I believe the way he put it was, 'My wife never could compare to you, Sallie Faye.'"

Sallie shook her head, "Lord, he even remembered that middle name. He made it equally clear he'd been divorced from her for fifteen years. I guess he didn't want me thinkin' he was committing adultery in his heart right then and there."

Billy asked, "When's the first date? You gonna invite him out here on Friday nights? You know Jaime stayed over the first night he came to dinner. Could be Santa Claus will do the same."

Sallie put to rest any such notion, saying, "Norman will not be spending the night on his first date. I'm not as easy to get as you."

Jean asked, "But you are going to give the poor guy a second chance, aren't you?"

Sallie exclaimed, "I've never discussed my personal affairs so much in all my life! I have no idea. As I say, he was amusing enough. I would be open to hearing what he's been doing for the past forty years. It won't take me long to fill him in on what I've been doing."

Betsy added, "I can confirm, phone numbers were exchanged."

To that Sallie responded, "And I can confirm, I'm a whole lot more excited that a curve-billed thrasher has taken up residence outside my quarters. I woke up to her song just this morning. I said to her, 'Well, hello there. I'm glad to see your momma and daddy finally sent some kin over here to get settled in.'"

I said, "I've noticed the swallows have found new territory here as well. I can confirm in both cases, we are still well attended to next door."

Betsy said, "And I can confirm those swallows still think every door needs a nest above it, but I do love watching them swoop around all day. I'm not sure there is a happier creature on the planet."

"Beyond those around this table, that might well be true," Bill offered.

Billy pointed towards the door. "Dad, you left the patio door open. Look what just walked in."

It was a cactus wren. I reflected, "He heard us talking about those other birds and thought he'd better remind us of his presence."

The little curious bird walked in about three feet, looked this way and that, and then hopped back outside.

Billy created an imaginary conversation with the bird. "He's gone back to the Mrs. and reported, 'Not a single cactus in there to sit on! Didn't look like home to me at all.' Then Mrs. Wren said back to him, 'They are fun to watch, but I wouldn't want to live with them—too cooped up for me. They'd be wantin' our little bitty eggs for omelettes."

Bill replied, as though it was a serious notion, "That'd take a lotta wren eggs to get one omelette."

Billy joked, "We could stretch it some by adding lots of kale to it."

Jean exclaimed, "You're a big help!"

Billy added, "I did have my wager that you couldn't fool Dad with that salad of yours."

Mary-Alice said, "Jean held out her long-shot odds against the rest of us."

Billy pronounced, "Jaime, you need to get in that kitchen and light up your dessert."

Of course, I did as the foreman instructed and presented my first public offering of Crêpes Suzette. I received modest applause as the flames ascended and the highest compliment possible from Bill. "Why these could put me to givin' up Twinkies for good."

Chapter Twelve

Back at the house, Billy said, "Well, ain't that something? Sallie's old flame has come back to her."

"She might not see it quite like that. You always wondered if she talked to you about regret from personal experience, or if she just didn't live by regret. After hearing that conversation, I'd definitely say it is the latter."

Billy asked, "Do you think they might rekindle a romance enough to actually fall in love?"

"I don't know," I replied. "I do believe it's never too late."

Billy added, "There was a time you'd never have believed it could happen at all for some people—including yourself."

"That is all too true," I acknowledged.

The phone rang, and Billy answered it. "Hello, Foreman Schlatter speakin' ... Yes, I believe he's here somewhere. Please hold."

Billy handed me the phone. "It's Zoey Mendoza."

Reflexively, I made a rather startled face.

"Zoey? Would it be okay if I put you on speaker? That was Billy who answered the phone in case you were wondering who Foreman Schlatter is. If you'd rather I not, that's okay."

Given her okay, I hit the speaker button. "Hi, Billy. Jaime, I have Mark on speaker on this end."

Mark piped in, "Hi, guys."

We said in unison, "Hi, Mark."

Then I asked, "How y'all doing?"

Zoey laughed, "It's hilarious to hear you say, 'Y'all.' You are an indoctrinated Texan, that's for sure. We're doing great. How is life on the ranch?"

"It's wonderful!" I added, "We just got back from a camping trip to Big Bend National Park. We had a great time. If you get out here, I hope we can spend a day or two down there just to show you some of the park."

Mark responded, "I'd love that, and I'm sure Zoey would too."

Zoey clarified, "I think we can safely say when and not if. That's why we're calling. When we saw how flying there still requires a long drive and driving there is quite a trip, we checked into Amtrak. We were surprised that it actually stops in Alpine. That's not that far from you, is it?"

Billy replied, "As we measure miles in Texas, it's right around the corner. We could certainly pick you up at the station."

Zoey asked, "Would we overstay our welcome if we spent two weeks over Christmas and New Year's?"

I exclaimed, "That would be wonderful!"

Mark said, "We needed to confirm now in order to get a sleeper on the train before they sell out. We may still have to shift a day or two on our plans until we get our tickets confirmed. We'll let you know as soon as we know for sure."

Billy noted, "I guess you know the Sunset Limited only rolls through three days a week."

"Yes, we saw that," Zoey replied. That's another reason we thought we'd better get moving on buying the tickets."

Mark asked, "Billy, are you really the ranch foreman?"

Billy clarified, "It's an honorific title I've inherited since Dad retired. I really only have one regular hand to boss around, and he sasses back about as often as he follows orders."

Zoey said, "I gather that one unruly hand is my brother."

I replied, "You gather correctly, though I'm about as unruly as a Cistercian monk."

Billy joked, "I think Jaime was heading for a life in the monastery before we Schlatters took him in, but we've turned him into a gen-u-ine cowboy instead."

I waited for Billy to make some comment about our "shacking up together," but he seemed to be avoiding some of his more playful comments.

Mark said, "I'm going to get off here and let Zoey talk to her brother."

Billy added, "Likewise here."

Billy left the kitchen to leave me on the phone with Zoey. We talked about an hour without dredging up the past. We just caught up on our lives. Neither one of us mentioned the three estranged members of our family. I wondered how we would talk about them when Zoey and Mark were here, or if we would even then.

After I hung up, I told Billy, "You were quite restrained for you."

"I didn't want to scare them off before they get here. I'll have two full weeks to get well acquainted."

"Yes, you will," I agreed, "and I'm pretty sure they will find you as amusing and endearing as the rest of us do."

Two weeks later when we were in town for the pantry distribution, we skipped lunch at the Slo Poke Cafe. Ernesto and Rosalinda were off on a trip to visit Chuy. We stopped for our usual mail run.

As he went through the mail, he stated, "We have a letter from Mark Mendoza." He didn't ask whether to open it or not—I heard him rip into it. "It's their itinerary. They arrive Monday, December 17 at 1:28 PM and leave on Thursday, January 3 at 1:05 PM."

I laughed, "I love those Amtrak schedule times. They print those schedules as though they run trains like the Swiss, right down to the minute. That'll be the day. I've got enough experience with Amtrak in California to know their schedule is way more miss than hit. We'll have to call throughout the day. We certainly don't want to sit up in the truck for twelve hours waiting for them to roll in. The Sunset Limited has been known to be a day behind schedule coming into LA. Still, one of the things I liked about California was riding up and down the coast on the train."

Billy replied, "I never have ridden the train. I'd like to sometime."

I added, "You're not going to get me to California anytime soon, but maybe we could take the train to New Orleans sometime. I've never been there and would like to visit."

Billy exclaimed, "Mardi Gras—here we come!"

"Yeah, I can see the two of us in those crowds of thousands down in the French Quarter. How about a quick trip over your birthday? It won't be hot that time of year."

Billy responded, "Two vacations in one year. I'm not sure the foreman can see his way clear to approving that."

I reflected, "I wonder how long the trip is from Alpine to New Orleans."

"Mark included the full schedule for the Sunset Limited. It shows it here. No matter which of the three days we leave, we pull out of Alpine early afternoon and arrive into New Orleans twenty-five hours later."

I noted, "We might want a sleeper car, too, like Mark and Zoey are getting."

Billy continued, "According to their tickets, they have a bedroom coming and going. I see in the brochure they included that they also have what they call roomettes—with two seats that face each other, and then the seats make into a bed and another bed folds down from above. The bedrooms have their own bath and the roomettes share a bath somewhere in the same car."

I suggested, "A roomette would be fine by me. I'm sure those bedrooms are pretty pricey."

Billy said, "Gosh, I remember how as soon as we talked about going to Big Bend you got excited even though you'd not thought about taking a vacation. I'm already excited about a quick trip to New Orleans."

"We'll have to coax our vacation staff to take over twice in one year," I said. "Could be that won't be too popular."

"You'll recall we weren't gone our full two weeks, so I don't think they'll flap about it."

I suggested, "We'd better follow Mark and Zoey's lead and make plans right away if we're going to go in November."

Billy concluded, "We'll talk to them tomorrow at lunch, and assuming we have our chores covered, we'll call Amtrak when we get back home and see what our options are."

"That sounds good to me," I said.

When we brought up the subject the next day, Bill asked, "Did we ever tell you what we did for our honeymoon?"

Billy replied, "You'd think that is something I would know, but if I ever did, I don't remember."

Betsy said, "I'm not sure we ever told any of you kids though I don't know why. We went to New Orleans on the Sunset Limited."

Bill added, "I enjoyed the train as much as I did our time in the French Quarter. When you're in New Orleans you almost forget you are in the US."

Betsy continued, "We were late leaving Alpine and late getting into New Orleans. And we left New Orleans almost on time and got into Alpine early. You have to be sure your hotel knows you're coming on Amtrak in case you arrive in the middle of the night. You don't want to get there and not have a room."

Sallie sat quietly as we discussed trains and New Orleans. Finally, she offered, "I never have gone on the train. That sounds like a nice trip."

Billy asked, "Why don't you come along? You could even bring Santa Claus."

Sallie stated in no uncertain terms, "Why don't we forget Santa Claus for now."

"Sallie, if you want to go, I can handle things for the few days y'all are gonna be gone," Bill assured her.

Sallie asked, "Jaime, since the trip was your idea for Billy's birthday, are you up for a cowgirl ridin' along?"

"I'm not only up for it, I think it would be great to have you come with us."

Billy laid out the options. "Sallie, it's a twenty-five hour trip each way if they are close to being on time. They have bedrooms, roomettes and coach seats. According to Jaime, the coach seats are wide with lots of leg room but don't make into a bed the way the roomettes do."

She asked, "What do you boys have in mind?"

He answered, "We were thinking a roomette, but we're not too high-and-mighty to ride in coach if you'd rather do that."

Sallie replied, "You don't have to worry about keeping me company on the train ride. We can always eat together. I'd be good gettin' my own roomette, so we can all have a bed to sleep in."

I said, "We'll let you know what we work out when we call Amtrak later today."

Betsy assured us. "You're going to have a good time. Bill, we might want to think about a second honeymoon there one of these days."

All Bill said was, "As long as it's not in the heat of summer or during Mardi Gras, I could be persuaded."

Chapter Thirteen

On the warmest days here, with few exceptions, the nights cool off quickly. In fact, something happens at this high elevation that I'd not experienced in California, though it may happen in the deserts there as well. As the sun sets, there is often a gentle breeze that comes across the land from the east. It is a quickly passing breeze that you can hear approaching as it moves across the grass. As it passes, you feel the temperature drop. The night air descends as though being pulled from some hidden cooler, unlocked by a light sensor once the sun is no longer present to illuminate it.

It is not unusual for our temperatures to swing thirty and even forty degrees from day to night here, and even in the winter when we've had a bright sunny day in the sixties, we find it hard not to sit out for part of the evening enjoying the moon and the stars and watching the meteors as they streak across the sky. The occasional meteor shower may keep us sitting out for hours. Sometimes, we just bundle up a little more and wait for the night air we know is on its way. Even in the warmest months of the year, we can get chilly soon enough if we haven't brought out a jacket or blanket.

Now though, summer was upon us. The days are long, and they heat up quickly. I believe it's safe to say it is not only my favorite season in this part of West Texas, but probably the favorite of just about everyone who lives here. It is certainly as true for the Geermann-Schlatters as it is for me. The summer is our rainy season—what there is of one—and the cumulus clouds build over the mountains until they finally become dark and heavy, dropping their rains upon the grama ready to spring back to life after months of dormancy.

The world turns a brilliant green, and except for the risk of a lightning strike starting a fire or hitting some living creature—be it human, bovine, antelope or deer—the thunder and lightning displays are awesome to behold.

On the ranch, I've observed something I hadn't noticed living in town but did see a time or two at the tomato farm. The thunderstorm would move to the southwest across the ranch, only to hit the mountains along its path and turn back around. On two occasions it made this back-and-forth trip three times before finally petering out. In between each pass of the storm, we would see a great double rainbow in the east as the afternoon sun that had heated up the show was beginning its descent. Billy and I would sit and stare as though not to do so would be a sin—a sin of ingratitude—and if we held one thing in common above all else, it was our genuine gratitude for the splendor of the world around us.

When the triple storm of late July passed us for the third time as it wound down its show for the day, Billy ventured into the unlikely. "I guess we could sell this dump and move to New York City. We could live an exciting urban life in the greatest city in the world."

I replied, "I know some elder Geermann-Schlatters who may have something to say about that, but sure, you and I would really fit in well. We might-oughta go over there right now and tell them New Orleans is off the agenda. New York City—here we come!"

Billy continued, "Just think, we could go to a gay bar besides the bar-stool bar in Jean and Mary-Alice's back yard. I bet two hot cowboys wouldn't leave alone."

I added, "We'd get some stares, I'll grant that."

Billy asked, "Do you think urban living would get old?"

I chuckled, "I think it's old already, and we've not gotten up out of these chaises yet. I can't think of anything on the planet I'd want to do less than live in a place like New York City. And I'd certainly rather sit in *La Capilla de la Rosa* in silence with your mom than boot-scoot in some gay bar or any other bar for that matter."

Billy asked, "No cruising chicks then either?"

"No. No cruising chicks either. My chick-cruising days are over."

Billy speculated, "You California boys could do lots of chick-cruising. We poor ranch hands in Van Horn didn't have any cruising to do at all except for the few cowboys who would go to the truck stop and hook up with any stray wandering through."

"Male or female?" I asked.

Billy answered, "As best I could tell, they weren't particular as long as they controlled the situation."

"You never did that or were never tempted?" I asked.

"Believe it or not, no. I was mighty lonely all those years, but to me, that looked like the perfect recipe to pile being miserable upon being lonely," he said.

"I'm curious, why do you think that was piling misery on top of loneliness?"

He clearly had thought it through. "Because I saw a pattern early on of the guys doing it, which seemed to start with some heavy shots of liquor, which then led straight into their brief carnal pleasure and right back to the bottle. It seemed to me if you had to get that drunk before, during or after, then I couldn't see what they were actually getting out of it. It wasn't love that's for sure—even of a kind, as you would say—and it didn't even seem to amount to much pleasure, however temporary. I just never wanted to hollow myself out in that way."

I repeated, "'Hollow myself out'—that, my friend, describes the ten years of my life to a 'T' before coming here. I never got addicted to the bottle, thank God, but I certainly could have because every miserable failure was best consoled by Jack Daniels. He was the only steady thing in my apartment all those years even though he was of little comfort. Every failure or fleeting one-night stand hollowed me out bit by bit.

"You were so young, I'm surprised you didn't get sucked into the games they were playing with their own lives—misery loves company."

Billy stated, "One or another would try to drag me into their games. I may have left because my mom lost her mind for a time, but Dad, Sallie and Grandma Geermann were with me in my thoughts every lonely day and night. I couldn't dishonor them. Not even for some temporary hope of a thrill.

"There would be guests at the ranch at different times who would come onto me—male and female, since I know you'll ask—but I wasn't going to risk losing my job over being some rich person's plaything for the few days they were on the ranch.

"I was sorely tempted with one woman from San Francisco, but I was spared the humiliation of it when I overheard her bragging about having me as her 'cowboy conquest' when she hadn't had me at all. It gave me a sick feeling just to hear her bragging the way she was. She was graphic in her telling of it and even had a place and time when it supposedly took place. I wasn't too worried about the owner hearin' about it and firing me, because I was with him during the entire afternoon she claimed it all happened."

I feigned deflation of my ego, saying, "So I'm the mess, and by all worldly measures, you are and have always been chaste."

Billy clarified, "Chaste, as the world might label it, but dishonest if I claimed it for myself. I've certainly never taken a vow of celibacy and never could really see the point. And if you are a mess, you're my mess. Besides that, livin' all my life on a ranch, I see not only the bull mount the cow or heifer but them steers mount each other all the time. As best I can tell, castration doesn't even take away the desire, and cattle must be as good an example of bisexuality as anything."

I added, "Reading about the eunuchs in the Bible, I thought it was supposed to take away 'desires of the flesh,' but I've thought the same thing as you about those steers.

"I've always known not to label you, and I love you enough to question my own labels. You've certainly taught me love comes in different ways to different people. In our case, it stands way outside the norm of what the marketing of sex in this country is supposed to look like."

Billy joked, "All a cowboy really needs after a long day of work is a good hot shower—some longer than others."

I chuckled and said, "Too true. Too true. I love that new tankless water heater." Then I added, "Of course for you, putting on a little show at the Slo Poke Cafe, and even acting up with your folks, is part of how you enjoy life."

Billy smiled, "I am playful, as you know better than anyone."

"Even when you're trying to teach a mess how to rope a steer," I added.

"Yup, Jaime, it's like I told you when you were first learnin' to rope. You gotta want them steers as much as you want me."

I replied, "I have to admit, I don't pick up a rope without smiling as I recall that day and those words, and how they turned me from an eyes-closed fool to a gen-u-ine cowboy. You're a masterful teacher, Billy-boy."

We had booked our two roomettes the same day Sallie said she'd tag along. We lucked into booking rooms right across from each other. For now, all we could do is wait for fall to arrive for our next big adventure.

I said to Billy one day, "Sometime while everything is green and we don't have much work to do, we ought to make a picnic lunch and go spend it up on the rock outcropping where you 'proposed.' Or we could go to that knob on that one mountain where it looks like some professional landscaper selected just the right plants and placed them there."

Billy responded, "I guess God was the landscaper for that garden."

I added, "I saw plants up there I've not seen anywhere else out here."

He had observed the same, saying, "There must be more around, but for sure they are pretty rare. Dad never wanted anybody to know about that spot for fear some environmental group would invade the ranch 'to protect it.' He'd say, 'I know they may mean well but, as best I can tell, most don't know their head from their ass when it comes to land stewardship.'"

"Your dad said that?" I asked.

"Yeah, Mom wasn't around, but Sallie was."

I reflected, "My guess is Sallie would have said it the same way."

Billy laughed, "I remember her saying back, 'Too true. Too true.' Then Dad added, 'For ten thousand years, bison roamed the grass from Alaska to the Gulf getting up to sixty-million—grass all intact. It took the government improvement program a few decades to get the number down to 541 and, after that, another 50 years to bring in the dust bowl—sins we have not fully learned from to this day.'

"He also told me that on the back side of the knob is where a lot of the owls nest. The ones we hear at night are comin' from there—at least that's what Dad says."

"He would know if anyone does," I observed.

"I love hearing the owls at night," Billy continued. "The coyotes don't give me any comfort. I always worry what they might be up to with the calves when they're first born, but the owls are a welcome companion in the night hours. They can scoop up all the mice and snakes they want on my account."

I offered, "I've only been up on the knob once. Let's take our picnic there."

"Sounds good," Billy replied.

A couple days later he set the wheels in motion. "Lookin' at the weather and our workload, today would be a good day to go on that picnic. Do you want to see if Sallie wants to ride along?"

"That would be fine by me."

He was off to call and extend the invitation. In a minute he was back. "She's gonna head over here shortly. What are we gonna throw together for our picnic? Maybe you want to whip up some Crêpes Suzette?"

"Those and kale salad, maybe. I made that chicken salad last evening. I guess we'll just take that. Sallie will be expecting peanut butter and pickle sandwiches, I'm sure. We'll surprise her."

Within the hour we were saddled up and on a slow trot to the knob. Sallie was the first to speak, saying, "It's been two or three years since I've ridden up to the knob. At my age, I'm inclined not to wander too far off the beaten trail in case old Nellie here gets spooked and throws me off. I ain't afraid of dying, but I'd just as soon not be helpless in the rocks before something comes along that thinks I look like dinner."

As is our nature, we rode silently the rest of the way there. We each picked a rock as a seat to make ourselves at home. Sallie was sitting next to one of the rare plants—its bright red flowers in full bloom. "I never have figured out what this here plant is, but it sure is beautiful when it's in bloom. I never have even plucked one of its flowers. I just leave it be. Looking at it is enough for me."

"It is a thing of beauty," I agreed.

We sat quietly for several minutes when I said, "I don't know why this just occurred to me, and I can't believe I've never asked about it before. How did Bill end up on this ranch in the first place? Isn't all his family more around San Angelo?"

Sallie replied, "The ranching world's a small world even if we cover a lot of territory. The Geermanns and Schlatters knew each other going way back to the old country. Daddy said they were Swiss. I'd always assumed we were German. I guess there isn't much difference. Momma said the Swiss like quiet while the Germans like beer. Of course, she was Church of Christ, so she would look at it that way. Daddy wasn't all that quiet and did like beer well enough—Church of Christ or not. She always said some German must have gotten in there somewhere."

I suggested, "I'm pretty sure the Swiss drink beer too."

Sallie continued, "Billy probably knows how his daddy ended up here. I'll let him tell it, and see if he's got it right or not."

Billy replied, "As the story has come down to us kids, the Schlatters and the Geermanns went every year to the Fort Worth Stock Show in February. Dad happened to sit next to Grandpa Geermann at one of the events and they hit it off. Before the week was out, Dad was offered a job by Grandpa as soon as Dad graduated high school which was that spring. How'd I do, Aunt Sallie?"

"That's how it came about. I remember the day your daddy arrived. My little sister was google-eyed from the moment she laid eyes on him. I remember Momma saying, 'I think you may have landed a ranch hand and a son-in-law in one catch.' The rest, as they say, is history. Sis about gave up on havin' any children. They were married ten years before this little bundle of mess came along. He came with a head full of that black hair, those big black eyes and fat cheeks front and back."

She tickled herself at describing him.

Billy just smiled, adding, "Adorable then—adorable still."

Sallie chuckled, "You gave your momma one hell of a labor. You were close to ten pounds when you were born."

Billy suggested, "I just made it easier for the next two."

Sallie laughed, "That's one way of lookin' at it, and true enough if the truth be told. She was barely in labor with the next two. Momma said she'd paid her dues with Billy, and the good Lord was givin' her a break from then on.

"Break out those peanut butter sandwiches, Jaime. I'm gettin' hungry."

"No peanut butter today, Sallie. Billy thought I should whip up some Crêpes Suzette, but I brought chicken salad instead."

I plated up the salad and potato chips and handed them both their plate. We returned to our silent-selves as we sat and stared out across the vast landscape that surrounded us up on that knob. We watched as a thunderhead slowly started to build on the highest peak a dozen miles or more away.

Sallie nodded her head towards it. "I reckon we ought to be headin' down just in case some bolt of lightning thinks we've overstayed our welcome up here."

Chapter Fourteen

We knew, by our standards, the end of the year was going to be a busy one. We had the trip to New Orleans, Zoey and Mark's visit, and by now, we no longer had to wait for an invitation in the mail to Ernesto and Rosalinda's New Year's Eve party—we were expected as regulars. I said to Billy, "Next time we see Ernesto and Rosalinda, we'll need to tell them about Zoey's visit. I'm sure they'll say to bring 'em along, but I want to hear them say it rather than assume."

We still volunteered as much as we could on distribution day at the pantry, which always led to lunch afterwards at the Slo Poke Cafe with Ernesto and Rosalinda, but it had been a long time since we'd seen Chuy and Lupe. I guess they were thinking the same thing about not seeing us, because on the first distribution Saturday in September, we found them waiting for us at one of the big tables at the cafe when the four of us arrived from the pantry. Lupe jumped up to give us both a hug.

"It's been way too long. You boys hide out on that ranch, and we never get to see you."

Ernesto went to Lupe to give her a big hug.

Lupe exclaimed, "Get off me, you crazy man! I see you all the time."

He responded, "I just wanted to hug my favorite sister-in-law."

Chuy added, "Given the competition, I'm not sure if that's much of a compliment."

I asked, "How's Chuy's retirement treating you, Lupe? Have you got him making quilts with you?"

Chuy responded, "You know what she thinks of my quilting stitches! The most trouble she lets me get into these days is doing the grocery shopping."

To that Lupe added, "I give him a list, and half of what I have on the list doesn't come home with him, and two bags of things I never put on the list show up."

When she saw us, Sara said much the same thing Lupe had said, "You two don't come into town much, or if you do, you're giving your lunch business to some other place in town."

Billy reassured her, "You get all our business when it comes to eating out in Fort Davis. Now that *Jaime* makes more than peanut butter sandwiches, we eat at home a lot."

I clarified, "A little too much credit coming my way. Billy grills steaks and does mean fajitas. We're both getting so domesticated."

Ernesto said, "We'd better come out and sample some of Billy's steaks. See if he can grill a steak as good as I can smoke a whole ribeye."

Rosalinda shook her head, "Nothing like inviting yourself."

I suggested, "Why don't all four of you come out next Saturday. Bring Elma if she's up for it."

Lupe replied, "I'm sure she'll be up for it. She's ninety-one, and acts younger than the old man here."

Chuy confessed, "I can't deny it."

I was glad all this socializing led Rosalinda to ask, "*Jaime*, didn't you say your sister and her husband were coming over Christmas?"

"Yes. They are spending about two weeks with us. They are coming in on the train from LA."

She asked, "Are they going to be here through New Year's?"

I replied, "Yes, they leave on the third."

"Well, you have to bring them to the party if you think they'd be up for it," she said.

Billy answered, "They'll be up for it. Count us in. Billy and *Jaime* plus two."

Lupe added, "I'm really looking forward to meeting your sister. I think it is so nice that she reached out to you."

I reflected, "I think it's interesting that a letter I could only have written having lived here a few years, and after having been adopted by the Cardonas and Schlatters as I was, brought about such a transformation in *her* life."

Lupe said, "You could almost consider it miraculous—that it arrived as she started a new marriage and faced her illness."

"Miraculous to me," I confirmed.

We continued to catch up with each other's latest news until Sara arrived with our lunch. She asked, "Did you hear John and James are opening that restaurant in Alpine they'd talked about?"

We all acknowledged it was news to us.

Billy jested, "I thought maybe they'd forget the restaurant idea and open the first gay bar in Alpine."

Lupe smiled, "I'm sure you thought that."

Ernesto added, "Billy's been buckin' to quit the ranch and have *Jaime* and him become hot cowboy bartenders. Instead of long Wranglers they'd wear cut-off short-shorts."

Lupe stated emphatically, "That would cure *Mamá* of saying, 'Oh, they're such nice boys!'"

Rosalinda gave Ernesto a good, hard jab. "You in your drag and now you're picturing these two in short-shorts. I do wonder about you!"

"Oh, you love me!" Ernesto replied.

"We all do," I said.

Sara had stepped away but was soon back. Rosalinda asked, "Where is this restaurant going to be, and what are they going to serve?"

Sara answered, "They are fixing up some building right downtown which I don't think is that smart. They are going to have a parking problem before they get their first guests. I guess it might be good for foot traffic."

Billy asked, "Have you turned in your notice to help them out?"

She roller her eyes, saying, "I think you know the answer to that."

She heard the bell in the kitchen and was off to pick up whatever was ready for another table. As she often did, she said loud enough for all to hear, "I hope they know what they're getting themselves into."

Rosalinda noted, "She never did say what they were going to serve. I guess we'll find out eventually."

As Sara came back out with the hot plates she called out, "They say it will be an 'upscale bistro,' to answer the other part of your question."

Billy smiled, "Ernesto, you're going to have to keep missing Mass to attend to your barbecue—no relief in sight."

Rosalinda said, "He's devastated."

Billy and Rosalinda both spotted two of Betsy's old church crowd coming in. Both women sat down at a table near the entrance and stared in our direction. I thought I was piecing together Billy and Rosalinda's looks at each other, and knew I had when Billy slid his chair closer to mine and put his arm around me. He even laid his head on my shoulder. It didn't take long for the rest of the table to clue in, as did Sara who was grinning from ear to ear.

I just said, "He's a mess."

My dinner companions replied, "But he's your mess."

Billy asserted, "Yes, I am."

Billy asked to whomever might feel inclined to answer, "Do you think if we moved our date next weekend to Friday evening Sara would come? Friday is one of her days off."

Lupe suggested, "You'd have to invite her husband too. You've probably never met him."

I asked, "Ernesto, could you even get away from work on Friday?"

"Not a problem this coming week. You should ask her."

Sara was back with the iced tea pitcher. Billy extended the invitation. "Sara, we're having steak night at the ranch this coming Friday. Would you and your husband like to join us?"

She jumped at it. "Whether he comes or not, I will."

Lupe said, "You could ride out with us or follow us."

"If Mateo comes along, we'll follow you. If he doesn't come, I'll ride along. What time is all this taking place?"

Billy replied, "You ought to be at the ranch around 5:30, so it doesn't get too late for y'all to drive back in."

Chuy added, "Sara, then be at our place a little after five."

"Wonderful," was all she said and was off to her duties.

Lupe said, "You know if *Mamá* comes with us, she'll have to bring her eggs. What else can we bring?"

I assured her, "Eggs are more than sufficient."

Rosalinda offered, "Why don't I bring a pot of pintos? I know you both like my pinto beans."

Acknowledging both offers, Billy responded, "Well, if y'all are going to insist, I guess we'll have to accept both the eggs and the beans."

I did say, "Elma doesn't need to do a cake. We'll take care of the steak, some guacamole salad or something, and we'll make homemade ice cream."

Billy added, "Just come around to the back when you get there. We'll be out on the patio unless it's raining or blowing like mad, which it shouldn't be doing either of those this time of year."

On the drive home Billy said, "After dinner, I think we should get the instruments out and play some music for them."

"I'm sure they'd appreciate it," I said. "We could play them some of the newer pieces including some of your dad's new lyrics we've set to music."

Friday night was quickly upon us, and the mini caravan of three pickups arrived promptly at 5:30—Mateo and Sara bringing up the rear. We were both glad to see Elma—not for her eggs, though of course she and Lupe had made enough for a small legion—but since we'd not seen her in some time. She grinned the moment she saw us, and we went up to give her a hug. Billy offered her his arm to walk her to the patio.

"How are my two favorite boys?" she asked.

I answered, "We're fine. How is our favorite *abuela*?"

She giggled, "Oh, *tu abuela es muy vieja*. I never thought I'd live this long."

Ernesto brought along pictures from their last trip to see Father Chuy in El Salvador. "When we were there, they had twelve of the fish tanks up and running and were building another twelve. We had some of the fish. They raise both tilapia and catfish—I gather, because both farm well and do well in the mountain water."

Rosalinda offered, "You never saw such happy people."

Ernesto noted, "We have a second copy of these pictures. Chuy said, 'Be sure to get a set to the Schlatters.' Consider my duties fulfilled."

He also brought a cooler full of beer, which we had already taken care of, but we didn't say anything. Everyone but Elma had one. Ernesto was on number two before I was halfway through number one. He smiled, "Don't worry. Rosalinda says she's driving home."

After dinner as I was spooning up the ice cream, Billy lit the fire in the fire ring, and we all moved to encircle it. Billy and I played all our new songs and a couple of their old favorites. No one seemed to be in any hurry to leave, so Billy asked, "Any requests?"

I interjected, "That's a little risky given our limits."

Elma asked, "Do you know 'How Great Thou Art?'"

I replied, "I'm sorry. I don't know that song."

Billy started to play it but stopped, "Ernesto, if you know it feel free to sing along."

Chuy piped in, "He knows it. *Mamá* used to watch Billy Graham crusades, and every time she'd hear George Beverly Shea sing it, she would say, 'He has a real nice voice, but not as nice as my boy's.'"

Ernesto said, "I only know a couple verses, so any you play after that you'll be on your own, Billy."

Billy started up the song again, playing his own improvised introduction, and Ernesto sang along when he got to the verse. I heard the words of that first verse and felt how they fit our life on the ranch.

When I in awesome wonder,
Consider all the worlds Thy Hands have made;
I see the stars, I hear the rolling thunder,
Thy power throughout the universe displayed.

I wondered if this was edging me towards a new theme song.

Chapter Fifteen

Our train adventure was upon us. We kept checking the status of the Sunset Limited and, so far, it seemed to be running only about thirty minutes behind schedule. The automated voice said trains can make up time—and since there was no stop between El Paso and Alpine, we thought we'd better assume they'd be pretty close to on time. All three of us figured that although we could sit at home and wait to leave, we could get there and wait just as easily. We called one last time before heading out, and nothing had changed in the estimated arrival.

We were the only ones there, which didn't surprise us. We thought we might be the only ones boarding in such a remote place as this. However, soon, others started arriving and sitting inside the station. We kept our seats out under the porch facing the track. A Union Pacific train went rolling through, not letting up on their horn most of the way through Alpine.

Sallie hollered over the horn, "THAT'LL WAKE YOU UP!"

Then a white van pulled in, and two conductors and an engineer got out with their duffle bags and went into the little office. They left the door open, and we could hear the radio from the train. They'd made up some time and would be in about ten minutes late —at least that's what we thought we heard. One of the conductors was back out to start looking at our tickets. He looked at ours first and told us exactly where to stand once the train came to a stop.

Sallie jested, "It looks like that first step will be a big one. I can't believe I never noticed there's no train platform here."

Billy added, "She doesn't get out much."

The conductor said, "We keep hearing we'll get one, but I've heard that for the ten years I've been on this line."

She replied, "I'm surprised to see y'all getting on here."

"Yes," he answered, "Alpine is a shift-change spot, as unlikely as that may seem. It just happens to work out right to get the next shift change in San Antonio going this direction. I go back and forth from there. We stay in a motel here, and they carry us to and from the station."

Billy commented, "I'm surprised to see this many getting on."

The conductor continued, "Alpine is more popular on the train route than anybody would ever guess. Sanderson on the other hand is a 'flag stop.' If we don't have a reservation or a drop-off we just keep rollin' through."

With that, he was off to check the tickets of those inside.

With the arrival of the train, we hoisted our way up into car two and made our way up the narrow stairs to the upper level. Sallie observed, "I'd hate to be on crutches."

We were met by our attendant, Yvonne, who showed us to our roomettes across from each other and wondered if we wanted to get in on the last seating for lunch. It seemed for breakfast we could just show up anytime after 7:00. The longer we waited after that, the more likely we'd wait for a seat. For lunch and dinner, we had to go at assigned times. We all agreed we'd skip lunch and go to the earliest seating for dinner. She handed us our dinner reservation reminder with the time 5:00 circled, pointed out the drinks next to the coffee pot and showed us where the bathrooms were.

"There's a shower downstairs," she noted. "Let me know about when you want your bed made up, and I'll be around to get it all set up for you. Let me know if you need anything."

"Sounds pretty civilized," Sallie offered. "A lot better than flying."

We heard two quick toots of the engine horn and the train started to roll out of Alpine. We didn't get very far. The train went off onto the next side track and waited about fifteen minutes before another Union Pacific freight train came rolling past.

I said, "I wonder if this line is all single track or just out here in the boondocks."

"If it's all single track," Billy replied, "that would explain why they can't keep a schedule."

We kept our door slid open as did Sallie. A few places the train rocked around pretty hard, and after one of those times she smiled and leaned forward to say to us, "Do you think this thing is gonna hop off these tracks?"

We looked out the window at the mountains we had just left behind and out onto the undulating, brushy desert floor that lay as far as we could see. About three hours into the trip the same conductor we'd talked to at the station came on the PA.

"In two miles we will be crossing the Pecos River. This bridge is the second highest railroad bridge in the country at 275 feet. You can get a great view of the canyon from either side of the train."

We heard a soft, "Oh, that's purdy," come from the other roomette. We jumped a bit when we heard a loud chunk-chunk in the middle of the bridge as our car's wheels went over whatever seam in the track could make such a clatter.

Sallie leaned forward again, exclaiming, "I guess she ain't comin' down, but she had me wondering when I heard that racket!"

Billy added his embellishment. "Jaime made the sign of the cross for the first time in his life thinking it was his last chance."

I clarified, "Sallie, as you might guess, that wasn't exactly my reaction."

She chuckled, "It'll make a good story though. You can both tell it to your grandchildren."

I looked at Billy. "She's as bad as you sometimes."

"Family trait—I get it honest," he replied.

It wasn't long before we heard on the PA, "The dining car is now taking 5:00 reservations. Please make your way to the dining car and wait to be seated."

We were the first to get there. Another woman came in and was seated with us.

"Hello," she said. "I'm Piper, and as you can probably tell, I'm not from the US. I'm from New Zealand, and I am taking a long, slow trip by Amtrak around the country."

Billy answered for us. "Now there's an adventurer. We got on in Alpine and are only going to New Orleans, and it's the first time me and my Aunt Sallie have ever been on a train. I'm Billy, by the way, and this is Jaime. He's originally from California and has ridden the train out there. Now he lives with us on our family ranch."

"Oh," Piper added, "I'm a ranch girl, too. My folks have a ranch on the south island of New Zealand which my brother mostly runs these days. I grew up on the back of a horse. I really enjoyed the train ride once we got into the mountains on both sides of Alpine. I had no idea Texas had any mountains."

Sallie offered, "Our ranch is just about an hour north of Alpine in the Davis Mountains. It's a beautiful place, and I'm guessing that stretch you saw is probably going to be the prettiest part of the Sunset Limited route."

"I got on in LA and can confirm that, so far, it has been the highlight."

Billy suggested, "I think we'd better be ordering before they bring in the next shift of diners."

We had studied the menu before going to the dining car. Billy said, "I don't think I'll try their flatiron steak. I can get that anytime. I guess, I'll get the baked chicken."

"I'm doing the same," I reported.

When it came time to order, the four ranchers seated together all ordered the same thing. Billy told them of our earlier decision, and they both said they had the same thought.

Piper added, "I did consider the fish, but seafood is another thing we are spoiled with in New Zealand. What can they do to chicken?"

Piper had also taken a train trip around Europe. She lamented her own country's lack of trains though was quick to say, compared to Germany, France and Switzerland, "Amtrak schedules are quite laughable and the connections near abominable."

She continued, "It makes it almost impossible to schedule getting from one long route to another. You're sure to need hotel stays between each just to ensure you get on the next train, even with daily departures."

We all speculated what kind of ridership could be built up if all Amtrak's long routes had at least two trains a day with ten to twelve hours between departure. And how double tracks would certainly help keep them on a schedule.

Piper adding, "Some poor towns are perpetually stuck with 2 or 3 a.m. arrival and departure times and then, on this route, only three days a week to catch it."

Sallie seemed to channel Bill just then, saying, "We can't afford the few billion it would take to try to build up the trains because we're too busy spending hundreds of billions on our 'security' which goes from disaster to disaster. I've lived with that stupidity all my life, and it only appears to be headed to more absurd levels with every passing year."

Piper responded, "Not to criticize my host country, but the US does lead the world in dragging the rest of us into their quagmires. Why we follow is beyond me."

Billy reflected, "Misery loves company."

I noted, "That explains why we drag them along. It doesn't explain to me why they follow."

We all loved our meal and skipped dessert for the sake of a good night's sleep over an all-night turning stomach. We bid our dinner companion a good night and excused ourselves to our roomettes.

We'd told Yvonne to make up our beds around 9:00, and she said we could wait huddled nearby or we could go to the observation car. We opted for the latter. As we walked down the narrow aisle in the car, we clearly went through a switch which rocked the car wildly.

Sallie chuckled, "Nellie, on a bad day, can't rock me around the saddle like this car does."

Just then we went around a curve, flying by Amtrak standards. She cried out, "Whoa! Hang onto your hats, boys. I think the right side of the train just lifted off the tracks for a second there. That engineer must be trying to make up time or fell asleep with the pedal to the metal."

We got back to the roomettes a little after nine to find them made up for the night. Sallie offered, "I assume since we're early risers we'll just meet in the dining car when they open at 7:00. That sound like a plan?"

I concurred, "That'll work. Goodnight, Sallie."

"Goodnight, boys."

Billy gave his aunt a big Billy hug.

"What's all this?" she asked.

"That's just for you being you," he replied.

She gave her little chuckle, adding, "Billy, it would be too much work to try to be anything else—a lesson you boys seem to have learned as well, somewhere along the line."

Billy responded, "We had a damn good teacher."

This time it was Sallie who gave the big hug.

I was in the top bunk looking on, when Billy turned back around he asked, "You want the bottom bunk? It doesn't matter to me. If you're claustrophobic you might get a little anxious up there."

I answered, "If I'm claustrophobic, I don't know it and might just as well find out. Besides, you're the birthday boy. You get the bigger bed and view out the window. Close the door, so I can get these jeans off and get comfortable."

"Strippin' for me, huh?" Billy joked.

"Yeah, somethin' like that," I said.

We'd both brought boxers and big loose-fitting shirts we figured we could wear in the aisle to get to the bathroom. As Billy put it, "Men wear speedos at the beach and show a lot more than these old boxers are gonna show."

We each made one last trip to the bathroom before locking ourselves in for the night. There was no conversation after that. I bet we didn't go two miles before the gentle rocking of the train had me sound asleep. I woke up a couple times only when we were stopped. With no window up top I had no idea if we were in a station or on a side track. I didn't want to wake Billy if he was asleep to ask what he saw out the window. But I never was awake long, and as long as we kept moving, I kept sleeping.

I was still asleep when I felt "big foot" down-under shake my bunk. "Mr. Cruz. It's gettin' up time."

I asked, "Did that train rockin' put you to sleep or keep you awake?"

He answered, "If I said, 'What train rockin'?' I guess that would answer your question. I wonder how I can get my bed at home to do that. I don't think I rolled around all night. I did wake up a couple times. Once they must have been fillin' up the engine. We were sittin' in some fuel depot past San Antonio. Other than that, I was conked out all night."

"Same here," I replied.

Once dressed, we left our door open. When Sallie emerged a few minutes later she declared, "I see in that little mirror in the room my hair is real pretty. I forgot to put a net on it. I'm gonna go see if it can be tamed, and I'll be right back."

When she was gone, Billy laughed, "I didn't know she wore a net on her head to bed, but I can see why she needs to. I never saw her look like that before. Her hair sticks out like Bozo the Clown."

"I wouldn't tell her that," I suggested.

He replied, "When she gets a look in the bigger mirror in the bathroom she'll probably say it herself."

She was soon back with her hair tamed more or less. "Lord," she began. "I looked like the love child of the Wicked Witch of the West and Bozo the Clown."

We both laughed, though we never told her it was because of Billy's Bozo comparison.

As we looked out the dining car windows, we watched the sun just beginning its ascent—ever-further in the southern sky as winter approached.

Sallie sighed, "It's nice to see *sol* comin' up, but wherever we are, it don't hold a candle to the sunrise at the ranch."

"You got that right," I agreed.

Billy asked, "Did the train rock you to sleep the way it did us?"

She chuckled, "What rockin'? I hardly laid my head on the pillow before I was asleep. I really thought, 'I'll never be able to sleep on a movin' train.' Boy, was I wrong."

I noted, "They are gonna want to give us our lunch reservation while we're in here, I'm guessing."

Billy replied, "I'd vote for skipping it. We're gonna want to eat a big meal our first night in the French Quarter."

Sallie agreed, "That gets my vote."

"Fine by me," I said.

We were about to order when Piper walked in. She passed by our booth to settle in one just behind us. She smiled, "I see the ranchers on board are all up and at it this morning."

Sallie concurred, "True, true—a lifetime of habit."

We'd noticed in the dining car the evening before, in the observation car, and again at breakfast, different people talking about Hurricane Katrina. It had been just over two years since the devastation of that storm, and some asked how people who'd lived through it had been impacted by it and how things had recovered by now. You could sense those caught in it still found it hard to even talk about, though that didn't stop complete strangers from trying to get them to open up about their experience. Only one man seemed to be pressing his tablemate a bit too much.

Billy asked, "Do I go over there and tell him to leave the lady alone?"

"Tempting," I replied.

I guess she'd had enough. She excused herself and, noting we'd watched the obnoxious and prying man, she rolled her eyes as she passed us.

Sallie shook her head in disapproval. "Boys, that man is an example where knowin' when to keep your mouth shut is a great blessin' to others."

Part III

Chapter Sixteen

Our three nights in "the Big Easy" went by quickly and were filled with too much food, too much café au lait and too many people. None of us slept nearly as well in our very nice hotel on Royal Street as we did in our little roomettes on the train. It probably seems odd, but one of our favorite things while there was visiting a couple of the cemeteries.

All the above-ground tombs were fascinating to us, and as Sallie had said, "These folks are a lot quieter than that bunch down on Bourbon. I must be leanin' toward preferrin' the grave over mingling with the masses of the livin'."

Billy added, "Yeah, and our 9:30 bedtime doesn't align too well with the night life of the big city. At least our early morning walks are relatively quiet."

We all had a wonderful time, but we were glad to get back on the train and headed for West Texas. Soon after, we'd be back at the train station to pick up Zoey and Mark. Also, we'd be seeing what Ernesto had in store for his guests on New Year's Eve. Perhaps he'd resurrect the Reverend Mother. Perhaps he'd give Sophia Loren one more try or perhaps he'd return to his old standby, Kate Smith.

Brett had booked in early to claim the bunkhouse for an uncharacteristic full week over Christmas. It would only be him, Pamela, one of her kids and Brett's youngest. The rest would be with "the other parent" over Christmas. Since we were hosting Zoey and Mark, we didn't feel comfortable inviting Jean and Mary-Alice to join us. We knew they were disappointed that they couldn't stay at the ranch over the holidays, but they got creative. They'd found a motor home they could borrow if we could figure a way to power it up. We hated to break the news to them. There was already a hookup—at the bunkhouse.

Jean responded, "Hey, that doesn't matter. He'll have his four walls, and we'll have ours. We'll see you all at Quiet Day."

Here it was upon us—the first Saturday in December would be another anniversary of that first Quiet Day. The gathering that inspired my letters to Zoey, my biological parents and brother—and later, the second letter to Zoey, and Bill's first and, to date, only letter to Brett. Brett never had mentioned it even in passing. I was surprised Billy never confronted him about it, but where Brett was concerned, Billy had a very aloof stance. I don't think he really cared whether Brett became closer to the family or not, even though he knew his parents hoped for as much. I could understand it. Once estranged, even a bit, it's just easier to stay that way. Brett never gave Billy the time of day and ignored him anytime both were in the same room. I sensed he knew Billy was the genuine article, and he himself was a facade masked by his own pretense.

We did know that Brett had "scheduled" the day after Christmas to meet with Bill, Betsy and Sallie. He made it clear that it was a confidential matter, and it was only to be with the three of them.

Of course, that got Billy's curiosity going on overtime. He said to his dad, "He must have given some hint of what is so top secret. And the fact that it includes Sallie, certainly, makes you wonder what he's up to. It must not have anything to do with the letter."

Bill replied, "I asked and got no answer. His only comment was, 'all shall be revealed.'"

Billy shook his head in disgust, "I know we always say he's clueless. It appears to me he's moved from clueless to being an ass."

"I'll reserve judgment on that," Bill stated flatly.

Over the past year, the faithful Quiet Day group had thinned out considerably. There never had been more than twenty on any given Saturday, but in the past year one had died, three had moved away, one had gone through a divorce and just quit coming, and two others had gotten in a squabble about something at church and quit coming. Betsy began to wonder if it was dying on the vine.

Jean offered her some reassurance. "I hear all the time from the ones who still come how important this day is in their monthly routine. Mom, you know how fragile these small church communities are out here. Our church in Marfa was on a growth spurt and now has lost all its growth and even declined some. It's the way of our world."

Mary-Alice interjected, "Wherever two or three are gathered."

Betsy smiled, "That's right. I still find solace in that chapel every single day. I'm not going to deny it for any who have even a bit of that same feeling."

Jean added, "If you want to know the truth, we'd give up on our church and just come here on Sundays like we do after Quiet Day now, but guilt keeps us going back. It's not that it's bad in any way. We just love it here more. And when it comes to Episcopal church politics with the Diocese, we've about had our fill."

Betsy responded, "*Tis the gift to be simple. Tis the gift to be free.* You don't have to be an Episcopalian to see how much the church could learn from that one Shaker hymn. Church politics are *never* simple nor free in any sense of the word."

Billy and I sat quietly listening to their conversation. He leaned over to whisper to me, "You and I avoided all that mess by being heathens all those years, and now we've gone straight into the Church of Mercy over Judgment."

I whispered back, "I think Jean hit the nail on the head—a lot of churches depend on guilt to keep 'em comin' back."

Billy, no longer whispering, said, "Good luck getting me to feel guilty about not going to church."

Jean asked, "Was that comment directed to me?"

"Not in particular," he replied. "Jaime and I were just discussing the freedom in keeping life simple."

I didn't think that was exactly what we'd talked about, but I didn't correct him—especially since I did agree wholeheartedly.

The next morning at Quiet Day, I sat reflectively as I tried to compose in my mind a second attempt at a letter to the three still estranged from me. When I wrote the first letters, it was as though I was taking dictation—which maybe I was in some cosmic, mysterious sense—from that great force of Love that somehow interacts with our created world, though is too often ignored. On this day, nothing came to me to say to those three strangers. What did come to me was this.

Entering the chapel in silence

—the chapel that came into my life
in every way unexpectedly—
I was flooded with a sense of belonging.
No estrangement from my past could
shake the certainty of the present time.
Such estrangements from my past
could not alter the reality of what I now know.
I am loved and I know it.
I love and those I love know it.
The silence enveloped me in peace.
The peace beamed from my soul
like the bright rays of the summer sun.
The light cannot now be extinguished
even when death comes to me.
Even when those I love join me
or precede me in their own death.
Love cannot die.
The light of love burns on.

I showed it to Billy afterwards. He smiled, saying, "The boy does have beautiful thoughts."

I asked him, "Do you think I should send this to my three estranged relatives? I know I want to send it to Zoey."

"She'll love it. As for the others, what do you have to lose?"

"Good point," I noted. "We'll cast seeds again to the winds and see what happens."

Chapter Seventeen

Our Quiet Day weekends have a routine, though that sounds dry and contrived, which they are not. They involve Jean and Mary-Alice coming out on Friday night, having a family dinner that night, another on Saturday night, and winding up the weekend as a family with our Sunday morning time in the chapel and lunch afterwards. After the Sunday lunch that anniversary Quiet Day, when Billy and I were back home for a restful Sunday afternoon, I said to him, "I hadn't thought about this until just this minute, but this family isn't big on Thanksgiving dinner like most people in this country. You ever thought about that?"

Billy responded, "We do have dinner together for whoever is around. Of course, for Jean and Mary-Alice that means a trip to Midland to be with Mary-Alice's family, which as you know, even Mary-Alice says is their annual visit to purgatory."

"I guess that's true. Brett almost never shows up and the girls have their annual obligation to the Miller clan."

Then Billy rightly noted, "We live in gratitude every day around here, and it's celebrated with the girls for an entire weekend every month—ever since Mom came to her senses, and you came into our lives. Besides, Dad doesn't like turkey. He says, 'You might as well eat gunnysack.'"

I jested, "Memo to self—cancel Christmas order for turkey-jerky for Bill."

Billy added, "He has been known to nibble on smoked turkey if someone puts it out, but only because he says it almost tastes like ham—and if you want something to taste like ham, buy a ham!"

Then I suggested, "Maybe we need to talk to Ernesto. He deep fries their turkeys and swears by it. That's what we had on the Thanksgiving when we were building the house. It was good."

Billy noted, "If Ernesto says it's good, it's good."

"Your dad does have strong opinions when it comes to food. I like when he fusses about vegans who want fake bacon, fake cheese and fake hamburgers."

Billy said, "As he would say, 'If your plants are so wonderful, why the *hell* do you have to try to make them taste like meat? At least my Twinkies aren't trying to imitate anything. They're sugar and flour from one end to the other—the way God intended.'"

I noted, "I think he's about sugared out. I see he's not only buying fewer Twinkies, but half the time he skips dessert altogether."

Billy laughed, "You know I say that's because he's warmed to the idea of growing old with Mom."

I added, "Ernesto, for all his craziness, always wanted us to eat mostly meat when we were hunkered down big time on a job. He'd say it was the only way we'd keep going all day. It was true, and Bill cuttin' down on sugar has inspired me to follow more his lead when dessert time comes."

"There go my Crêpes Suzette," Billy reflected.

"We ain't gettin' any younger. Better to start of our own accord than by some doctor's orders after we land in the hospital for one thing or another. Once they get their hooks in you with their 'medication cocktails,' they expect you to be hooked for life."

Billy added, "I wish it wasn't as true as you spell it out, but I know it is." Then he jested, "Memo to self—cancel Christmas confectioner's basket ordered for Jaime."

I continued, "I don't know about you, but even as hard as we work, my metabolism has taken a hit. I can see from the scales and the mirror that the last ten pounds I've put on aren't muscle."

He observed, "Sorry to say, it's at least fifteen for me. We really gonna do something about it?"

"I think we've just answered that question."

Billy added, "True enough—we ain't gettin' any younger, but we are young enough we don't have chronic complications to make it harder."

I settled it, "Well, then starting tomorrow, we're going to begin —however falteringly we may go about it."

"I'm in," he agreed. "Of course, I might get so svelte you won't be able to keep your hands off me."

"You'd like that."

Billy reflected, "Well, better yours than most people's who come to mind."

I asked, "So I can crawl in your sleeping bag next time we go down to Big Bend?"

Billy exclaimed, "I'd better enjoy it!"

I jumped from my end of the couch to his and replayed that Slo Poke Cafe scene with Ernesto and Rosalinda after I'd worn his borrowed shirt. I put one arm around him and took the other hand and said, "Look at the face. Isn't it cute? He's like a little puppy dog. Just adorable!"

Billy laughed, "I think you've remembered that word for word."

I asked, "How could I forget it? I'd never been snuggled up to by a man before—and in a public place on top of that!"

Billy enjoyed the recollection. "And that one wasn't even done for the benefit of Mom's old church crowd. That was pure spontaneity."

"Ernesto inspired, no doubt. He's as crazy as you."

Billy replied, "But *he's* not your mess."

I agreed, "No, he's Rosalinda's. She and I are equally blessed in that regard."

Billy responded, "I'm glad to know after four years you still think of me as a blessing."

I smiled, "I'm pretty sure, if it doesn't give you the bighead, I'll still think it after forty years."

Demurely, Billy added, "I guess we'll reevaluate in thirty-six years then."

"I guess we will."

His mind shifted to new territory, "Hey! Speaking of puppies, you said we weren't getting any other animal to care for until you knew how to take care of the ones you already had. Well, I say that you've accomplished that beyond anything even your foreman would have set as a standard. Are we ready to get a dog or two? I don't really want no cats unless that's your thing."

I responded, "I suppose two cattlemen could consider getting two cattle dogs. Could be our Christmas present to each other in place of that confectioner's basket you canceled earlier."

Billy stated, "Since the Cardonas know and are related to most of Fort Davis, they might know where we could get a couple red heeler pups."

First, I asked, "No blue heelers then?"

He replied, "I like the red heelers better. I think they got more dingo in 'em."

Then I asked, "Are these dogs gonna be in the house?"

"Hell, yes! One can sleep with you and the other with me."

I asked, "What if they both want to sleep with only one of us?"

He replied, "It says in the Bible, 'Bring them up in the way you would have them go and when they are old they will not depart from it'—or something like that."

I noted, "It hasn't worked too well for your parents with Brett, though I guess he isn't old yet. He could still come around. And it doesn't say the puppy might not be disobedient in the meantime."

Billy stated, "I'm willing to risk it."

"I don't suppose we can say they need to come housebroken already."

Billy replied as though he would know, "From what I've heard, red heelers are real smart. They come pretty naturally housebroken."

"I doubt that, but the way your planning always works out, I'm guessing if there are two on the planet that could come that way, those are the two we'd get."

Billy gave the first "dog command" but it was to me. "Go call Chuy or Ernesto and get them working on the adoption."

"I can see we're going to give this thoughtful consideration before acting—all because I grabbed your face and said you were cute like a puppy."

All he said to that was, "Get off your almost-a-butt and go call."

I slowly eased up off the couch and mumbled as I went into the kitchen to call, "*Jawohl, herr kommandant.*"

"I heard that," he mumbled back.

Part of me hoped this would be a lengthy process. I figured of the two, Chuy would be least likely to know if there were any options currently available or pups about to be born. Ernesto's out-and-about too much. I figured he'd have seen some momma dog somewhere, and cattle dogs in Fort Davis aren't exactly a rare breed. They appear to be bred into half the dogs around town.

Lupe answered. "Hey, Lupe. It's *Jaime*. The boy's got his heart set on gettin' a couple red heeler pups. He said I should let the

Cardonas know in case they know of a couple sometime down the road."

Lupe replied, "Hang on." She hollered, "Chuy! Come to the phone. *Jaime* and Billy are looking for a couple red heeler pups." Then she said, "I think he may be able to help you out."

"That quick?" I asked. She was off the phone and Chuy was on.

"Hey, *Jaime*. You want two or ten?"

"Billy says I want two."

Chuy continued, "I'm not sure you know this, but I've started volunteering at the new animal shelter that's in Fort Davis. We ended up with a very pregnant momma dog. It looks like multiple fathers may have been involved, but half the litter look like purebred red heeler and momma dog is a damn fine dog. I don't know how anybody could have dumped her off. We actually think it was someone from Alpine drove up here and tied her to the front door. At least that's what one of the neighbors reported. I don't know how she knew they were from Alpine. My guess is they just knew it wasn't anybody's car they'd seen around Fort Davis.

"You should come by and take a look. It was a litter of six, and I think we may have homes for the four bigger ones. There are two that aren't real runts but people seem to look at them like they are, which is why they're still unspoken for. Personally, I think they'll grow up to be really good dogs, especially if they have good masters like you and Billy. They are the two that look most like purebred red heelers."

I responded, "Good lord! I didn't know you could sell used cars. You missed your calling."

He relayed my comment to Lupe. Then he said, "Maybe I'm just late finding it. The shelter staff say I can get dogs moved better than anyone else there."

"I believe it!" I exclaimed.

He continued, "If you and Billy can meet me there tomorrow at ten we could wrap up this adoption. They are weaned, have their shots and are ready to go. You'll just need to get them fixed when they are a little older unless you plan to breed them."

"We do not," I answered, though of course we'd not discussed that. "I doubt I need to confirm with the foreman. He'll want us there at ten. We'll see you then."

When I went back into the living room Billy had disappeared. I had been surprised he hadn't eavesdropped when I was on the phone. I looked back in his room and he wasn't there. I looked out on the patio and he wasn't there either. I thought, "Where in the Sam Hill did the boy go?"

I put on my around-the-house loafers and went to see where he'd escaped to. He and Sallie were out with the horses.

When he saw me headed their way he said, "Look what the cat drug in."

I replied, "You just said you didn't want a cat."

"Sallie came over to go for a ride, and I told her you were on the phone getting us a couple red heelers."

Sallie suggested, "They'd be good dogs for out here. With some training, they'll be in hog heaven helping y'all move cattle from section to section."

Billy continued, "Sallie has assured me that when their top secret meeting with Brett is over, she'll wind up having to do something over here, and we'll get the scoop then."

I noted, "It could be she'll have to take a vow of silence like your dad made Ernesto and me do when your mom left the church."

Sallie feigned a super-serious tone, "Could be if Bill asked me that, I would. Could be if Brett does, I won't. Y'all are welcome to ride along. I thought it was too pretty a day for December to just sit and watch my sister read all afternoon."

Billy responded, "I'm up for it unless Jaime says we have to pick up two puppies."

"For the moment, we can squeeze in a ride. I'll tell you about my phone call once we're saddled up."

I laid out my true intentions of electing to call Chuy first and how that fell right into Billy's usual luck for such things going his way.

His first reaction was, "Hot damn!"

Sallie's was, "I always knew you two would adopt if you couldn't have your own."

I asked, "Sallie, what would your sister say to such a statement?"

106

She chuckled, "Well, fortunately these days she would just laugh. I sure like her better now that she's come up to speed with the rest of us as far as facing life with some joy and good humor."

Monday morning, we were off to look at puppies. By the time we arrived, the other four and momma dog were all adopted. Momma was still there but due to go to her new home the same day. Chuy took us to their kennel. I saw how short-haired momma dog was and speculated, "Maybe since they are short-haired dogs, they won't shed so much in the house."

I should have read the signs when the used car salesman responded, "Yeah, maybe."

Billy sized up their anatomy, "*Jaime*, we'll finally have two females in residence."

I responded, "They are going to get fixed before we have a whole house full! No tellin' what stray will come sniffin' around, and we'll have another typical hit-and-run daddy leavin' us with the young'uns."

We did all required to complete the adoption, and were on our way back to the ranch. I drove and Billy played with the pups.

I suggested, "That littlest one is going to have to grow into her looks, I think. She looks kinda like she came out half-baked."

"She'll be beautiful!" Billy pronounced.

I conceded, "Well, momma dog was, so she might be too."

He asked, "What're you gonna name yours?"

"I didn't know there was a yours and mine except for sleeping arrangements. You have any names in particular now that you've seen them?"

He replied, "The bigger one has a kind of little bear face. She looks like a koala bear, so maybe Koala for her."

"And the other?" I asked.

"How about Kola. Those go together good."

I said, "Let me try 'em out. See if they respond. Hey Kola!"

I couldn't believe it. The "runt" turned her head to look at me. "Kola it is," I said. "And if she's Kola the other one has to be Koala."

Billy smiled, "I can see already they're smart—just like their masters."

I replied, "I can already see their daddies are gonna spoil 'em rotten."

I was ordered to turn right when we got to the ranch. "We gotta show Mom and Dad their new grandchildren and introduce them to their great aunt."

"You're a mess," but I did as instructed.

When we went into the house with them, Billy set them down on the floor. "Meet your new grandchildren, Koala and Kola. Kola's the little one."

Bill took one look, "I could see from that face on that other one, she was Koala."

Betsy asserted, "I don't want those dogs peeing on my floor."

Billy fibbed, "They peed outside. Jaime says red heelers come housebroken."

I noted, "I don't believe I was the one who said that, and I'm sure the one who did was engaging in wishful thinking."

I picked up the dogs before one of them did pee on the floor since the only outdoor peeing, so far, would have been at the shelter.

Sallie heard the commotion and came up from her office in her wing of the house.

She grinned, saying, "Well, well, aren't they the spittin' image of their daddies. That little one looks kinda like you Billy and the bigger one like Jaime."

Bill jested, "Now that you mention it."

Billy shook his head at both of them. "We don't want to expose the children to such sarcasm. Let's take 'em home, Jaime."

Billy took the puppies from me and said, "Say goodbye, kids." He took a paw of each and waved goodbye.

Chapter Eighteen

Billy lucked into being almost right about Koala and Kola being housebroken. It took about one "accident" each before they clued in that such necessary functions were to be taken outdoors. He also seemed to be right about bedmates. Koala slept with him and Kola with me. Of course, even on the ride from his folks' place that first day, he said it would be Koala that wanted to sleep with him. When I asked why that was, he responded, "'Cause Dad says he looks like you, and you've always wanted to sleep with me."

"If you say so."

I tried not to be too happy about the one thing that happened that Billy hadn't predicted with his doggie nirvana. We had run over to talk to Bill and Sallie about selling some cattle, and we were gone a bit longer than either of us thought we would be. When he opened the door, I heard him holler, "What the hell!?" I stepped up the pace and looked inside to see what surprise lay in store for us. I was expecting more than a pee or poo accident given the reaction. I immediately expected couch stuffing everywhere. What I saw was one boot, of his only expensive pair of cowboy boots, chewed to smithereens.

I actually think I witnessed true anger in Billy for the first time. I decided to withhold the little bit of pleasure I was getting out of it, since I knew I shouldn't be experiencing pleasure in that moment. And he couldn't blame Kola because Koala was there chewing away still.

I did say, "Damn, we should have gotten some rawhides to throw around. I don't know why we didn't think about that."

Billy fumed, "Well, we need to put up anything leather that's for sure!"

He couldn't hang onto his anger long. He was over scooping up Koala, looked her in the face and said, "What did you do to my boot, you naughty dog?"

I said, "She's getting a message of firm rebuke now!"

"Well, look at her," he replied. "How can you stay mad at a face like that?"

"About the same way I could stay mad at yours if you ever made me mad."

"Have I ever made you mad?" he asked.

"You do recall how that kinda question drags on for a while once we get to considering the possibilities. Let's take 'em outside."

Kola liked to lie in my bathroom for some reason, and I called out, "Kola!" She came running full-steam—fishtailin' in across the hardwood floors toward the door. "She certainly knows her name," I said.

Billy stated flatly, "I never wear them damn boots anyway. Too fancy for going to Fort Davis." He set Koala down on the patio and she quickly went to the gravel and peed. Kola followed suit.

"You did wear 'em in New Orleans."

He replied, "If we ever go back, I'll go incognito and wear tennis shoes. No one will know I'm a cowboy."

I suggested, "I think we're both gettin' bowlegged. Could be that'll give us away."

I could see he was pleased with what popped into his mind. "They'll prob'ly be lookin' at my ass since I won't have those fancy boots on, and they may not notice the bowlegs."

"That's one possibility, I suppose."

Christmas was upon us, and with it, the two most anticipated events of the season—Zoey and Mark's visit and Brett's hush-hush meeting.

We took the pups with us to meet the Sunset Limited. When we left the ranch, the update from Amtrak was for the train to be thirty minutes late. It was more than an hour after that when the shift change of conductors and engineer finally showed up at the station. We knew it had to be rolling in soon.

Billy said, "You stay with the pups. I'll go see why it's running late."

He was soon back. "The conductor said some passenger started causing trouble and smokin' on the train. They stopped as close to Van Horn as the train gets and put him off. He ran up in front of the train and laid across the tracks before the train could get rollin'. They had to wait for the sheriff to show up to get him out of the way once and for all."

"Exciting!" I exclaimed. "We'll hope it wasn't Mark."

From the ticket information Mark had sent us those months earlier, we knew what car they'd be in and, from our own trip, where to stand to wait for them.

Billy asked, "Think you'll recognize her?"

"Even if I don't, we can probably assume it's them when a couple our age gets off at this spot. I just hope she doesn't look too much like either of my parents. I never thought we took after them, but I'm not sure kids ever notice that even if they do look like 'em."

Billy laughed, "I know Mom never foresaw me being the spittin' image of her dad."

We heard the train's horn coming from the west before we saw it round the corner coming into downtown Alpine. The railroad gates' bells started to chime and the arms came down. The big diesel engine went bellowing past us and car number two stopped with its door right in front of us. The conductor on board opened the door and threw out the yellow step stool onto the gravel base below, stepped down to straighten and level it as much as one can in such a bed and held his hand out to those getting off. The first few got off with no luggage.

Billy suggested, "Smokers probably."

He was right. All three quickly lit up cigarettes.

Next, was an old man with a suitcase and apparently traveling alone. Billy noted, "I think I know him though I can't remember his name. He was mayor of Alpine when I was growing up. Victor somethin' or somethin' Victor. Maybe they missed the train."

I replied, "These could have been on the lower level. And smokers are lined up way before the train is near the station. Mark and Zoey are up top, of course."

"True," Billy agreed.

Then we both saw a bright smile on a dark-haired woman who looked thin as a rail but, as the afternoon sun hit her face, we could see was just as bright-eyed as her smile. She didn't say a word but just reached out and hugged me. I could hear her sobbing. With a long sniffle she pulled back and exclaimed, "We made it! Jaime, this is Mark, as you will have guessed." And then hugging Billy, she added, "I don't need an introduction to this one. You're Billy, and you're adorable."

"I'm glad you noticed," Billy responded. "You and I are going to get along great as I see you're a hugger. I didn't think Cruzes knew how to hug and Schlatters generally aren't any better. I always have to show them how it's done."

We meandered to the truck and found the two pups busily gnawing away on the rawhides instead of the front seats. We put our guests' suitcases in the back, and I hopped in to drive.

Billy asked, "You want me to drive?"

"You know the way in and I know the way home. I'll drive."

I really had just hopped in out of the habit of driving home, but I didn't see any need to switch. I figured Billy could entertain them better in the truck than I could anyway.

He picked up Kola, "Kola, meet Auntie Zoey and Uncle Mark." Then he repeated the same for Koala. He asked, "Which one do you think looks like Jaime?"

Zoey replied, "I didn't see any immediate family resemblance, but then I haven't studied Jaime's face or even seen it for years. I'll have to get back to you on that."

Mark interjected, "You know anything goes in California. Are you two gay cowboys?"

"Mark!" Zoey exclaimed. "Maybe that's not a question you should ask. It's not really any of our business."

Mark said, "But you did say, 'I wonder if they're gay.'"

I thought I'd better answer before Billy got creative. I replied, "We are playful and don't like labels—but if you want to know if we sleep together, no we do not, though Billy has threatened to crawl in my sleeping bag on one occasion."

Billy added, "The only stipulation if I did was Jaime had to enjoy it."

Mark asked, "You could have guaranteed that, couldn't you, Billy?"

Zoey laughed, "I can see this is going to be a fun time together. Clearly, you boys have no intention of pretense in any direction."

I sighed, "That would pretty well describe our life both on the ranch and with our friends in town. Billy, you best tell them what they are in for if they go with us on New Year's Eve."

When he recounted our first and subsequent parties there, Mark pronounced, "I'm not missing that for the world!"

Zoey added, "Ernesto sounds like Mark's kindred spirit. He was in a drag act in college and has the pictures to prove it. I think I'm Rosalinda."

Then she said, "Billy, hand one of the pups back here."

She eased it towards her face to be sure Kola wasn't going to snap.

Billy assured her, "You can tug and pull on their lips or put your face right into theirs—they won't do anything but give you a little lick."

Mark said, "I've never seen dogs that look like these. What are they?"

Billy answered, "Cattle dogs—red heelers. There are a lot of them around here and all have Aussie roots. I don't know how the first ones got out here."

I added, "They are called heelers because they nip the heels of cattle as they move them. Of course, ours are too small to mix with cattle just yet, and I have no idea how we're going to train 'em. Trust instinct mostly, I guess."

Billy said, "I forgot to tell you this, but when I first got to Van Horn there was an old man there who trained cattle dogs. He was truly a master—won competitions and everything. That was a long time ago, but he did show me the basics."

"Good to know!" I replied. "Since you brought up Van Horn, you might as well tell them that whole story, starting in the kitchen. That ought to take the rest of the ride home. By the way, guests, you're about to enter the mountains, and it's a pretty drive the rest of the way."

Mark asked, "Have you ever gone west out of Alpine on the train?"

"No, why?" I asked in return.

He explained, "The last few miles before you come into town were without question the best part of the trip. The rock and colors in the canyon you pass through are amazing."

Zoey added, "Literally, breathtaking for me."

Then Mark said, "Before you start your story, hand me that other one. What was her name again?"

"Koala," Billy answered.

Mark laughed, "I think I see a little of Jaime in this one."

113

"Bingo!" Billy shouted. "And that's the one that sleeps with me. Draw your own conclusions."

Zoey said, "Jaime, I can see why trying to describe Billy in a letter is an impossibility."

"I tell him all the time, 'You're a mess.'"

Billy added, "And to keep the record straight, I say to him, 'But I'm your mess.' Even Mom and Dad tell Jaime, 'Take this mess home. He's yours now.'"

They both laughed and then Mark reflected, "Billy, it seems like you and I both have managed to have a little hand in pulling these two from sad and sorry lives. Look at them now. Tell us about Van Horn, and when we get to the house we'll tell you about our one Van Horn story—but it can wait. I believe Jaime left you somewhere in the kitchen."

Before he started his story, Billy pointed out towards the driver's side windows. "That's Mitre Peak. Now, we're coming into the Davis Mountains. You should see this mountain up here on the left when it's green from the summer rains. It's incredible."

I was deliberately driving slower than normal, not just to give Billy adequate time to tell his tale, but to allow our guests the opportunity to look at the mountains and ask about anything in particular they might want to know about along the way.

As we came up the rise where Ernesto and Chuy's *papá* had died, Mark saw the sign for High Frontier. "Is that a family ranch there?"

I had always assumed it was and had never asked anyone about it. Billy answered, "A ranch for wayward teens. I'm not sure who qualifies exactly, but it is a coed boarding school of some kind. I think they do drug and alcohol recovery, but I'm not sure. It opened here when I was in elementary school—I do remember that much."

We stopped in Fort Davis long enough to grab the mail and asked if they wanted a late lunch.

Zoey answered, "We had an early lunch on the train so, unless you two haven't eaten, we're good. We certainly don't mind if you want something."

"We're good too," Billy replied. "Your brother has put me on a diet."

"Of a kind," I noted. "Carry on with Van Horn, Billy."

He sorted mail and told them about the twenty years away from home, and managed to get to the whole house-building miracle before we reached the ranch.

He concluded, saying, "That's sorta the 'CliffsNotes' version, but you get the idea."

I asked, "You wanna drop the mail now or later?"

Billy answered, "Now is good. I told Mom we'd probably stop in to drop the mail and let them meet Zoey and Mark."

"Okey-dokey," I acknowledged as I cut to the west cattle guard. "Welcome to the Geermann-Schlatter ranch. For the next few miles you'll see what this foreman oversees."

Mark replied, "It's beautiful. I feel like I left urban life a million miles away."

"I know the feeling," I concurred.

We left the pups in the truck. Billy stuck his head in the door, "Anybody home?"

I smiled, "That's his ritual. When we see the car and trucks here, it's not like we don't *know* they're home."

By the time we stepped in, Bill was there to greet us. "So, these are the California dreamers. Welcome. I'm Bill and this is my wife, Betsy, and her sister, Sallie. I expect you've heard something about all three of us. I can assure you, if it's from Jaime it would all be true—and if from our firstborn, probably highly embellished though not an out-and-out falsehood. The boy can't tell a lie, for which your brother, Zoey, bears the brunt."

Zoey said, "All I know is Jaime and I have of late fallen into families neither of us conceived possible. We've already been persuaded by Billy that he is adorable."

Sallie chuckled, "That would be Billy. Of course, he gets that more from his aunt than his mother."

She reached out and shook their hands like the old cowgirl she is. Her handshake alone made our two guests smile widely and look at each other in delight.

Bill had a fire going, and Betsy, the great hostess, suggested they sit and take the chairs by the fire. Then she added, "Billy, if those pups are in the truck, as I suppose they are, you can bring them in."

She didn't need to say that twice. Then she went into the kitchen, opened the refrigerator and was soon back with a big tray of meats, cheeses, celery and olives. "The boys are on a diet, of a kind, and we're doing much the same."

Bill asked, "Do you want a beer, iced tea or water?"

They both said a beer would do nicely, and Billy and I had one too. Billy said, "We'd not talked about beer on this diet, but the little we drink, I don't guess it would need to be a hard and fast rule."

I agreed. "I concur with that."

Bill observed, "The train must have been late getting in."

Mark replied, "We were actually doing pretty well on the schedule the entire trip until we got near Van Horn. Then some nutjob started causing problems back in one of the coach cars who, according to our coach attendant, not only tried to smoke on the train but was high on something as well. The conductors put him off the train as close to Van Horn as they could and the crazy guy ran ahead of the train and laid on the tracks."

"Good lord," Bill replied.

Mark continued, "I'm sure the conductors would have pulled him out of the way if they could have figured out how to do that and get back on the train. As it was, they already had radioed in to get the sheriff out there to arrest the guy. It just took a while for them to show up, and so we had to sit there and wait."

With the full version of the Van Horn events now told, the ranch foreman announced, "We've got to go. We've a few chores to get done before it gets dark. Mom, holler when you need us to come help you eat dinner. We don't want you three missin' us for too long."

She answered, "We'll probably be calling you before we miss you, but you can count on dinner over here real soon."

Billy suggested, "It's like you say to Jaime, Sallie and me about getting you your Christmas tree—sooner is better than later."

Bill shouted from his chair, "Goodbye, son!"

Chapter Nineteen

Now that our guests were settled in, I needed to settle Christmas Day plans. I described what constituted our Christmas Eve with the service in the chapel and family gathering afterward. What we did on Christmas was up to us. Betsy made it clear we were welcome there, or if we wanted to stay home that was fine as well. I was a bit surprised how strongly Billy lobbied for staying home until I thought about Brett being there on Christmas Day as well as seeing him the night before. Once that sunk in, staying home sounded a lot better to me, too. I would make both offers to Zoey and Mark without tarnishing the second option with our opinion of the second Schlatter son.

Mark was up for either. Zoey said, "I don't want to offend them, so I'm okay either way as well, but I wouldn't be heartbroken if it was just us."

Billy cried, "Thank the lord! Right answer, Zoey. You'll meet my brother on Christmas Eve, and taking him two days in a row isn't my idea of a merry Christmas."

"You could have just said you preferred to stay here," Zoey offered.

"Your brother made me take a vow of silence," Billy replied.

I laughed. "Vows of silence run in the family. Before that all comes about, Billy and I have us booked into the lodge down at Big Bend this Friday night. When we booked it, we didn't have the pups, but I don't guess it matters if we take them along."

Billy added, "I told Jaime we could just cancel the rooms and rough camp in the big tent we have. He said he wasn't sure Mark would want me crawling is his sleeping bag to keep warm, and Zoey might not want to sit up on the Porta Potti in the back of the pickup—being it can get a little chilly this time of year."

Zoey replied, "Good decision, Jaime. I'm not that into roughing it, nor am I ready to share my new husband."

I noted, "We won't be able to see a lot of the park in that amount of time, but the lodge is in the Chisos Basin which is a highlight and we will, for sure, hike into *Santa Elena* Canyon while we're there."

Billy added, "We plan to go through Alpine on the way down, past Cathedral Mountain, and then take the river road home which goes through Presidio and Marfa. You'll get nearly the full road tour that way."

I recalled, "Sallie told us her dad always said that God took all the leftover rock from creation and dumped it down there. You'll see what he meant when we come back via the river road."

Mark asked, "So, the river road runs along the Rio Grande?"

Billy replied, "The road winds right along with the river. You can't call it an express route, but it is pretty spectacular as far as we're concerned."

I added, "Since you both mentioned that canyon west of Alpine, I'm sure you'll love it down there. I don't think we can oversell it."

While it was still dark, we loaded up the pups and guests on Friday morning to catch the sunrise on the ride down to Big Bend. Billy wanted to time the drive so the sun would be coming up as we got south of Alpine, saying, "They've seen the Davis Mountains on the way to the ranch and will get other chances while they're here. I'd like to catch the sun when it first hits Cathedral."

The great planner and foreman timed it perfectly. The sky was illuminated with bright pinks and purples in the east as we wound up the mountains south of Alpine. As Cathedral came into sight, the sun hit the top and slowly lit up the mountain as we approached. We all gawked out the window—not saying a word.

As the day brightened and the colors faded, Zoey exclaimed, "Oh my! That was the most spectacular sunrise I have ever seen in my life."

"Ditto that!" Mark replied.

Billy responded, "All in the plan."

I added, "If I said that Billy exaggerates in this instance, I wouldn't be telling the truth. Somehow his plans and nature's acts seem to coincide more than not."

Billy's humility kicked in enough to say, "Out here, nature provides the food for the soul. We just have to get out of bed and outside to appreciate it. If we'd left a couple hours later, the show would have been there, but we'd have never seen it."

"Never was a truer word spoken," I said.

When we got to the lodge, we saw we weren't the only ones with dogs, and ours were smaller than some. The little bit of fretting about having them along, whether justifiable or not, was dismissed. Given the cooler temperatures, it was not a problem leaving them in the pickup when we hiked into *Santa Elena* the next morning. From the canyon, we headed out of the park and onto the river road. Billy had to show them the cemetery in Terlingua and we stopped for an early dinner at his favorite restaurant in Presidio. We'd made two full days of it, and were sure it would be a highlight of their two weeks with us.

We told Mark and Zoey what our normal Sunday routine was, giving them the opportunity to join us or decline.

Zoey noted, "We're here for the whole experience. We attend the Episcopal Cathedral which requires an hour-long drive for us each way. Of course, Sunday traffic is as light as it gets, so it's an easy drive. Mark likes going there because he loves pipe organs and they have a grand one."

Mark added, "I grew up Catholic and another thing I like about the Episcopal service is we sing all the verses of the hymns."

Billy asked, "So, you sing?"

Zoey answered for him, "He has a lovely voice. I mostly mumble along, but I do like all the music at the Cathedral. They have a splendid choir."

I said, "*Manaña* will be about as humble an offering as you can imagine, but the simplicity of it, thanks to how Betsy puts it together, is lovely."

"You'll get to meet Jean and Mary-Alice too," Billy added. "They are bringing their borrowed motor home out today to get set up for the week ahead."

I noticed he didn't include Brett's arrival time. I added, "Brett isn't coming out until Monday and he's staying the week."

Billy muttered, "Top secret plans included."

I thought they'd be wondering about that comment, but since they didn't ask, I left it alone for the time being.

Zoey said, "I think we were a bit out of it after the long train ride. That first day neither of us said anything about that lovely tree at your folks' place."

Billy enlightened them, "Jaime, Sallie and I were under strict command from the *Kommandant* to get a big piñon off the ranch right after our December Quiet day. It's been a tradition since they moved in."

I suggested, "You might want to sing them the traditional song you've adopted when the three of us return with the tree." I knew it wouldn't take any persuasion on my part. He broke into song,

We three queens of orient are
bearin' yer tree we've cut from afar.
Sap and needles, bugs and beetles —
Rattlesnakes left behind.

They laughed and Mark said, "God broke the mold after you, Billy."

I can usually catch my tongue before it blurts out something maybe it shouldn't. In this case I heard myself say out loud, before the words had been analyzed whether proper for conversing with our guests or not, "I think it was the other way around—that ass broke God's mold."

I thought Zoey was going to fall out of her chair laughing so hard. Mark laughed as well, adding, "Jaime, I couldn't help but notice he puts you and me to shame."

Billy recalled our night in the chaise lounges, "I said to Jaime one night when we were completely tuckered out, 'Since I was sixteen years old, I've done nothing but work my ass off.' Jaime replied, 'Clearly, that is not true.' I had to admit I could have picked a better analogy."

We all laughed until it hurt.

I recalled, "Sallie says he came out that way—front cheeks and back as big as any baby could have. She says they must be from some recessive gene."

Billy sighed, "I sure love Aunt Sallie. I wouldn't be me without her."

I confirmed, "I believe that to be true with all my heart. She sure missed him those twenty years he wandered off."

Silliness set aside for a time, I confirmed the schedule for the next three days. "Sunday, we will have our chapel service and lunch afterwards with the family. After lunch, 'we three queens,' along with any California Dreamers who want to help, will decorate the chapel. Then at 6:00 on Christmas Eve, we will have our service in the chapel followed by another family gathering afterwards. Christmas Day we stay hunkered down here for our own Christmas together. Sound like a plan?"

"Sounds perfect," Zoey replied.

Billy preferred his harmonica over his fiddle, but the last two Christmases he had, as he put it, "put up the fiddle for a violin." He had worked on and mastered a violin solo of "Ave Maria." This was now part of our Christmas Eve service in *La Capilla de la Rosa*. Somehow it seemed especially appropriate in the chapel of the rose even for its Protestant members. With my inexperience with church, I didn't realize until Billy explained it to me, the stumbling block Mary presents between Protestants and Catholics.

He had a rather Billy way of summing it all up. "Dad says when you put a shit-ass with someone who wants power you get a politician, and I said to him when you put a shit-ass with someone holier than thou you get a theologian. Both cause lots of trouble—especially where politics and theology get tangled up together."

Made sense to me. History seemed to be strongly aligned with the Schlatter men's theory of power and its abuse thereof.

As we always do, and most Christians across the world I would guess, we concluded that Christmas Eve service in the chapel, each holding a candle as we sang that most famous carol of all.

Silent night! Holy night!
All is calm, all is bright
Round yon virgin mother and child!
Holy infant, so tender and mild.
Sleep in heavenly peace!
Sleep in heavenly peace!

Silent night! Holy night!
Shepherds quake at the sight!
Glories stream from heaven afar,
Heavenly hosts sing Alleluia!
Christ the Saviour is born!

Christ the Saviour is born!

Silent night! Holy night!
Son of God, love's pure light
Radiant beams from thy holy face
With the dawn of redeeming grace,
Jesus, Lord, at thy birth!
Jesus, Lord, at thy birth!

"...the dawn of redeeming grace." For me, that line defines my life here now. I feel so entirely redeemed, and I could see from Zoey's face as I sat across from her, the redemption she too has come to know.

I noticed as well a fine boy soprano voice as Noah, sitting between his grandmother and Billy, looked and sounded like the angel we were beginning to understand resided somewhere inside the shy boy from the peculiar family that was Brett's. His face seemed to glow, not only from the candle he was holding, but from some mystical comfort that comes to him when he is near his grandmother—and now, it seemed to me, being near Billy as well.

Chapter Twenty

On the "second day of Christmas," Billy made no secret of his eagerness to get Sallie's report on the top secret meeting with Brett. They were all to meet at 11:00. That was the first thing that got his ire.

As he put it, "What the hell! Everybody on this ranch is up by six at the latest. He can't get his ass in gear before eleven?"

I replied, "That's a city boy's idea of offering an accommodating schedule."

"Bullshit!" was all he said to that.

Mark seemed to think he needed to offer us some privacy when Sallie did come over. "Zoey and I will make ourselves scarce when she gets here. We'll just go in our room with the door closed."

Billy piped up, "Not on my account you won't. And I doubt seriously that Sallie will care either. You're gonna hear it all secondhand if you don't stay and hear it firsthand."

I didn't want him getting his expectations any more on edge than they already were, so I suggested since the meeting was so close to lunchtime, that might delay Sallie that much more.

"Shit," was all he said to that.

Sallie arrived just before noon. Her first words were, "I told them I'd accepted an invitation for lunch over here and had to run."

Billy responded, "Firstly, thank you for doing this and gettin' over here so quickly afterwards. Secondly, unless you mind, I told Zoey and Mark they could hear it firsthand from you. And thirdly, get to it!"

Sallie began, "I don't care if Zoey and Mark hear it. The only reason it was so top secret was because you and Jean would have wrung his neck before he got two minutes into his spiel. I don't know how the boy sells as much real estate as he does. Desperate buyers or somethin'. He can't read a room, and says things that do not help his case, but I'll get to that later.

"He went on and on about the virtues of the booming housing market and how he had leveraged all his assets to buy into mortgage-backed securities. He had so many examples of this and that I tuned him out completely for that part. He was there to 'change our future and offer us a lavish retirement.' Now does that give any indication that he knows us at all?"

We knew that was rhetorical and just listened in amazement.

She continued, "If we would sell the ranches, then with his 'guidance' we could easily double our money in a year or two and double it again after that—plowing more into these mortgage securities.

"I could see your dad's ass bitin' into the chair and steam building in my sister's head. She was getting redder every minute, and like I said, he sat there clueless as to their state of mind. I didn't even figure I needed to be outraged or say anything. I just sat there lookin' at him and thinkin', 'Thank God you're not my son.'

"Then he made his worst misstep of all. I think up to this point he actually thought they were warming to his ideas. How, I don't know, but it seemed like he was getting more excited all the time. Maybe he just thought if we were going to shoot it down, we'd a done so early on. The only reason we didn't was we agreed before he came into Bill's office, which is where we met, that we'd listen as patiently as possible to whatever it was he had to say. We all figured it involved inheritance or a big loan or something.

"Where Bill had had enough, and my sister and me too, was when he said, 'What future does this ranch have anyway? You gonna let that fruitcake run it for you the rest of your lives?'

"Now, I know I should have waited for your momma and daddy to speak first, but I couldn't help myself. I leapt out of my chair and went and stood right over him. I shook my finger at him and said, 'Let me tell you something, you *jackass!* That *fruitcake* is ten times the person you'll *ever* be and knows as much about this ranch as Bill and me put together!'"

She smiled and looked right at Billy. "Now, I'll grant that might have been a little bit of an exaggeration, but that's what came out. Anyway, I went right on. 'And if you don't know how much love that boy has in his heart, you're not only the jackass you've proved to be today, but the *dumbass* I've long suspected you are!'

"Then I sat down and said, 'There—I've had my say, and as you can see, I won't be investing in your *damn* mortgage-backed securities.'

124

"I figured Bill would say something next, but it was your mom. 'Brett, I'm sorry if I dropped you on your head or something when you were a child. I must have and don't remember it, but to sit there and try to slight your brother is a new low, even for you. You are usually just a bore. Today, you crossed over into sinning against this family. If you can't see that, then maybe you need to start by rereading that letter your father sent you and keep reading it until it gets through that thick skull.'

"Brett just sat there with a stunned look on his face. Finally Bill asked, 'Did you receive my letter?' 'Yes,' was all Brett said. 'Did you actually read it?' Bill asked.

"He just sat and never did answer yes or no."

Sallie looked at me and Zoey, "I know Jaime said he never knew his grandparents or at least not well. They might have been nice folk. Brett's a good example how one can stray so far from how he was raised. Could be your parents were the one-offs of a good family, and all they did was pass their misery on. I sure hate to think what Brett is passing on to those kids of his and all the stepkids who come in the package."

Billy asked, "Did Dad say anything else?"

Sallie replied, "He stood up, went to about where I'd stood in front of Brett and said, 'This conversation is over. You'll always be welcome at our table, but we'd better *never* hear of selling this ranch, or you saying anything against Billy again—or your sister, if you're inclined to disparage her because she's made her life with a woman. They've both made good lives for themselves, and I think it's your envy that makes you try to belittle your own brother. And let there be no mistake—Mary-Alice and Jaime are this family as well. I'd better never hear even a mumble under your breath about them.'

"We all walked out and left him sitting there in the office. He might still be there. I didn't hang around and got right over here."

I said as much to myself as the others, "Well, holy shit."

Sallie added, "I'll bet he leaves that office, packs up that brood with him and heads back to El Paso."

In this situation, I didn't know what to expect from Billy. I couldn't foresee him going over there and getting in a fight like they would in most movies. He was a bigger man than that and too secure in his own skin to let the likes of Brett get to him beyond the usual irritation. He confirmed my best instinct for him when he got up from the chair, went to Sallie—who never had sat down through her telling—hugged the daylights out her, "My God, I love you!"

Sallie replied, "You can let loose now. I ain't goin' nowhere. Jaime, I told them next door I was coming over for lunch. What're we havin'?"

"Zucchini carbonara—a recent addition to our diet and one Billy loves."

Koala was back on Billy's lap the instant he sat down. Sallie noted, "I guess that other heeler is back in the bathroom as usual whenever I come over. She called out, "Kola!" Kola came fishtailing across the hardwood to the patio door, assuming she was going outside. Koala leapt down by her sister.

Billy directed, "You're gonna have to take 'em out now. You've got 'em all excited."

"We shall return shortly," Sallie announced, and was out the door right behind the dogs.

Zoey came to help me in the kitchen. I looked out the window and Sallie was lighting up a Swisher Sweet. "Look, Zoey. There's the old cowgirl as I first knew her. She doesn't smoke much these days, but after the morning she's had, I'm not a bit surprised to see her light one now that it's over."

Zoey replied, "What a gem she is."

"A delightful character and a gem. You can see why we love her so much."

Billy went out onto the patio with his aunt and the pups— quickly becoming dogs—and Mark joined us in the kitchen. He looked out the window, saying, "She may not be the boy's mother, but that lioness knows how to tear apart anything trying to get at her adopted cub!"

Then, as she took a long drag from her Swisher Sweet, he added, "I used to think I had some cool aunts. Sallie has upped the bar considerably."

I had things on the stove ready to serve whenever the other two came back inside. We all three looked out the window at the two of them. Billy had picked up Koala and Sallie was holding Kola as they headed back in the house.

126

Mark put his arm around his wife, "Honey, if I ever *was* gonna get in a sleeping bag with another man, it would be that crazy cowboy standing out there."

She smiled, "I might beat you to it."

"It may sound funny," I said, "but I'm glad to hear you both say it. His magnetism is somethin' else, isn't it? And you can see where he gets it from."

Sallie's prediction that Brett would cut his plans short and head to El Paso came to pass. We got a call from Jean on her cell just as we were sitting down to lunch.

Billy answered. "Our brother has packed up and left. I wonder what that's all about. Things must have gotten tense."

Billy advised, "I suspect if you run up to the house, you'll get an earful from Mom and Dad. Sallie is over here for lunch, and she had quite a story to tell. But I gotta go now. Jaime has lunch on the table."

I noticed he didn't even say goodbye—just hung up.

He sat down and asserted, "I'm not lettin' my carbonara get cold going through all that with her. She'll have to get it firsthand for herself."

Chapter Twenty-one

We'd aimed for Thursday or Friday for our ride around the ranch. Since we had enough horses for six but not for eight, Billy and I were reluctant to cast the net too widely. We knew Betsy wouldn't come, but we thought perhaps everyone else would want to. Jean and Mary-Alice were still there.

On Wednesday, we'd decided we'd take everyone to the Slo Poke Cafe, and were surprised when we saw Jean in the motor home and Mary-Alice following in their car.

When they came in, Billy asked, "I thought you were staying through New Year's?"

Jean replied, "That was the plan, but we decided we'd just as soon get back to our own beds and out of the motor home. We could move into the bunkhouse, but somehow that seemed like more trouble than it was worth since we'd first have to change and wash all the towels and sheets that Brett left for whoever comes in next."

"He did have to get out of Dodge quickly," Billy noted.

I could see Billy working out now being able to invite Bill and Sallie on the ride. Billy and I had already agreed that we wouldn't bring up the subject of Brett, and if Jean happened to, we'd keep quiet—figuring that his folks would just as soon not talk about that with Mark and Zoey still there. We would have plenty of time once they were gone to talk more.

Mark looked around and asked Betsy, "Are there any of your old church group in here to get Billy lovin' on Jaime."

She smiled, "I don't even need to turn around and look. If they were, he'd already be carryin' on. You're taking a big risk sitting on the other side of him."

I thought maybe Mark would share his comment about how, if he was going to crawl in a sleeping bag with a man, it would be with Billy, but he never did. I wasn't going to tell Billy about it until they were safely on the train back to California.

Jean said, "Oh, I can't believe we forgot to bring this up earlier. We'd been puttin' off sayin' anything until we had a little more confidence that it was going to come together. Dad, we didn't forget about you wanting us to look into the fair trade co-ops and how to get hooked up with the farmers in El Salvador. Conchita has been most diligent about helping to get this going."

"Ernesto would kick her butt if she didn't," Billy rightly noted

Mary-Alice laughed, "That's what she said word for word—except for the pronoun."

I added, "That wouldn't be word for word if Ernesto had said it. He'd have used a different word for the body part kicked, for sure."

Jean continued, "Conchita has been back and forth a few times to El Salvador on Ernesto and Rosalinda's dime, and she knows a couple in San Angelo who are opening up a roasting business. She's trying to line up a couple more around the state, all under the same label—built on a co-op model rather than franchises. They plan to sell the coffee under the brand "Mountain Bean Roasters of Texas"—hopefully no longer open to a name change as they've built a website to sell online and ship to anywhere in the US. The first beans have left the farms and are in transit as we speak."

Bill responded, "That is great news—that is *really* great news. I had no idea y'all had made that kinda progress."

"He's been dying to ask you about it," Betsy added, "but I told him, 'When they have news, you'll know.' That's wonderful, girls."

Billy suggested, "When we get ahold of some, we should get Sara to talk to the owners, and they could serve it here with those little triangle things you set on tables to advertise the coffee and website."

Mary-Alice replied, "That's a good idea and one Jean and I could do—checking with other restaurants."

Billy asked, "Do upscale bistros serve coffee or just wine? The guys who bought the old homestead opened up a bistro in Alpine."

"Of that we are aware." Jean answered. "They came to us to set up the books and do payroll."

I noted, "What little I know of the restaurant business you'd better always get paid in advance. There was one new restaurant I went to in California when they first opened, and I thought I'd support them. A week later there was a sign on the door, 'Closed two days—remodeling.' They never did unlock their doors again."

Bill said, "Since they seem like nice men, we might ought to make a list for them of who *not* to hire. We could all put at least two or three names on *that* list!"

Sara overhead that, informing us, "I've already given them a dozen names of those who make the rounds."

I commented to Mark and Zoey, "Sara's like family. She takes good care of us, and we try to do right by her—which she probably heard me say. She's got ears like a bat."

"Yes, I heard that," she remarked from halfway across the restaurant.

When she came back by the table she asked, "Did you all leave Sallie home alone?"

Betsy answered, "She's in Alpine having lunch with her old high school sweetheart, Norman, who moved back earlier this year."

Bill added, "And no, you won't hear wedding bells ringing anytime soon. He'll be lucky if she consents to more than the once a month lunch they've been having."

Billy noted, "But she does drive down once-a-month like clockwork."

"That is true enough," Bill conceded.

Then Billy said, "She needs to be courteous enough to have him out at the ranch, so we all can meet him."

Betsy laughed, "That would send a signal she is reluctant to send out just yet. I've suggested it. She forthrightly said, 'No way, José.'"

Mark jested, "Given her brother-in-law and nephew, I'd guess Norman might have an uphill climb to come close to measuring up."

Billy exclaimed, "Dad and I are real catches which Mom and Jaime well know!"

Bill replied, "Good lord."

Betsy added, "You've said the boy can't tell a lie."

"I'm staying out of this one," I said. "Back to the fair trade coffee, I'm surprised Ernesto and Rosalinda haven't said anything about Conchita making such headway on the project."

"I don't think they wanted to jinx it," Jean explained. "Once it's officially up and running, I'm sure you'll hear all about it. They were in the office with Conchita a couple weeks ago, and Ernesto said, 'When Chuy sends pictures of the farmers loading up their beans for exportation, we'll get your folks copies, as I know they like to keep up with everything going on down there.' You should get them anytime. I know the beans are on their way."

Bill's inherent bond to Ernesto's youngest was evident. "That boy sure has done a lot for those farmers and villagers. He's gotten more done in four years than most clergy ever accomplish in a lifetime."

Betsy tagged on, "Or even try to get done."

Mark stated flatly, "They are accomplished at getting good pension and insurance plans."

Bill responded, "That's true enough, and you can see how unimportant that is to Chuy."

Billy and I had told Mark and Zoey about the fish tanks but not who'd funded them. I said, without giving away anything in front of them or anyone within earshot in the restaurant, "Between Elma's prayers and the generosity of others, it shows what's possible."

Bill surprised us all, and no one more so than Betsy, when he offered, "Maybe instead of taking that second honeymoon to New Orleans, Mother, you and I should take a trip to El Salvador."

Billy interjected, "If you're planning that for your fiftieth, you'd better plan it pretty quickly. You don't even have passports, and Groundhog Day is right around the corner."

"I don't think it matters if we are there on our actual anniversary," Bill replied. "Anytime in the year would work if your mother wanted to make the trip."

Betsy responded, "Now that I've recovered from the initial shock, I think it's a wonderful idea."

Bill added, "Since I don't think a second honeymoon was ever about rekindling our romance, you could invite your sister to come along if you wanted to. She's certainly as interested in Chuy's work as we are."

"When you decide it's something we are really going to do, I'll ask her."

Bill stated in his matter-of-fact tone, "I thought we just did."

Billy turned to Mark and Zoey, "When the people in this family have a good idea they don't second-guess it."

I verified, "That is true enough."

"You realize, Mr. Cruz," Billy continued, "that their fiftieth means I turn forty next year, and you're only six months behind me."

"We can't deny middle age any longer," I said. "It is upon us."

Mark added, "That makes four of us. I hit forty in June, and you know your sister hit the mark already."

"She *is* my much older sister."

Zoey responded, "Granted, but you have a little gray hair coming in."

"I'd say Ms. Clairol helps you in that department. Your hair wasn't that black any time in your life."

She replied, "Once it grew back out after chemo, I did cheat a little—I thought I earned it."

"Sorry, Zoey, I didn't even think about that."

She took no offense. "No need to apologize. After all, you and Mark did get me through it. Now, I have the gift to actually *be* middle-aged."

Bill asked, "Anybody ready to head to the ranch and Marfa?"

No one answered. We just got up to go. Sara met us at the cash register and asked if Billy and I were picking up Mark and Zoey's lunch. Billy declared, "We're treating everybody today. Ring it all up together."

Sara asked, "Betsy, I gather Norman is from Fort Davis. What is his last name? Does he still have family here I'd know?"

Betsy answered, "You do know everyone. No, his family is gone, but your mom and dad will remember them. Your dad and Norman might have even graduated together. His last name is Case. Norman left after graduation and never was heard from until he moved back here a few months ago. I don't remember why or when the rest of the family moved away."

Sara responded, "I do remember seeing his picture in the senior class in Dad's annual."

Billy laughed, "Now he looks like Santa Claus—white beard, little wire-rim glasses and, according to Mom, even a poochybelly."

Then Sara asked, "Are you taking your guests to the big Cardona New Year's Eve party?"

I replied, "Mark says they can't wait."

"Mateo and I got invited this year. I credit you for having us out for dinner."

Billy noted, "That was a fun evening. We will do it again if y'all are up for it."

"We'll be up for it," Sara replied.

When we got back to the ranch, I went to let the dogs out, and Billy herded our guests toward the stables.

He announced, "In preparation for our ride, you'll both need to have a roping lesson in case we get caught up in a stampede, and we need all hands on deck to bring the herd under control."

He pulled out a bale of hay, grabbed a lasso and asked, "Who's first?"

The dogs and I were there by then. "What the Sam Hill are you up to now?"

"Preparing them in case of a stampede."

"I see." Rather than spoil his fun, I went along with it.

He handed his volunteer, Mark, the lasso and instructed, "Now this is the most important thing about roping. Keep your eyes open."

Mark replied, "I was planning on it. That seemed a given."

Billy said, "Jaime assumed eyes-closed was a best practice for starters until I moved the bale."

"It's true," I admitted.

"He was good at lassoing his own neck but not much else until he finally got his motivation clear in his mind," Billy explained.

Zoey asked me, "What was that?"

"I'd rather not say." Of course, I had my doubts it would end there.

Mark made his first toss and came pretty close to getting it around the bale. He pulled the rope back and tried again— successful on the second attempt, but he wasn't up on a horse yet.

"All right, that's good enough for now, Mark." Billy took the rope and handed it to Zoey. "Zoey, it's your turn. Let's hope you don't need the Cruz motivation like your brother did, although in your case I know a reasonable substitute."

She replied, "Okay, I've got to know what the Cruz motivation is."

"After I chastised Jaime for having his eyes closed, he tossed the rope towards me and got a perfect catch. I told him, 'See, you just gotta want those steers as much as you want me.'"

Zoey skipped the bale and tossed it first time right over Mark!

"Well done, Zoey!" Billy exclaimed. "That was the reasonable substitute I was going to suggest."

"I guessed it was." Then she added, "I'm just speculating here, but we don't need to worry about stampedes, do we?"

"Pretty unlikely," I replied. "We can barely get 'em up and moving from one section to another. I suppose if a mountain lion came on the scene they might spook, but if they did, we aren't about to go chasing after them."

As we started back into the house Kola put her nose on the back of my ankles and then the other. Koala did the same to Billy. Zoey exclaimed, "Look! How cute! The pups are herding them back into the house."

I added, "Billy, I think it's time to begin training our cattle dogs. Clearly, they both have the instinct."

He noted, "I thought they would actually bite at our legs as they herd us, but they just barely touch. Pretty cute."

"It's adorable," Zoey said.

Billy plunked on the couch and gave one tap to his leg. Koala was up in his lap. "All their puppy fuzz is gone. They have real dog hair now."

Kola was up on my lap too. I noticed how much hair was coming off as I scratched her back. "Yeah, they have their dog hair, and the used car salesman skirting my comment about short-haired dogs proves to me we're going to be dealing with dog hair for a long time if they shed this much in winter."

Billy added, "Kola finally looks all the way baked. She's getting really pretty." He clarified for our guests, "She was the smallest of the litter and real splotchy-looking. We said it looked like she came out before she was all the way baked."

Thursday morning at breakfast Billy announced, "The forecast says, 'Perfect day for a ride on the ranch.' Sally and Dad are coming along. They should be here shortly."

We ate, tidied up and headed out to saddle up. Billy asked me, "Do you think we could let the dogs tag along?"

"No, we need to let them get a little bigger and take them just with us, so we can always come back home if we need to without ruining the ride for everyone."

"Good plan," Billy replied.

We soon had the six horses saddled and ready to go. Bill and Sallie came over, and we headed out. I soon figured out that Billy was headed to the knob. I guessed the tour would include the rock outcropping on the way back so he could share his proposal story.

Billy turned in his saddle and asked our guests, "How's it going? You ready to slap their asses and get 'em in a full run?"

Mark answered for both "The slow trot's just fine."

As he turned back around, Billy replied, "Well, all right. We'll mosey along then."

We rode along quietly—only speaking to point out something or answer a question about the ranch. We tied up the horses and headed to the top of the knob.

On the way up Bill said. "This is the one spot on the ranch we don't bring anyone but family, and to be honest, I've never even brought Brett up here. There are rare plants up here, and I don't trust some do-gooder group coming in here to protect them. They survived a few million years on their own, and we intend to keep it that way. It is also home to a number of great horned owls who nest in the crags on the south face."

When we got to the top Zoey declared, "Oh, my—this is lovely."

We all picked a rock to sit on and just let our thoughts be informed by all the beauty around us. We'd been there at least half an hour when a male painted bunting came and sat on a rock right in front of Sallie and just bobbed its little head looking right at her.

Sallie spoke softly, "Well, you beautiful creature. What are you doing here this time of year? You should be in Mexico by now."

The bird just sat there looking at her.

She waited a bit and continued her conversation with the bird. "Oh, is that right. Well, okay then. Say hello to the Mrs. for us."

A moment later, he flew from his perch on the rock.

Bill asked, "What'd he say about why he wasn't in Mexico?"

"He says he had it on good authority that it was going to be a mild winter and didn't need to hurry and scurry down across the border. They'll be heading that way after New Year's. He just came around to say goodbye."

I sat there believing, however incredible, that Sallie's conversation with that beautiful bird was real. It is inexplicable, I know, but she has some gift with the natural world few of us can conceive. Perhaps it is just a failure of imagination on our part. I do believe Billy has much the same gift and will, with little doubt in my mind, equal his aunt's gift as his years advance. She has had a lifetime to tune her mind to the world around her. He's still growing in that direction—growth I see from year to year.

We rode next to the outcropping as I'd predicted, and indeed, Billy showed them "the exact spot" where he had "proposed." Then he said, "Jaime, we should recreate the hug at the end."

I stood up from the rock where I was sitting and went to him. I held him tight in my arms as I had longed to do that first time, and my willingness this time caught him off guard. He did as he had the first time. He began to weep. When I let loose of him, his dad obviously recalled his own embrace when he heard Billy say—after being told about the new house and the healing of his mother's relationship—'When it's done, I'll be there.'"

I watched Bill hold Billy tightly with Sallie now hugging the two of them. I recalled Bill's exact words as he told us Billy was coming home—"When I heard those words, I never hugged a boy so hard in all my life, and I couldn't let go."

Zoey, Mark and I held each other in our own embrace. Here we all were—six souls respecting the serenity and grace of the moment as each celebrated the restoration of the onetime estrangement each had known in some context. Love made manifest on a mountaintop in far west Texas.

Chapter Twenty-two

Two little red heelers were sitting at the patio door eagerly awaiting their run into the back yard. We were getting used to the two little faces waiting for us. Koala was the lazier of the two. She'd lie down and let Kola stand guard. I'd see her and say to Billy, "Kola's at the door." And I'd no sooner say it when Koala would then stand up, and I'd add, "Koala's at the door." We'd open the door and they'd take a quick nip at our legs, signaling we'd been gone longer than they thought we should have been; then they would tear off to do their business. It seemed they could go all day if need be without any accidents in the house. Since we stocked up on rawhides, we no longer had to worry about chewed boots or anything else of value. They were growing into great companions.

We all settled in the living room after the quick bathroom breaks we needed as badly as the dogs.

Mark was the first to speak. "I'm pretty sure I wasn't the only one up on the knob who thought Sallie really could talk to that bird."

I replied, "I *know* you weren't, and I wouldn't be a bit surprised if Billy couldn't hear the bird as well. He and Sallie have some extraordinary gifts when it comes to understanding the natural world."

Billy added, I believe only *half* jokingly, "I caught part of what Mr. Bunting was saying."

Zoey said, "I've always considered myself an urbanite, and I realize now how little thought I've given to the lives of the people and creatures of a place like this. As redeemed as my life has been over these past months, I felt a certain weight of sin this afternoon— I don't know another word for it—for being so *ignorant* to the world around me. A sin, I must say, that was redeemed as well in the moment it was acknowledged."

Mark confirmed, "I didn't know how to put it into words, but I know now I can say that I experienced exactly the same—both the sin and the redemption."

I was just sitting there with the back of my head resting on the couch and eyes closed. "I understand it completely. I awakened here."

Billy didn't say anything. After returning from the mountaintop, he remained in a reflective mood the rest of the day. He quietly got up and said he'd take care of the few chores that needed tending while I got something fixed for dinner, adding, "I don't think we need more than a snack unless y'all are hungry. I've been fed pretty well just by the day together."

He went out the door with the dogs following. I said, "He's something, isn't he?"

Zoey didn't say a word, but just put her arm around me as she and I went into the kitchen to get the snack Billy had rightly predicted was all any of us really was hungry for.

Friday, we sat out back and watched Billy give his first lessons to the dogs on the basic commands he wanted them to learn. If you can call two or three acknowledged commands in one day good progress, he made good progress. It seemed to me, that was all that could be expected of them, and Billy didn't push them beyond that. Clearly, both were smart dogs.

Billy was back to his more playful self. "Now, you see how much smarter these dogs are at 'reading the room' than that jackass brother of mine. I barely change my expression and these dogs react."

We both had observed how a look or the slightest tap would be picked up by them as a signal for this or that. They were also getting to the playful stage with each other. They would bare their teeth and go for a leg to try to throw the other off balance. They could look downright mean, but they always gave themselves away when they'd look at us to be sure we were watching the show. Then they'd go right back at it to the point of standing up on their back legs, jaws wide open and front legs tangled together in a fight to the finish.

They put on a good show for Mark and Zoey after their training session with Billy.

"Good grief!" Zoey exclaimed. "It looks like it will end with bloodshed, and yet neither ever actually bites down on the other. What a show!"

Mark added, "Too bad politicians can't learn to do the show without the blood."

"Amen," I said.

New Year's Eve was upon us. I said to our guests, "It's crazy how much we look forward to this—just to see Ernesto and hear whatever it is he selects as his song to bring in the New Year."

Mark commented, "You said you didn't think you could oversell the Big Bend, and you were right about that. I'd say the same is going to prove true for this party. We've looked forward to it from your first telling us about it."

When we were ready to head into town, Billy softly asked, "Dogs go for a ride?"

Two heelers leapt from the couch and were at the door. I smiled, "I guess they're riding along."

Billy stated, "They'll be fine in the truck."

Each did her "business" and then popped up into the front seat. Both could already leap up onto things you'd think their little bodies would be incapable of conquering.

The long-awaited moment had arrived. Who would greet us as the door opened?

"Well, hello, Dolly!" I exclaimed.

Ernesto responded, "Welcome to the best little whorehouse in Texas."

He was in a full-length, bright red dress with puffy things on each sleeve—I'm sure someone knows what to call them. None of us did.

Then he added, "I tried to get Rosalinda to dress up as Sheriff Dodd, but she said she didn't want to steal the show."

Rosalinda was there to greet us as well. "That, and my mustache isn't quite heavy enough to pull off looking like Burt Reynolds. I do have the build to pull it off, though."

Ernesto continued, "I don't know why it took me so long to come into my own as Mona Stangley. I've always loved that movie. As you can see, I make up real good as Dolly."

Billy agreed, "We didn't have to think twice who you were— that's for sure!"

The whole evening seemed even crazier than usual, if that was possible. It must have been the red dress.

Billy joked, "Mona, you'd better not come near any of our bulls with that thing on. They'll come chargin' at you just like those bulls in Madrid come at the matadors."

Ernesto had his own surprise when midnight finally arrived. He hushed the crowd. "Now I have something to say before I do my traditional New Year's song. This required special permission from *mi esposa*. She said it seemed appropriate given Dolly's presence tonight. I'll be doing *two* songs this evening. The second is dedicated to Rosalinda. Billy, the first is dedicated to you. You and *Jaime* come stand here by me."

We did as ordered, though I suspected we were likely to turn as red as his dress when we heard what he had in store. He usually sings a cappella. He hit the play button on a boom box which started the karaoke accompaniment. He broke into song.

Why'd you come in here lookin' like that
In your cowboy boots and your painted-on jeans

He altered the lyrics a good deal including flipping "big ideas and a little behind" to "little ideas and a big behind" and making every reference somehow fit Billy's antics with me in the Slo Poke Cafe. He was nearly drowned out with laughs and applause a dozen times, but that strong voice prevailed over the roar of the crowd. I was wrong about us turning red. Oh, I turned as red as that dress, but Billy ate it up and didn't turn even the slightest shade of pink!

Once the applause died down, he motioned to Rosalinda. "Now you come here, my chickadee." He went back to a cappella and sang to her, "I Will Always Love You." He changed up those lyrics as well—this time making them all words of their fidelity for all their years together. No one was leaving for the sake of the other in his rendition.

Zoey leaned over to me, commenting, "He and Billy have one gift in common—they can take you from laughter to tears in a minute flat."

Rosalinda embraced her crazy husband, and when she let loose she came over to Billy and me. "He couldn't get away with what he did to you two with anyone else in town. You're good sports."

Billy declared, "I loved it!"

She responded, "I could see you did and knew you would. That's what makes you Billy. And *Jaime*, you and I both know they're worth it."

"Yes, we do."

Then she added, "Something tells me Kate Smith may now be permanently retired. Dolly has played enough roles in movies, I think those big, fake breasts and blond wig are going to get lots of use in the coming years."

We had joined up with Sara and Mateo after the singing, and they were having a great time—how can you not? Ernesto came over to our group and said to Mark and Zoey, "I hope our little Fort Davis New Year's wasn't too big a disappointment for you Hollywood glamour types."

Mark laughed, "Ernesto, you make most Hollywood performers look like they are part of a two-bit sideshow!"

He replied, "Oh, I'm just a big fish in a little pond."

I shook my head in disagreement. "I don't buy it. You're a big heart in a big man in a big world. And this may be a little pond of a town, but even with just you and Billy, per capita, it puts most of the world to shame."

He and Billy looked at each other. Ernesto smiled, "We can live with that, can't we, Billy."

"Damn straight," Billy replied.

Back in the truck, Mark said, "Well, that is a night I shall never forget. I wish I had a video recording of Ernesto singing those two songs—with you and Billy standing up there for that first one. Jaime, you got a little red!"

"And you noticed how Billy didn't," I replied.

Billy said, "Jaime, you need to get the words from Ernesto and sing that to me for Mom, Dad and Sallie."

"I don't think I *need* to do that. Telling them about Ernesto doing it will humor them sufficiently."

As per usual, Billy had driven in and I was driving home. He turned to Zoey and Mark in the back, saying, "I just can't get him to sing me a love song."

Billy and I each had a dog head lying on one leg. He added, "These dogs are ready for bed and so am I."

We all went quiet for the rest of the drive home.

Betsy had planned a New Year's Day luncheon for us, and we knew they'd be eager to hear about the party. Little did they know that Billy and I would figure into it so prominently.

When Billy told them about it, Sallie declared, "I can't believe I missed that!"

Bill added his usual response to such things. "Good lord."

And his mother replied, "Little shocks me anymore. It sounds like the crowd loved it."

"Oh, they did," Mark said. "There is no exaggeration to Billy's telling of it."

Bill responded, "Well, that part's a first. Usually you get the truth plus a healthy bonus of the boy's imagination."

I confirmed, "No embellishment needed. Ernesto is the one person in town who can give Billy a run for his money."

Bill agreed, "That is a fact."

Billy added, "We're kindred souls 'of a kind' to borrow Jaime's descriptor."

Sallie asked the question I would have liked to and didn't feel comfortable bringing up just yet. "Speaking of 'of a kind' have you heard anything from that 'son of a kind' since our little meetin'?"

"Nothing," Betsy replied. "And to be honest, I am more troubled than I ever have been as pertains to him—which is saying something. Though it's not really about him. It's about that youngest of his, Noah, who was here with him this trip. What must he have thought when they packed up and left so abruptly. What's Brett saying to him?"

Sallie said, "I understand that, Sis. Of Brett's children, what little I've actually observed of them over the years, that Noah seems to have Momma's quiet heart. He looks like an angel."

Billy added, "He sings like one too. I could hear him singing those carols on Christmas Eve. I even told Jaime afterwards that he and I needed to practice a piece for next year if he is here for Christmas."

Betsy expressed her concern, "Now, I worry if we'll ever see him again. Maybe we handled it all wrong."

Bill said, "All we did was give Brett the strongest message we could that he'd crossed the line and wasn't gonna get away with it. Nothing from that day precludes us from trying to connect with Noah. He is the only one of the grandchildren I feel like I know at all, and maybe we need to try harder with the others even though their mothers have made that next to impossible. Seeing Brett as we did, I can begin to understand why they might be so reluctant to get us involved in their kids' lives."

"I suppose that's a part of it," Betsy acknowledged.

He added, "I don't think Zoey and Mark need to hear our family woes. They've only got a couple more days here. We've got months to sort out the Brett mess." Then he asked Billy and me, "Have you even sung for your guests? I think you should fetch your instruments and I'll get my mandolin. We'll sing for supper even if it's just lunchtime."

Betsy and Sallie said in unison, "That sounds good."

On our way out the door to do as instructed, Betsy added, "You might as well bring those dogs. Sallie can tell them not to shed while they're here. If they'll listen to anyone, they'll listen to her."

Chapter Twenty-three

Two cowboys, two urbanites and two red heelers headed to Alpine to meet the Sunset Limited on its route to Los Angeles. From L.A., Mark and Zoey would take a cab to where they resided near Oxnard. I'd only seen Oxnard on the few rides I took on Amtrak's Coast Starlight route. I'd never gotten off the train there or visited the town.

As we pulled into the station in Alpine, Mark said, "I've always liked Oxnard—even the greater L.A. area if you can believe that. But after our two weeks here, it's just not going to look the same to me."

Zoey added, "My life as an urbanite has been severely disrupted. I'm sure I'll return to the groove once home—life being defined so much by habits as it is. But Mark is right, the ranch, the mountains, your family, the Cardonas—all have left an indelible mark on our lives. I don't think either one of us slept more than two hours last night. We weren't even talking to each other except for an occasional check-in to confirm the other was actually awake. We just kept replaying our time at Big Bend, the ride on the ranch, Sallie's conversation with the painted bunting, Christmas Eve, New Year's Eve and yes, it must be said, Sallie's telling of the meeting with Brett and Betsy's worry over Noah as a result of that meeting."

Mark confirmed, "I did think of *all* those things as Zoey says, but for me there was one other thing that lodged in my mind—keeping me awake. That was the fact that the Cruz siblings, who lived the entirety of their years together in both toxicity and estrangement, could now appear as two halves put back together in some mysterious fashion."

Billy interjected, "That mysterious fashion is the power of love in the universe."

"Yes, I'm persuaded that is wholly true," Mark responded. "While we weren't here for Betsy's Quiet Day, being on the ranch, in their home and spending the time we did in the chapel, I can say, 'I get it.' Jaime, I understand how transformative you have found your life here, and how you were able to pass it along to Zoey in the one way that was needed for her to be transformed."

Billy shared our oft-cited line, "Mark, you have beautiful thoughts."

I said, "Enough beautiful thoughts. The crew is pulling in now. They'll be checking tickets and the train should be along shortly. Looks like you'll be getting an on-time departure for your long ride home."

"Hopefully devoid of any drugged-up nutjobs this leg of the trip," Mark added.

As we walked to the station, I heard the train's horn east of town. "Getting in early even. I hear it coming."

Zoey replied, "It could be a freight train."

"No, I know an Amtrak horn. It's the Sunset Limited."

Billy looked down the tracks and, pretending to be an excited boy shouted, "Daddy, Daddy! The train is coming! The train is coming!"

I looked at Mark and Zoey, shaking my head. "He's a mess."

They replied in unison, "But he's your mess."

I added, "I see you've been fully indoctrinated into our world."

"The delightful world it is," Zoey said.

"The delightful world it is," I echoed.

Within minutes, they were on the train. We stood by the nonexistent platform until the two toots of the horn and the gentle rolling forward of the train towards California. In this midday departure, they'd get another look at that canyon that caught their eye coming in.

I thought then how I hoped some ill-informed bureaucrat wouldn't change the schedule to someday make the mountains, the trans-Pecos desert and the Pecos River high bridge all nighttime passages, depriving Sunset Limited riders of the most beautiful sights of the journey. Part of me was oddly resigned to the inevitability of it, though I had no reason to think such would come to pass.

When the train went around the westward bend and we could no longer see it, we went to the pickup. Billy instructed, "I'll drive home. You can gawk out the window. That's about all you'll be good for right now."

I didn't say anything, though as usual, he was right. I petted the two loyal companions now part of our life, and once back in the mountains, stared out the window—nothing but contentment filling my thoughts.

As we neared the ranch, Billy started singing something I'd never heard before but knew the basis from which it was drawn. I had heard the story on Lupe's Bible story CD she'd given me those years before and even a heathen, like me, knew something of the story.

Noah found grace in the eyes of the lord.
Noah found grace in the eyes of the lord.
Noah found grace in the eyes of the lord.
And he landed high and dry.

"What brought that on?" I asked.

"Oh, I was just thinking about how Noah will work into our lives somehow. He'll land high and dry in the Geermann-Schlatter family."

"Your mother trusts your and her sister's instincts for such unforeseeable and seemingly impossible things. You should share it with her. It will help ease her troubled mind."

"I will," was all he said.

With our guests safely back in California, our days returned to our standard routine. Making the rounds on the ranch, we found a small calf that had hurt its leg. Billy rode back to get the truck and trailer as I kept an eye on the calf. Once safely in the barn, we kept a watchful eye on him, so at the first opportunity he could be returned to the herd. Once his leg had healed up, Billy decided it was a good opportunity for the dogs to meet their first steer face-to-face.

He stuck his head in the door. "Dogs go outside?" They came tearing from the bedrooms in back, across the hardwood and flying out the patio door. After a quick pee, Billy and his companions were walking my way towards the barn.

I asked, "Do I just open the gate and let them in?"

"Open it up!" he instructed.

Koala sheepishly started into the pen looking at the new creature before her. Kola waited to see what happened to Koala.

The calf put its nose down to sniff at Koala. She stepped back a bit but curiosity got the best of her and she went right up to the calf's nose. Kola slowly approached and followed her sister's lead.

I had shut the gate to keep them from running right back out, but was prepared to open it quickly if things went awry. The calf snorted a bit, and both dogs jumped back a couple steps and gave their own half-bark-half-growl snort. Then they were back to having a face-to-face encounter with the calf.

I asked, "I take it we're off to a good start?"

"Looks pretty good to me," Billy replied.

Then Kola got playful and went around to herd the calf across the pen—touching his back legs just as she does ours as we walk. The calf didn't kick, but did skip across the pen as Koala lay on her belly between us and the gate as though to steer him in the direction Kola was driving him.

"Now, that's a very good sign, I'd say," Billy said as we watched in some amusement.

Billy issued his command to stand down which consisted of two short whistles. Kola moved next to her sister and lay down beside her, poised to spring into action if called to do so. One whistle and he expected both to spring up, waiting for the next command. He gave the one whistle. Both sprung to their feet. Two whistles and they were back down on their bellies.

I spoke for Kola. "Kola's thinking, 'Tell him to make up his mind.'"

Billy said "Let's just watch 'em a bit longer and let the calf come to them or ignore them—whatever he has in mind. The dogs should stay put unless the calf gets aggressive."

This small microworld of the animal kingdom seemed to be in good harmony. The calf returned to the dogs, and did a little skip-around trying to get them to respond—but neither dog moved.

Billy continued, "Open the gate and you know what to say."

I opened the gate and said in a very ordinary voice, "Come."

Both dogs got up and left the pen.

"Good dogs," we both said—their tails wagging with glee from the praise they'd just earned.

Billy added, "With no adult dog to show them, it will be slow going—slower than it probably seems right now. But it looks to me like they've got all the cattle dog instinct to enjoy going out with us when we move cattle. Workin' dogs like to work, and we've got two good workin' dogs."

I laughed, "And I can see already when Kola gets full-grown she's gonna be drivin' me over in bed to stay on 'my side.'"

Billy replied, "Koala thinks my extra pillow is just for her. She plops right in the middle of it. I might have to get her her own."

I added, "Neither one seems to want under a blanket. I don't think it can be too cold for them. They must be from the antarctic side of Australia."

Ever since Chuy's retirement party, Jean and Mary-Alice had been exchanging an occasional email with Brett's wife, Pamela. It just seemed to be normal for the three of them, once acquainted, to keep in touch. With little of importance in topics, they rarely mentioned it, and none of the rest of us thought to ask very often what they'd heard from Pamela. After "the departure" following "the meeting," we were all suddenly more interested.

Jean and Mary-Alice were back in the bunkhouse for the weekend of the February Quiet Day. At dinner that evening, Betsy asked the girls if they'd heard from Pamela or dropped her a note. I noticed Betsy finally was calling her by her name.

Jean informed us, "We got an email from her when they first got back to El Paso saying that when Brett got back to the bunkhouse he said, 'Pack up. We're leaving.' 'Right now?' she asked and he said, 'This minute.' As best we can tell, she still doesn't know why he was hell-bent on leaving in such a hurry, and we had the distinct impression she didn't even know what he was meeting y'all about that morning."

Bill muttered as much to himself as us, "He always was a great communicator with his wives."

Billy asked, "Did you tell her he left because Sallie chewed his ass out, and Mom and Dad followed suit?"

Betsy said, "I'm not sure we need to phrase it exactly that way."

Sallie replied, "We all know the boy can't tell a lie."

Betsy added, "Yes, but a little less blunt would be okay by me in this instance."

Jean replied, "I've been reluctant to say anything about it. While we feel friendly enough with her, we don't have any real clue as to their dynamic as a married couple."

Mary-Alice added, "We do know enough to know she has frustrations with him making decisions on his own. We suspect that might well have to do with his great investment strategies. We don't know if she realizes he's leveraged everything he's got."

"I wonder if he has his money and she has hers?" I asked. "Given their marriage track records, I'd think they do, but you never know. As Billy says, 'Misery loves company.'"

Bill state matter-of-factly, "If she's thrown in with him and she doesn't know how leveraged they are, any blip in his mortgage-backed-security scheme is going to pop their joint finances like a ballon."

Jean added, "There is one thing she mentioned that I don't recall Brett saying anything about when he was here—maybe he did to you. She said Noah's mother has a new boyfriend who does not want kids around. Noah's been staying with them most of the time unless the new boyfriend is out of town, which apparently he is with some frequency."

Billy broke into his song.

Noah found grace in the eyes of the lord.
Noah found grace in the eyes of the lord.
Noah found grace in the eyes of the lord.
And he landed high and dry.

"I told Jaime, I have a feeling that somehow that boy is going to land safely in this family. It's just a gut feeling."

Sallie commented, "One I suddenly had myself when you sang that song. I didn't before then."

Betsy responded, "Where you two are concerned regarding gut feelings, I've learned to think there must be something to them. I hope you're right, though I can't imagine raising another child at our ages."

Billy countered, "You do have two other children—both quite responsible."

Bill noted, "Be careful—that could be construed as an offer to take custody of a child."

Billy replied, "We've adopted dogs. Maybe a boy is next."

Bill responded, "You might want to consult Jaime on such a notion or have you already?"

I confirmed, "He has not."

Billy asked, "Well, there's Jean and Mary-Alice too. Don't lesbians like to adopt children?"

Jean replied, "We hadn't foreseen that in our crystal ball."

Mary-Alice had a rather horrified look on her face at the thought of it all, but she didn't say anything.

Jean added, "Besides, you need someone from the next generation to take over when Billy and Jaime are old and decrepit. The boy ought to grow up on the ranch."

Bill said, "I'll concede that would be a strong argument for wanting this to go that way if Billy and Sallie are right in their instincts. But I'd say for now, we're gettin' *way* ahead of ourselves. His mother might well drop the boyfriend and want the boy back. Even if she gave up custody altogether, Noah would still be with Brett in El Paso one would presume."

He looked at his wife's face and asked, "Why do I think your prayers in the chapel are gonna be wishin' that boy is raised across that other cattle guard?"

"I didn't say a word," she replied.

Chapter Twenty-four

During the short ride up the ranch road to cattle guard west, across the narrow ranch road to cattle guard east, and back down another ranch road to the place we now called home, I thought about the raging argument that might well be ensuing, when one "mate" publicly brings up such a wild notion of taking in a child without any discussion beforehand with the other "mate." And while we aren't "married," bringing a child into the home can hardly be anything but a fully joint effort on our part. Billy's earlier notion, that somehow Noah would land in the family, didn't exactly spell out plans for an addition to our home as had just been postulated. Here, we were merrily rolling back home without even the slightest hint of irritation, let alone rage.

In my mind, I replayed that evening months ago when we discussed what we could argue about, and then ended with wondering if we ever had disagreeable moods. As far-fetched as it may sound, the only honest answer is, Billy and I don't argue, and I can't recall either one of us in a mood that could be construed as being disagreeable to the other. He has his disagreeable moods towards Brett, and I certainly have mine towards one thing or another—but not towards each other.

I said, "You have no idea how this is going to all come about, yet you have every notion that it will."

Billy replied, "I thought that was shaping up to be a question but in the end, it didn't sound like one. Was it supposed to be?

"I'm not sure," I said.

He asked, "What are you sure about?"

"I'm not sure." I repeated.

"That's not like you."

"You sure about that?" I asked.

"I'm not sure."

We both started to laugh as we got out of the truck and went into the house. We settled in our respective ends of the couch, each with a dog on our lap.

I continued, "It's hard for me to see how a mother in El Paso—however involved with some man who, going in, doesn't accept the woman's own child—along with a father who lives in El Paso are both going to somehow place their mutual offspring here on the ranch with a fruitcake and his live-in.

"That said, I don't doubt for an instant your instinct, and now Sallie's as well, that somehow this may indeed come about. My only point is to say how totally improbable it seems when I look at it from the biological parents' perspective.

"If I can read a room better than Brett, it seemed pretty clear that Jean and Mary-Alice are not going to put themselves in the mix for consideration as Noah's guardian or whatever legal filing would actually take place. Your parents said flat out they didn't want to take on a boy at their age. You are the logical mentor for him if he ever was to take over the ranch, though it must be said, the day might come when Noah has other plans for his life other than living out here and working as hard as we do. It is not for everyone."

Billy responded, "For all my gripes about Brett, I have thought, overall, he hasn't been the worst dad—nothing compared to the bad husband he has been in his ongoing cycle of wives. Hearing about what Pamela knows, or it seems more likely doesn't know, I hear the clock ticking already on marriage number four. Maybe he'll finally give up and just live in sin."

I replied, "That's such a funny notion—living in sin. Isn't the sin not loving? Plenty of people have marriage licenses and no love. Plenty of people have genuine love and no license."

Billy noted, "Like us, you mean."

"Of a kind. Though we never have gotten around to the sinning part despite what the good church women think."

He asked what he already knew the answer to be. "Do you think that kind of love is sin?"

"As your beloved aunt would say, I don't believe love comes in one package as defined by somebody else."

Billy said, "She's a wise woman. I just wanted to see how you'd put it."

"Yes, she is. Did I pass?" I asked.

"A+," he replied. Then another thought hit him. "I bet Mom will be drafting Elma to pray to get Noah out here. You could tell, even though she doesn't think the two of them should raise a boy, that she'd sure like to see him live out here and learn the ranch life."

I replied, "Yes, you could see her countenance change at that very notion. Whatever comes of it, you gave her a hope to pray for to counter the guilt she she's been carrying about the fallout of that meeting."

He asked, "Can two heathens like us believe in the kind of prayer that Mom and Elma believe in?"

I answered, "Best I can tell, whatever label we might have worn as heathens is pretty well shot at this point, but the question you pose is a sound one. I don't know the answer. I can't chalk up any part of my life here as my own doing, or just coincidental or some happy accident. I've never felt led at any given time and yet, when I look back, I feel I've been led all the way. Is that answered prayer?"

Billy said, "You're right. As heathens we are pretty lame— going to the chapel every Sunday and singing, and celebrating creation and having hearts full of gratitude. That you and I can describe our life in such a way, prompts me to see some mysterious force at work. How we communicate with it, I'm not sure. I remember you saying the first prayer you ever made was in the casita on your first night in Fort Davis, and you didn't know if you were praying to a god, to the cosmos or if there was any difference."

I added, "We do know your mom and Elma think their thoughts and words are heard directly."

He noted, "And Sallie either just takes the world in silence or talks to herself and every creature—pretty much practices you and I both follow. That's the way she prays, I guess."

"I'd say so," I confirmed.

"So, to each his own," Billy said.

"So, to each his own," I echoed. "Though in our case, it seems to coexist in some form not our own but truly shared."

He smiled, "You do have beautiful thoughts."

I asked, "What beautiful thoughts are we going to put to the cosmic, mysterious force of love for an eight-year-old boy's sake?"

"You've heard Dad say that the odds in our family and yours seem to fall two out of three to the good. At this point, whether the eight year old ends up here or not, I just hope there is at least one in four in that bunch who falls to the good—and as we both know with one to the good, another may follow, like Zoey followed you. I

153

figure that's all the praying we can do for the time being for the boy — that he falls to the good."

"You do have beautiful thoughts," I replied. "As a wise man said earlier today, 'Noah found grace and landed high and dry.' That my friend was your first prayer for him and I don't think you even knew it."

"I know I didn't!" Billy declared. "Things sometimes just bubble-up, don't they?"

"Indeed they do."

In winter, we're in no hurry to get up and get out in the dark to do the daily, needed chores. It is our one time of the year to be a little lazy in the morning — with the foreman, the lazier of the two. He is far from lazy the other three seasons of the year. This time of year, I am up and making breakfast before he's out of bed. Now, I've added dog duty to my routine and, once the refrigerator door is opened and the bacon comes out, there is no going back to bed for two red heelers. They lie in the kitchen, under my feet, waiting for bacon or cheese to come their way. Both can smell any meat coming out of the refrigerator — cooked or raw.

Once Billy smells the fair trade El Salvadorian coffee — that is now the Geermann-Schlatter staple — and bacon frying, he shuffles into the kitchen like an old man, rubbing his forehead and eyes. He and I could both benefit from one of Aunt Sallie's hairnets, as our heads of hair tend to go every which way with our rolling around at night. We both just mat it down with both hands as best we can and cover it all up with a cowboy hat or stocking hat — if it's cold enough out — both of which will mat it sufficiently for the day.

The only one to ever call early is Bill if he has some cattle business he wants to discuss before we get out of the house. On this particular February morning, Billy had not yet shuffled in, though the bacon was now heating up and it wouldn't be long. The phone rang and caller ID showed it was Jean's cell phone. My immediate thought was, this can't be good, since she hardly ever calls and has never called this early.

I cut off the heat to the skillet and answered the phone. "Hey, Jean. What's wrong?"

She asked, "Does something have to be wrong for me to call?"

154

"No, but this is a first for an early morning call. It caused me some reason for concern."

"Fair enough," she admitted. "Is Billy in there with you? He'll want to hear this."

"Hang on ... Billy! Jean's on the phone. Get in here."

The unusual timing of the call didn't alter his entry into the room. He came slowly shuffling both feet along the floor, still in his slippers and bathrobe, rubbing his forehead and eyes like he'd just awakened.

"He's here now and you're on speaker," I relayed to Jean.

"Good morning, brother."

"Good morning of a kind, I guess," Billy replied. "What are you calling about, so early?"

"Pamela sent us an email late last night. I just saw it this morning. I would forward it to you, but since you two haven't caught up to the twentieth century and don't have email, I'll just have to read it to you."

Billy corrected, "It's the twenty-first century."

She said, "Exactly! You two have never even caught up with the last century yet."

Billy replied, "If it ain't broke, don't fix it."

She said, "Well, anyway, I'm just gonna read the email.

Jean and Mary-Alice,

Brett had been very quiet ever since we left the ranch. I had no idea what was really going on inside his head. I suspect you know that he isn't the best communicator even when he's in a good mood. And he is moody. His meeting with your mom, dad and aunt put him in an obvious funk.

We weren't home two weeks before he announced he was going to Phoenix for business. He wouldn't elaborate. He was gone a week and back home a week before leaving again. This evening he called and said I should get the house in order; he'd put it on the market. We never even discussed this!

Having been through two marriages myself and him three, we did have iron-clad prenups before getting married. The house is only in his name, since as you know, it predates our marriage. Legally, I can't do anything about him selling it, but it would have been nice to discuss it, all the same.

He announced we were moving to Phoenix—that he's taken a job there and already made an offer on a house contingent on the sale of the El Paso house. He's sure this house will sell quickly. I think he knows it will, because I'm guessing he's already been working it. The market is pretty hot here, in part because of the violence in Juarez and people there buying homes on this side of the border. As you know, we've got one of the most violent cities in Mexico on one side of the river, and one of the safest cities in the US across the other side.

He ought to know I can't just pick up and leave the state. I've got court-imposed custody orders I can't just ignore. And I have no idea how he plans to deal with his own custody arrangements, though since he's not the primary custodian, he can move out of state. Typical Brett—thinking of himself, all else be damned.

Billy interjected, "Is that you saying 'typical Brett' or is that Pamela?"

She replied, "I'm just reading her email word for word with no editorial comments, however tempting."

She picked up where she left off.

Typical Brett—thinking of himself, all else be damned.

You already know, Noah has been spending more time here than usual since his mom's new boyfriend is such a jerk. Brett doesn't seemed to have thought that through at all. When I asked him about it, he said, 'She'll either have to give up custody or take him back.' Of course the older ones can fly out for visits, but you can't split an eight-year-old fifty-fifty between two states, or two cities for that matter.

I'm gonna ring his neck! Sorry to dump on you with my rant, but I'm just hoping someone in the Schlatter family can help intervene for the sake of his own kids. I hate to think I'm done with another marriage, but there is no way I'm moving to Phoenix. If he doesn't stop this craziness, I'm going to file for divorce and never marry again!

Pamela

We were both silent. Jean asked, "Well, you gonna say anything?"

Billy responded in a very questioning tone, "Holy shit?"

Then he added, "I'm not sure you should read that email over the phone to Mom and Dad. They need to read it for themselves."

She replied, "I know that. I'm going to head out there shortly assuming they'll be around this morning. I just didn't want to call them this early."

Billy asked, "Do you want me there, too?"

She responded, "I'll let you know what time I'm going to get there, and it would be good if you and Jaime showed up about twenty minutes later or so. I'd rather not descend on them together."

I added, "I think that's a good plan. Have you responded to Pamela?"

"I did a quick reply to let her know I'd seen the email this morning, how sorry I was for having an asshole for a brother, and that we'd talk to Mom and Dad about it as soon as possible. I didn't think there was anything else to say at this point."

"I would agree," I said.

Billy told her, "Adding the asshole part was a nice touch. Call us when you know what time you're coming out. Jaime needs to get breakfast on the table. These two red heelers have been staring up at that skillet the whole time we've been on the phone. I heard Kola say to her sister, 'My stomach thinks my throat's been cut.'"

Jean responded, "Probably the same thing your stomach thinks. I'll call you shortly."

I had the fire back up on the range before she hung up. I said, "That's one mell-of-a-hess."

Billy responded, "Pamela summed it up with that one line— 'Typical Brett—thinking of himself, all else be damned.'"

"I'm already worried for your mom and dad. They are going to be weighted down by this like nothing he's pulled before."

"You're absolutely right. Exactly what they are going to be able to do about it is beyond me, and beyond them, too, I'm guessing, which is what will make it so burdensome."

I continued, "Some people get in a spiral of stupidity and can't get out. I know, because I lived it myself though, thank God, my stupidity never impacted any children. I spiraled out of control all at my own expense. That was the one great blessing of those miserable years. Brett—all I can say is 'lord, have mercy.'"

We were just finishing breakfast when the phone rang. Billy answered. It was a quick, "Hello ... and Okay."

"She's gonna be there by 10:00."

We arrived right at 10:20. Billy skipped his customary "Anybody home?" and just walked right in. Betsy was sitting there with a copy of the email in one hand and a handkerchief in the other—obviously still trying to recover from her initial tears. I could see that Jean had printed out copies for her mom and dad and Sallie. No one was saying a word.

They were all seated around the dining table, and we sat in our usual chairs.

Bill looked right at me, though I figured he just needed to look somewhere and I was the handiest, I guessed. "*Now* what are we going to do?"

Not surprisingly, no one said a word but continued to let it all sink in—and hope for some hint of an answer to come to one of us to his essential question.

Finally, Sallie spoke. "I don't think any length of phone conversation is gonna do it. You're both gonna have to go to Phoenix to confront him. But if you do that, you need to go realizin' your efforts are probably not gonna change his mind. If you don't do it, you'll always wonder if you should have. Your trip would be for your own due diligence."

Betsy replied, "You are right, of course."

Chapter Twenty-five

Following the initial shock of the email from Pamela, the next steps few quickly came together. Bill and Betsy phoned Pamela that same morning and had a long talk with her about the mess their son was making. They got ahold of Brett long enough to find out where he was, and to state they would be there in two day's time, whether that was okay with him or not. They just hoped he would still be where he said he was by the time they got there. Both went in with eyes-wide-open to Sallie's notion that they would most likely fail in convincing Brett of anything, but that the effort on their part was necessary.

They didn't know whether to call the ex-wives at this point or not, as they had no idea what they might or might not know about what Brett was up to. They decided the exes would have to wait, though they did try to arrange to see Noah while they were in El Paso. As usual, the mother found it too inconvenient, and she complained that Brett was supposed to have Noah right then and that he had made excuses about why he couldn't pick Noah up. They also called the other ex-wife in El Paso to try to see the second youngest of Brett's kids. She, too, found it too inconvenient.

Sallie tried to offer some comfort on this point—if it can be called comfort. "You have to realize, they are projecting Brett's behavior onto you. None of those wives of his, save this last one, ever got to know anyone in this family besides Brett. They just assumed he gets it honest."

When Bill and Betsy returned from Phoenix, a family meeting was called. The first sight of them was distressing, to say the least. None of us had high expectations for the trip, but to see the dejection in their whole being was terrible. We didn't have to ask if they'd had even a remote possibility of success. Abject failure seemed to be the order of the day.

Bill laid it all out for us. "Mother and I didn't want to repeat this multiple times, so we thought it best to sit you all down together.

"Brett is oblivious to the hurt he is causing. He is high on his 'riding the market up' on these damn mortgage-backed securities he was peddling to us. 'El Paso is too small a pond for a big fish like me, and Phoenix is where the action is.' I wish that was my exaggeration of what he said but, as Mother is my witness, those were his exact words. He was just sorry that we couldn't see the big picture and believe in him. He's persuaded himself that Pamela will work out her custody issues and join him soon enough—after all, he's 'bought her' a new five-thousand square foot house with a pool. According to him, she'll not be able to say no to that.

"As to the problem with Noah's custody, he told us he's already given the mother an ultimatum—either take him back or give him up."

At that, Betsy started to cry.

Bill looked at his sobbing wife and continued, "I sat there thinking, 'Good Lord, tell me what to say to get through to this boy that what he's doing is wrong not just to his children but to himself as well.' All I got back from the good Lord was a sudden stream through my mind of all the dysfunctional families in the Bible. I didn't know if that was supposed to comfort me or just resign me to the fact that divine intervention was unlikely at this time."

Bill actually gave a little smile then, saying, "I didn't think about how funny that would sound until I actually said it out loud."

He was quiet for a minute, gave a long, deep sigh, culminating with, "Ah, *shit!*"

We all just sat there. I couldn't imagine what to say and knew it was not really mine or Mary-Alice's to do or say anything. I questioned if it was Jean or Billy's to do either. It seemed the elder of the bunch might know the words, though I had sympathy for Sallie, knowing she probably had placed the burden on herself to think of something.

Bill spared all of us for the moment by saying, "We don't expect anyone to have wise words or even comforting words for this mess. We, assembled here, are in this together, and that's enough for Mother and I—we want you to know that."

Jean spoke to say, "I do have some unsurprising news I need to tell you about. Pamela, it turns out, could say 'no' and has filed for divorce. At least the two of them never had children together."

Betsy, in the softest voice I ever heard her use, said, "That's one small mercy to be thankful for."

Part IV

Chapter Twenty-six

For the Geermann-Schlatter family, the year 2008 started from bad and went to worse. Brett not only moved to Phoenix, with Pamela divorcing him in the process, but as Bill and Betsy had learned on the intervention trip, he wasn't even selling real estate. He'd gotten some job in the mortgage industry, and neither of his parents understood exactly what he was doing.

As Bill put it, "I sat there not making heads or tails of it but thinking if it wasn't illegal it ought to be."

As he had long said since the deregulation of the banking industry, "If what the banks are doing isn't illegal it ought to be."

Now their son was into it deeper than ever and seemed to have placed all his eggs in one basket.

The few times Brett would actually answer his phone when Bill and Betsy called, he would always brag about something and how wonderfully everything was going. He told them that his two oldest would be flying out during their summer break for a month's visit. Child number three was coming the month after that. When they asked about Noah, since he'd not mentioned a visit from him, he replied, "For now his mother says it would be too unsettling to send him to Arizona." We all thought that was probably right and wondered if she had dumped the no-child-wanted boyfriend. Maybe she was a better mother than we at times had given her credit for being. Since all the information was filtered through Brett, we had no way of knowing for sure about any of his children or how they were doing.

Bill suggested Brett could fly to El Paso and visit Noah, given the mother's reluctance to send the boy to him, to which Brett responded, "I'm way too covered up in my new job to get away anytime soon."

Bill noted, "I couldn't help myself. I said to him, 'If you're lucky, a boy about to be nine years old, living with a pretty bitter ex-wife, might not hate you for being covered up in that new job you didn't need if you'd have stayed put.'"

Billy asked, "What'd he say to that?"

"The same answer I got when I asked if he'd ever read the letter —silence."

All the family ever knew about Noah's mother, Olivia, was that she was originally from Minnesota, and during her brief marriage to Brett, no family visits were ever taken in either direction. They had married in the courthouse, so neither family was present for the wedding. They had seen Olivia exactly two times during the marriage and none since.

Pamela had seen her more than any of the family since she and Brett would either go by and pick up Noah, or Olivia would drop him off. Brett had a prenup with her as well and kept the house he owned; so she was on her own to find a place to live when the marriage ended. It was Pamela's view that the most recent choice of a man centered around his apparent prosperity. She knew no details, of course, but did note that he drove a BMW and gave off a prosperous look with how he dressed. That was the extent of what we knew with any confidence. Anything Brett had said of her over the years was always taken with no more than a grain of salt.

About the time Billy was to celebrate his fortieth, Brett's world and Noah's both came crashing down. The market crash in September quickly put the completely leveraged Brett in a world of hurt, and his new wonderful big-fish-in-a-bigger-pond job came to an abrupt end. He had no emergency fund and was quickly on the phone asking for a bail-out.

Bill said, "I told him, 'If you get me the details of your child support, I will see to getting and keeping that current. But Son, you can sleep in your car, if that hasn't been repossessed, before I will bail you out of the mess you put yourself into. You'll have to do like the average American and get whatever job you can. If it's baggin' groceries, then bag groceries. If it's workin' at one of the home improvement stores, then you'd better get in there before all the other people hurt in this crash get in there and take the job you might have had.'"

"I guess there was silence then?" Billy asked.

Bill replied, "No, there was a recitation of the facts to be dealt with regarding all his child support orders. And, no, there was not a 'Thank you, Dad' in there anywhere. I'm sure he hung up and cussed me good for not offering to wire the fifty-thousand he said he needed to 'get by.'"

Sallie interjected what I know we were all dying to say, "Just fifty-thousand? What's wrong with you, Bill?"

The last Friday of November, the sheriff showed up at the ranch. We knew who he was, of course, but he was in no way a social contact who would drop in for any reason. He came to our house thinking it was the main ranch house which, of course, it still was technically. We led him over to the new house and debated whether to go in with him or not. He didn't seem to want to say what his business was—just that he needed to see the folks.

Billy led him into the house and sent me to see if Bill happened to be in his office since that is where he would normally be that time of day. Bill's first question was, "Did he say what he wanted?"

I answered, "No, just that he needed to see you and Betsy."

"This can't be good," Bill replied.

When we got in the house, Sallie had come out from her office when she heard a strange voice, and the sheriff looked at Sallie, then Billy, then me. Looking at Bill, he said, "We might want to speak in private."

Betsy responded, "This is as private as this family gets. Tell us why you're here."

No one was sitting down. I guess having been overturned on the privacy topic, he figured suggesting sitting down if we weren't inclined to do so was just more wasted effort when he knew he needed to get to the matter at hand.

He fiddled with his hat brim, turning it in circles, as he held it in front of his potbelly and finally started in. "There has been an incident with your son's ex-wife in El Paso. The El Paso police have tried to reach Brett, but they don't seem to be able to track him down. The phone number they tried is disconnected."

Bill asked, "Which ex-wife and what kind of incident?"

He answered, "The woman is Olivia Schlatter and I believe she and Brett had joint custody of one boy, is that correct?"

Bill replied, "Yes, that is correct. What kind of incident?"

The sheriff continued, "There's no easy way to say this. She was murdered." He put his hat up a bit as if to forestall panic adding, "The boy is all right, and the men in custody. We've got to get ahold of your son before the boy falls into the state's custody."

Bill told him, "He's gone down with this economic crash. I don't know that we can get ahold of him to do anything about it quick enough. I assume we can drive to El Paso and get temporary custody right now, couldn't we? Though I suppose we'd need to talk to her folks first."

The sheriff said, "I don't know anything about her family at this point."

He handed Bill a slip of paper. "This is the detective in El Paso you need to talk to. I know they were trying to find any of the woman's relatives when they called me."

Bill asked, "How in the world did they know to call you to get ahold of us? How long ago did this happen that they dug up enough to track us down?"

He replied, "It just happened late last night. They didn't have to dig because there was a check from you on the kitchen table she'd not yet deposited. The memo said child support, so they knew you were family."

Bill said, "Well, thank you, Sheriff. There must be some perks to your job, but breakin' this kind of news certainly isn't one of them."

The sheriff shook Bill's hand and started to the door. "That detective can be a lot more help to you than I can. It's a terrible situation. That's about all I can say."

"Of course," Bill agreed. "Thanks for drivin' out to tell us."

Bill went straight to the phone while the rest of us still stood in disbelief. He called the number for the detective.

"Sir, this is Bill Schlatter. The Jeff Davis County sheriff gave me your number and the news of Olivia's murder. I've got my family here. I'd like to put you on speaker."

There was a pause after which Bill responded, "No, there aren't any children present."

The detective continued as we all listened in, "I'd like to confirm a couple things before I get into the details of the crime. The sheriff may have told you, we found a child support check from you. Is this for your son Brett?"

Bill confirmed, "Yes, he's out of work and living in Phoenix."

The detective responded, "That explains our difficulty in tracking him down. He should have updated the courts on his location, as his child support orders still show an El Paso address to a home he no longer owns. I'm glad your check was there, so we knew where to start."

Bill interjected, "We want to know about the boy, Noah. Where is he? Did he witness the murder? We're worried about him!"

He replied, "Of course you are. He was not hurt physically, but he was home when the shooting occurred. He was quite literally under his bed when the officers arrived on the scene."

Betsy let out an emotional, "Oh, my God!"

Bill said, "We would like to get temporary custody immediately if that is possible. What about her parents? We don't know much about her family, only that she was from Minnesota and an only child."

The detective continued, "We are still confirming details on her side of the family, but it appears her parents both were killed in a car accident a year or so ago. At least you have been able to confirm there are no siblings to try to find.

"We will work with you to get the boy in your care. Your sheriff has already assured us that such a course of action would be best for Noah. I would suggest you head here as soon as is reasonable for you to do so. You will need to meet with social services and a trauma therapist before they will release Noah to you. I can't say how long that might take, but every day delayed up front is only going to add another day or more on the other end."

Bill assured him, "We will be on the road within the hour. I have your address from the sheriff. Is that where we should come?"

"Yes, come here—911 North Raynor," he confirmed. "If you have a cell phone, call me when you are about thirty minutes out."

Bill replied, "We do and will call you."

Bill hung up. "I guess we were done. I didn't really ask him, did I?"

Sallie and Betsy said in unison, "That poor boy."

Bill shook his head, "It's an awful thing. Billy, do you want to come along with your mother and me?"

"Don't worry about anything here if you do," I assured him.

Billy answered, "If you want me to."

Bill said, "Unless your mother thinks otherwise, I'd like you to."

Betsy responded, "Of *course*, I'd like Billy to come along."

I added, "We'll run home real quick and wait for you at the cattle guard."

Bill replied, "All right, Jaime."

We left. Billy packed. The dogs rode along. We waited at the gate. Billy rubbed the dogs' heads but neither of us spoke a word. As Bill and Betsy rolled over their guard, he jumped out, closed the door, grabbed his bag from the back, opened the door again and said, "Hold down the fort. Bye, Jaime. Bye, dogs."

"Bye, Billy."

I felt a momentary sense of gratitude despite the dramatic circumstances that sent those closest to me on their most peculiar and worrisome trip of their lives. It was gratitude for the realization that neither Billy nor I felt the need to cram in a bunch of "be-sure-tos" before he left. Billy telling me to be sure to do this or that on the ranch. Me telling him to be sure to call, to be careful, to do this or that while he was gone. Instinctively, I would let him manage his own trip, and he allowed me, just as instinctively, to manage the ranch in his absence. My first instinct was to go back over and see Sallie. I assumed Bill or Betsy had called Jean but wanted to be sure.

When I got there, she was on the phone with Jean. I just gave her a quick wave and said, "Holler if you need anything."

She waved back and gave an affirmative nod of her head.

I wasn't home long when Sallie showed up. She stuck her head in the patio door, and despite seeing me sitting there in the middle of the couch with a dog on each side, she called out, "Anybody home?"

I hollered back, "Let me check!" I waved her in.

She said, "Scoot to your end. "I need a dog to pet right now."

I moved Kola to make way for my move to my end, and she sat down were Billy sits. Now, we both had a dog to pet—both a little too big to still call lapdogs though they didn't seem to know it.

She asked, "Anything you gotta do today you want my help with?"

I replied, "I'm moving the big herd of steers over a section. The dogs are pretty good help now, but I'm not going to turn down your help."

"Well, let's go get it done, then."

We'd gotten to where two quick clicks of the tongue signaled the dogs that we were going to work cattle. I gave the two clicks, barely audible, and they jumped into action.

Sallie asked, "Did they just do that because of the double-click sound you just made?"

I confirmed, "Billy taught them that signal as unique to rustlin' cattle. They know now we're going to work and not to dawdle around sniffin' every little bit of grass they come across."

She smiled, "I already feel better." She petted each head now standing at the door waiting on us. "They get those tails goin' any faster and their little butts are going to lift off the ground."

Both dogs drank heavily while we saddled up. I noted, "See, they like to fill up before we head out. They know it might be a while before they get to drink again."

We trotted along to where we needed to get the herd moved, opened the gate where we wanted them to move through, and rode slowly around to one side and stopped.

"Now the show begins," I said.

I gave the one short whistle to alert them to be ready to move. They stood there tails pointing straight up. Then I gave the one, long whistle which signals them to start moving cattle. They took off trying to see who could haul ass quicker. Once behind the cattle they split up and each started moving them toward the open gate.

Sallie chuckled, "I don't know why I ever hired men. These dogs get the job done without any gripin' and are a lot more fun to watch." She asked, "I guess we just sit here?"

I confirmed, "We're just here to close the gate when they're done. Billy would have them do that, too, if he could figure out how."

We rode slowly behind the dogs as the cattle moved past us. Sallie said, "Wither they goest, we will go."

"Yup, wither they goest, we will go."

She added, "Kinda like a cowboy I told you once would follow wherever you go."

"That's givin' me a little too much credit. He's got me and you and the dogs goin' right where he wants us."

She gave her little, customary, head-shaking chuckle and adding, "Wither he says goest, we shall all go. Too true. Too true."

With the steers moved and the horses put up, I said to Sallie, "Come on in. I'll fix some vittles."

She asked, "Canned tuna and kale salad?"

"Sorry, fresh out of tuna and kale. How does chili and cornbread sound. I've got plenty of both."

She replied, "I could force it down if I had to. Do these dogs eat chili?"

I laughed, "As you'll recall, they'll eat cowboy boots. Yes, they love chili—the more cheese the better."

As we sat down to eat, Sallie looked at her watch. "They ought to be there by now. I wonder if they will get to see Noah today. Did you ever know anything like this when you lived in California?"

I replied, "Of course, murders were in the news all the time. I never knew anyone personally who was murdered or murdered anyone. I knew someone whose son was murdered, and I was in a hotel once where someone was shot dead in one of the elevators.

"I'm sure, like you, I just keep seeing in my mind that boy hiding—crammed under his bed. What a nightmare."

Sallie responded, "None of us had any idea Noah was in such a dangerous situation. Did I tell you? Jean said she would let Pamela know what happened."

"Oh, good idea. It's easy to forget who ought to be told. Did Bill or Betsy have any ideas about tracking down Brett?"

Sallie answered, "They thought now that they had given the El Paso police some idea where to look, the Phoenix police can track him down."

I said, "Thank goodness Bill's check was lying there."

She added, "Let's hope the boy can come back with them. I'd hate to think he gets caught up in the system. Think how many kids have nowhere else to go. It's so sad."

I served up the chili and put the heated cornbread on the kitchen table. As we started to eat the dogs sat across the room looking at the two of us.

Sallie nodded her head towards the dogs. "Look at those pitiful faces. Kola just asked, 'Where's ours, Dad?' I guess you didn't hear her."

"I thought maybe I did."

Chapter Twenty-seven

Sallie was just about to leave when the phone rang. It was Bill and Betsy's cell, and I figured it would be Billy.

"Hey."

"Hey." It was Billy. "It looks like we'll be here a couple days, but they are supposed to let us see Noah in about an hour."

"Oh, that's good. Did they find Brett yet?" I asked.

"Not that we've heard," he replied.

"Sallie's here. Anything to say I should put you on speaker for?"

Billy responded, "Go ahead and put me on speaker. Hey, Sallie, you over there eatin' my chili and cornbread?"

She answered, "How'd ya guess. I came over here to force Jaime to let me help, to get my mind off things a bit. Those dogs do all the work. We just watched."

"Ain't they somethin'?" he asked. "I don't have much news other than Brett is still MIA, so far as we know, and we should be seeing Noah soon. He's naturally pretty shaken up, and we'll be meeting him with a trauma therapist or psychiatrist or something. The police have gone through the house trying to find Olivia's personal papers, looking for a will and guardianship directives—stuff like that. The detective said so far they haven't found anything."

I asked, "Any idea what set all this off in the first place?"

Billy replied, "If they know, they're not saying yet. There seemed to be some possibility that he was involved with drug trafficking, which I guess is why Pamela thought he had money and, obviously, why he had a gun."

I said, "This is Texas. Who doesn't have a gun?"

"Good point—well a gun he'd use to kill without a second thought. Hopefully, that's a little less common in Texas."

Sallie piped in, "Hopefully, as you say. Is your mom and dad calling Jean or should Jaime and I?"

"They'll call Jean when I get off here, which I need to do."

Sallie said, "Take good care of them, Billy."

"Will do. Bye, y'all."

Sallie and I said in unison, "Bye, Billy."

Then Sallie sighed, "If *our* Noah found grace in the eyes of the Lord, his landing high and dry is one *hell* of a rough landing."

I replied, "I guess the first Noah had a hell of a time, too, for a while. Still, the rainbow came."

"Still, the rainbow came," she echoed. "I'm off to home. Do I need to take Koala with me, so she doesn't have to sleep alone with her daddy gone?"

She chuckled and was out the door. I looked at Koala and said, "She shouldn't offer unless she's serious, isn't that right Koala?"

No answer that I could detect. Probably she said something, but I just don't have the gift. I was glad to have the dogs. This was the first time since moving to the ranch that I would be here all alone. Of course, I was alone for years. That seemed like another life. It *was* another life.

It was a long evening. The days were getting short again, and without Billy's presence, the big house seemed pretty empty. When I was alone in the casita, as Billy had put it, a chihuahua would've had to give me warning if he'd wanted to turn around. A hundred chihuahuas could overtake this house, and we'd still all have room to turn around. I knew I was thinking about the chihuahua just because Billy wasn't home. For the first time since becoming part of the Schlatters' lives, the bizarre events surrounding Brett's life were disturbing my life in a way I'd not felt for a long time. I'd forgotten what real anxiety about life's problems felt like.

I thought I might as well turn in early. I let the dogs out one last time for the night, turned out the lights in the living room and headed down the hall.

The phone rang in the kitchen. I went in and answered, knowing it had to be Billy again.

"Hey," I answered.

"Hey—just thought I'd let you know we are at Western Union wiring money to Brett. He has been tracked down, but he didn't have any money to get here. Dad's trying to get him on the first flight here in the morning."

"Have you seen Noah?" I asked.

He answered, "Yeah. He is actually with us right now if you can believe it. I'm standing in the parking lot, and he and Mom are in the truck. I didn't want him to hear me talkin' to you. He ran right up to Mom and hugged her like there was no tomorrow—which I guess, given the events of the past twenty-four hours, he might well have thought was going to be true. Anyway, the city's employees could see he felt safe with her, and thought it would be better than any alternative they could come up with."

"Thank the lord," I replied.

He continued, "He sat right next to me in the back seat all the way coming over here, holding my hand the entire time."

I said, "That's a very good sign. I thought he might be scared of men at this point."

"Me too, but he seems to be fine with me and Dad. Sallie is probably in bed by now, but Mom wanted you to update her first thing in the morning. I need to call Jean now and fill her in. I'll talk to you soon. We love you."

"I love y'all," I said.

I turned out the light and started down the hall—Kola following, Koala not quite sure what to do. "Come on Koala! My pillow is as soft as Billy's."

Perhaps, Sallie and Billy *are* rubbing off on me. I thought I heard Koala say, "Well, all right then." She beat me to the bed and was on the pillow.

"Over, girl. This is *my* side of the bed."

Chapter Twenty-eight

The next morning I drove over and updated Sallie as requested. We decided we should do a mail run later that morning, and we thought we might as well eat lunch at the Slo Poke Cafe while we were in town.

On the drive in, she said, "I've had one of the other restauranteurs ask me what he had to do to get some of the Geermann-Schlatter business that always goes to the Slo Poke Cafe. I told him he'd have to get a job in their kitchen and not screw up the food."

I repeated Billy's line, "If it ain't broke, don't fix it."

Sallie repeated, "Yup, if it ain't broke, don't fix it."

Then she added, "I guess based on your update, they will probably be back home sometime tomorrow—maybe even late today. It all hangs on what happens with Brett at this point."

I asked, "Do you think there is much of a chance of him taking Noah back with him to Phoenix?"

Sallie replied, "Only if Bill bails him out. He hasn't got the income right now to support himself, and you know it's only a matter of time before they repossess that five-thousand-square-foot house of his."

I said, "Bill made it clear he wasn't about to bail him out, but that was before murder was part of the equation."

"Exactly!" she responded, "But if Bill asked for my opinion, I'd still say it would be a mistake. Bill and Sis are better off getting temporary custody and letting Brett crawl out of the hole he's put himself into on his own. He's already far luckier than most now that Bill's paying all that child support—and at the high amounts the court set when he was making plenty of money."

We'd said about all there was to say on the subject and drove the rest of the way without saying a word. I saw Lupe's car when we pulled into the parking lot.

I said to Sallie, "That's Lupe's car. She and Chuy are probably both here. I guess I can tell them about the murder, but I'm not inclined to say anything about Noah possibly coming out here."

"I'd agree," she replied.

Indeed they were there and motioned us to join them.

Chuy asked, "Where's Billy? I've never known you to leave home without him—he's like your *American Express*."

"He, Bill and Betsy are in El Paso. Brett's youngest, Noah—his mother was murdered in their home. We think by the boyfriend who the police think is a drug trafficker. We don't really know much of what's going on yet. It just happened night before last. The police found Noah hiding under his bed."

Lupe made the sign of the cross saying, "*Oh, Dios mío!*"

I continued, "The good news is, Noah was able to stay with them last night. When they went to child protective services to see him, Noah ran to his grandma, and as Billy put it, hugged her like there was no tomorrow. The employees saw right then and there that he was better off with them than anything they could come up with."

Sallie interjected, "That boy is an angel."

Chuy asked, "Where was Brett during all this?"

I answered, "We haven't seen you in a while. We never got the chance to tell you Brett had moved to Phoenix in pursuit of his fortune, and that fortune came tumbling down with the market crash in September."

Chuy responded, "Holy shit."

Sallie said, "Holy shit is right. The El Paso police didn't know where to even go looking for him. They thought he was still in town. Fortunately, the sheriff here came out to break the news to us, and Bill told them where to go looking for Brett. None of us could reach him by phone. The number we had was disconnected. The Phoenix police tracked him down, and Bill was getting him on the first flight to El Paso this morning."

"Good grief," Lupe said.

I added, "And that's all we really know at this point. We're not sure when they'll be back home. Maybe tomorrow."

Lupe noted, "You know when *Mamá* hears the news, she'll be saying extra Rosaries for poor Noah."

Sallie said, "When it comes to Elma's prayers, the members of this family are true believers. Her prayers would be most appreciated."

"Amen to that!" I replied.

174

It was Sara's day off, and Alicia had been busy with a large table that was taking forever to order. She made her way to our table and immediately asked, "What'd you do with Billy?"

I just told her, "He's in El Paso with his folks," and hoped for now that would be enough. Since we're far more regulars with Sara, I didn't have any great compunction to go any deeper. I knew the affair would get mentioned in the weekly local paper once more details of the crime were released.

Once she was back in the kitchen, I asked, "Will you let Ernesto and Rosalinda know what's happened?"

"Sure." Chuy asked, "How old is Noah?"

"He turned nine in June."

Lupe shook her head, saying, "What a thing for a child to deal with. I'm sure he'll have nightmares for a long time."

Sallie said, "Not if Betsy and Elma's prayers have anything to do with it."

I added, "There is that."

Chuy assured us, "Noah and Brett will certainly be in our prayers. And I know even that crazy brother of mine will be praying for y'all."

We picked up the mail and Sallie assumed Billy's sorting duties. She said, "Billy's got a card here from the Mendozas of Oxnard, California."

"Well, that will be his birthday card. I'm sure they sent it on time—we're just late gettin' the mail. We could open it. We're not big on privacy."

She responded, "We'll save it for him. How are they doing?"

"They're doing great. She goes for tests to make sure the cancer hasn't come back, and her last report was she didn't need to come back for another year."

"That is good news," Sallie said. "So, do they have any plans to come back out anytime soon?"

They'd like to come during our rainy season. I suspect we may see them next August."

She replied, "I hope they come. I really enjoyed spending time with them. You and your sister look a little bit alike. Who do you take after?"

I added, "Neither one of us thought we looked like either of our parents, but then as we agreed, it's been years since either one of us has seen them. I wonder if we saw them now if we'd recognize them."

"That must seem strange," she rightly noted.

"I can say this—when Billy first made his way home, I had some inexplicable longing to hold him tightly in my arms. I have no such longing when it comes to my own parents. Do you think that is a sin I'm hanging onto?"

Sallie added, "Instinctive survival, I'd say."

"Yeah, I suppose you're right—as usual," I said.

She asserted, "I've been wrong more times in my life than I can count. Keeps me humble. But on this particular point, I'm pretty sure I *am* right. We can't let others drag us down, and you certainly have found your way to love. That's not something to give up for anyone."

"Amen to that."

When we got to the ranch, we were surprised to find Bill's pickup and an unknown car at the house. Sallie said, "That car must be a rental for Brett. Looks like they're home sooner than we'd expected. I'm glad I left a note where we were going just in case."

I smiled, "I did the same next door."

Sallie said, "This is bound to feel a little awkward. I don't have experience dealing with murder's aftermath."

"I know what you mean. I kinda hope Billy pulls us aside and catches us up to date."

She added, "If he doesn't, I'll drop a big hint in that direction. I'd just as soon hear from him without Brett in the room."

We walked into the house to find all five of them settled around the fireplace—a nice fire crackling away. They'd obviously been home an hour or so.

Sallie and I both offered rather subdued "glad your home" greetings and Billy met us, saying, "Let's go back to Sallie's office. I want to talk to you two."

We both looked at each other with a sigh of relief in our look and followed him to the back of the "Billy wing."

I closed the door behind us.

He started, "How was the Slo Poke Cafe? Did they miss me?"

I answered, "Chuy and Lupe were there so, yes, you were missed. We told them about the murder but didn't say anything else about Noah maybe staying here."

"Break the news a bit at a time—that's good," he agreed. "It's been interesting to say the least. Firstly, it turns out it wasn't the boyfriend who did the shooting. Some drug trafficking associates of the boyfriend came looking for him and kicked in the front door. The boyfriend went running out the back, and they fired several times, missing him but hitting her. She didn't stand a chance. She took two to the chest and one to the head.

"Noah was upstairs when he heard the door kicked in and that's when he crawled under the bed. The police who found him and coaxed him out said he was shaking like a leaf. Noah told me last night that he didn't like his mom's boyfriend, so when he was around he stayed in his room. His mom would even have to bring up his meals to him. Isn't that pitiful? What the *hell* was she doing with that man!?"

We both knew no answer from us was required. We just listened.

"Anyway, the neighbors heard the shots and called 911. A couple officers were just a block away, so they got there a lot quicker than usual. Since gunfire was suspected, they waited for backup but saw the boyfriend trying to slip away. His Beemer was parked out front, and the black SUV the shooters were driving was still there too. They had the shooters trapped inside the house—one officer covering the back and the other the front.

"The officer in the front got the boyfriend cuffed and in the back of their squad car thanks to the help of a neighbor who came out with his rifle. The police said the neighbor saw the boyfriend trying to hide in the bushes and flushed him out saying, 'I'm retired Marine Corps. You wanna see if I can still kill with one shot?'

"When two more officers arrived, they called whoever was in the house to come out. Two men surrendered and the rest you pretty well know. The only other thing we know about the boyfriend is that there was a duffle bag full of cash in the trunk of that Beemer which is probably what the other two were after. It was obvious they'd started tearing up the house looking for something.

"Noah stayed in my room at the hotel last night. We gave him the choice of staying with his grandma or me and he said he'd stay with me. Then I let him decide if he wanted to sleep in the second bed or sleep with me, and he wanted to sleep with me."

Sallie interjected, "That's a good thing."

Billy agreed, "Yeah, I thought so, too. When he first got in bed, I asked him if he was scared—and I told him that if he wanted me to hold him it would be all right to say so. He didn't say anything, but he did lie right next to me with his head on my chest. I thought I might have to lie awake all night just to let him stay there. You know how I say I roll around all night when I sleep. He seems to be a roller too. He was soon rolled over on one side and was asleep, and I was soon rolled over and asleep myself. I know at least one bad dream woke him in the night, but otherwise he seems to be doing all right—all things considered.

"This morning, Mom and I stayed at the hotel while Dad went to the airport to get Brett. He wanted to be able to talk to him without Noah having to hear it. We pretty much knew what Dad was going to say to him. He'd said the day before that he wasn't going to bail Brett out. Then he said, 'I'm going to tell the boy, temporary custody is not up for negotiation. Noah is coming home with us, and Billy is going to be named his legal guardian for now. You *will* sign papers to that effect, and we will get this boy in a stable home as early as possible. He will live with Billy and Jaime. Sallie, your mother and I will do everything possible to help, including working out his schooling, which you don't seem to have even considered when you moved to Phoenix.'

"I assume that's how it all went down. We've not had any alone time away from Noah to talk about it. Mom and I figured Noah would ride out here with his dad, but there was no tearing him away from me and Mom. Brett even asked him, 'You gonna ride with your dad to the ranch?' And Noah just shook his head and hung on to Mom's hand with one hand and mine with the other.

"I think that catches you up to date. Jaime, it looks like we'll need to get into the twenty-first century after all. Mom thinks, and Dad and I tend to agree if you do, that we should homeschool him for now at least. We don't want him running into any bullying in school, and taking him in every day would be hard anyway. Sallie, Mom volunteered you, too. In addition to his two schoolmarms, we thought we should get connected to the Internet and get him enrolled in one of the online academies for homeschoolers. Mom said, 'As long as we stick to an academic focus—and not some Christian values group that would try to lead him where it led me— I think it would help deepen his education beyond what we can offer him.'

"Jaime, it's probably time for us to replace that computer of yours too. Dad says we should get two—one for here and one for home. Same with the satellite connection—one for here and one for home."

I assured him, "I can get going on that. I'll call Jean and make arrangements to go to their place, so I can look online for what we need and get everything ordered. I can even look for some academies, though we can all review those together once we get connected out here."

"That sounds real good," Billy said. "I guess we should go join the others. Maybe we can run to Jean's first thing in the morning. Noah and the dogs can ride along."

"Brett?" I asked.

"Oh, I do suppose we'd have to invite him, too, if he sticks around that long," Billy conceded.

Sallie asked, "What did Bill do about his return flight back to Phoenix?"

Billy responded, "Ah, I did leave that part out. When Dad was on the phone to Brett about wiring the money, Brett said he was going to have to file bankruptcy and couldn't put if off. He was going to have to get back to Phoenix pretty quickly. He is using his SUV for some kind of delivery service and was hoping he could hang onto that since it is used for his work. The most he could get off this early on without losing that job was to be back day after tomorrow."

Sallie exclaimed, "He's gettin' a-hell-of-a servin' of humble pie from every direction!"

Billy responded, "The one sign of that to the good is, I haven't heard him brag about anything yet."

She reflected, "Well, that's a first."

Chapter Twenty-nine

When we joined the others, Billy informed them of our plan to go to Jean and Mary-Alice's the next day to get moving on the computers and satellite services. Billy extended a remarkably generous invitation, given their history, for Brett to join us. Brett didn't say anything which I thought was strange, but then it is Brett.

Noah chose to stay with us rather than with his dad in the bunkhouse. When we got to our house, I said, "Kola's at the door... Koala's at the door." They almost greeted us, but were too interested in the new arrival. They went sniffing out Noah, who I was afraid might be frightened by them but, instead, he just giggled.

Billy made the introductions. "Kola and Koala, this is Noah. Noah, the littler one is Kola and the one that looks like Jaime is Koala."

Noah looked at me, then Koala and giggled again.

We have two spare bedrooms in the house. Billy took Noah's little suitcase the police had packed from the house and put it in the room that would be Noah's. He told Noah, "You don't have to sleep in here alone until you're ready, but this is *your* room now."

"Thank you, Uncle Billy," Noah responded.

"Would you like to take a hot shower?" Billy asked.

"I guess."

Billy continued, "You've seen where the bathroom is. Holler if you need anything—otherwise, I'll leave you to it."

Noah was in there a while. Billy noted, "Another long-shower taker. I hope he's not in there crying and letting the noise of the shower cover it up."

I said, "I'd think he's gonna have a good cry from time to time. If the shower is his time to do it, that's okay."

"Good point," Billy replied.

Noah put on his pajamas and reappeared in the living room where we were eating popcorn. The dogs are commanded to the floor when we're eating popcorn, and we throw them one to catch about every ten seconds. What one misses, the other snatches up. Noah sat between Billy and I on the couch.

I said, "Sittin' there you'll have to hold the bowl."

Noah just looked at me and smiled.

I added, "You got a hole there in the front."

He answered, "I just lost that tooth on Sunday."

Billy asked, "Did you get any money from the tooth fairy?"

We got the first glimpse of the Geermann humor that Sallie and Billy shared when he smiled and said, "If I had, that man of mom's would have been snatching it from under my pillow while I was sleeping."

Billy risked it and asked, "He wasn't very nice, huh?"

"A creep!"

Then he started throwing the dogs' popcorn and I said, "Looks like you just earned your first chore on the ranch. We'll let you throw the dog's popcorn from now on."

He gave us a big smile.

When bedtime came, Billy asked, "Where you sleepin'?"

"I'll sleep in my room, but you might wake up with me in yours or Jaime's."

"That would be fine," Billy assured him. "I should warn you, Jaime says he rolls around a lot at night."

Noah smiled and said, "Uncle Billy, so do you."

The next morning as we were about to go pick Brett up at the time Billy had appointed the day before, Brett pulled in. He came into the house, saying, "I wanted to come say goodbye to Noah. My flight has been moved up to this afternoon, and I need to leave for El Paso in just a little bit."

Billy asked, "Do Mom and Dad know you're leaving?"

"Yes, I went to talk to them before I came over here."

"Good," was all Billy said.

Billy made up an excuse about him and me checking something in the barn to give Brett some time alone with Noah. Once well away from the house, he said, "I guess if Noah comes running out here, we'll know it didn't go well."

I replied, "They don't really seem estranged, but I'm sure Noah is still trying to figure out why his dad left El Paso, especially with that boyfriend around."

"That is the problem, or at least one of the problems," Billy noted.

Noah came out holding his dad's hand—to our relief. Brett knelt down to his level to give him a hug, of a kind, and a kiss on the cheek. The three of us stood there and waved goodbye as Brett went heading back into his crumbling world. I suppose one of us could have given assurance to Noah that he'd see his dad soon, but as neither of us are inclined to offer such unfounded assurances, neither of us did. Instead, Billy opened both doors of the passenger side of the crew cab, called the dogs and loaded up one boy and two dogs for a trip to Marfa. I drove us in and back home again. Me and the dogs in front. Billy and Noah in the back.

When we got back from our computer and satellite ordering at Jean and Mary-Alice's, we had a missed call from Billy's mom and dad. I returned the call and Bill answered. "Jaime, when you get a chance we'd like to talk to you—with Billy staying there with Noah, so we can talk freely."

"Now?" I asked.

"It doesn't have to be now, but now is fine with us," Bill responded.

I answered, "I'll come right over."

Noah was on the floor scratching two dog bellies. I made a general gesture in his direction and said, "I'm gonna run next door and talk to your dad for a minute."

"Okey-dokey."

When I got there, Bill, Betsy and Sallie were sitting by the fire. Bill said, "Jaime, we wanted to talk to you about a couple different things. We'll let you pass this along to Billy when you can.

"First of all, Mother and I made one thing clear to Brett—clear enough, I think it even got through *his* thick head, which may be thinning as a result of his misfortunes. That is, until we see that he is able to work out a good relationship with his other three children, and only if it is apparent that he can be a full-time dad to Noah, the boy is not going anywhere.

"My concern for this rather hard line I've set for him is the impact it will have on you. You didn't exactly sign up for raising a boy when you said you'd come make a life here with us on the ranch."

I stopped him there. "I'm not going anywhere. As far as I'm concerned, Noah is now a part of our family. And while I wish his dad the best, I rather hope Noah is with us to stay."

Sallie interjected, "I assured them where you were concerned, there was no need to fret."

Betsy added, "Bill and I thought such would be the case, but we could see when the conversation first came up those months ago that our daughter and her partner weren't keen on the prospect of taking Noah in. We didn't sense any of that apprehension from you."

"And rightly so," I said. "I had no apprehension then, and I have none now."

"That's wonderful," Bill responded. "What'd you sort out in town?"

"I have two computers ordered and orders for the satellite service. I gather they will have to show up first just to look around and then later to install. I didn't have a lot of confidence that they were going to rush right out."

Bill said, "At least the ball is in their court. Thanks for doing that. Ordering computers made me wonder—you still design a house for Ernesto every now and then don't you?"

"Yes, sir, though Ernesto is slowing down some and is content to have a fairly long dry spell between big jobs."

Bill responded, "They've got to get their trips to El Salvador in."

"That's right." I agreed, adding, "And you haven't gotten your trip in yet."

"Doesn't look like we will now—at least not for a while," Bill said. "How did things go with Noah last night?"

"He sat between us on the couch, and when he threw some popcorn to the dogs, I told him that would be his first chore on the ranch—taking over our popcorn-throwing duties. He smiled from ear to ear. Then Billy told him he could sleep in his own room or with one of us, though Billy warned him that I say I roll around a lot at night. His answer to that was, 'Uncle Billy, so do you!' Noah said one of us might wake up with him in our bed, but neither of us did."

Sallie noted, "You'd have to take that in whole as a good sign."

I replied, "I know we thought so."

When I looked to Betsy, I saw why she was so quiet. She was there with handkerchief in hand, and I don't believe she could have said anything had she wanted to.

Bill said, "I've always taken it as an article of faith that Saint Paul tended towards two seemingly opposing characteristics. One to overgeneralize and one to be overly dramatic. One area where I thought he overgeneralized was saying that all things work together for good. Yet, here we are staring right into murder and somehow things are working out for the good of that boy. I may have to cut Paul some slack goin' forward."

Besty managed to say haltingly, "That boy is an angel."

Sallie looked at me and clearly thought of Billy as she added, "The angel is in good company next door."

Bill muttered, "Amen to that."

Chapter Thirty

While we were all still faithful to Quiet Day, it must be said that for Billy and me, our faithfulness to helping at the food pantry had become pretty sorry. We didn't even really have a good excuse. Somehow, with Noah now part of our lives, we just didn't seek out the connections the pantry had once provided. We probably would again, but, so far, in 2009 we hadn't shown up at all. It was now time for my birthday and Billy suggested a family camping trip to Big Bend. Noah was all for it. He certainly seemed to be a lot more like Billy than like his dad. I suppose the boy couldn't help but be drawn towards Billy's inherent magnetism.

Now that both homes had email, Brett used that more than the phone to keep in touch. He'd hung onto the delivery service job and his SUV. By May, the foreclosure on the big house was a done deal as was his bankruptcy filing. If he had any notion that the final judgment on that filing would ease up his finances, he faced a reality check with the payment schedule he had to maintain.

Bill continued the child support payments without ever seeking a reduction based on Brett's current situation. One thing the two remaining ex-wives realized was that they had a good thing going and they'd better go along with it. For the first time, they began to find it convenient for Bill and Betsy to visit their grandson and granddaughter in Odessa and their grandson in El Paso. They even seemed amenable to the children spending a couple weeks during the summer on the ranch. That had not come to fruition yet, but summer was approaching.

When we asked Noah about his half-brothers and half-sister and how well he knew them, he told us, "They always said I was just a baby, and they'd never play with me."

I asked, "What did you do to entertain yourself since they wouldn't let you play with them?"

He answered, "I drew."

Billy asked, "You drew? We've never seen you draw."

Noah stated matter-of-factly, "The police didn't pack my pencils and paper."

Billy asked him, "Why didn't you say something? We'd have gotten you paper and pencils."

Noah replied, "I haven't really needed them here. You two don't ignore me the way they did, or my dad either."

Billy and I looked at each other wanting to roll our eyes.

Then Noah added, "I suppose if I got some for Christmas, that might be all right, but I don't want them before then."

I said, "Memo to self—put colored pencil set and paper on layaway."

Billy added, "Memo to self—cancel new bike ordered for Christmas."

Noah giggled, "Memo to Uncle Billy—cancel previous cancellation—keep bike on order."

I shook my head, saying, "Colored pencils, paper *and* a bike for Christmas? We're spoiling you!"

He replied, "Memo to Uncle Jaime—might want to throw in some watercolors to spoil the boy rotten."

Billy and I simultaneously gave the boy a good rub of the head.

"I guess you love me?" he asked, looking at me.

"Just a little," I confirmed.

Then he looked at Billy and asked, "I guess you do, too?"

Billy answered, "I guess I do. I guess you love us?"

Pleased with the answer that popped into his mind he said, "I'm holding out for Christmas Eve to decide for sure. Till then you're under evaluation."

I responded, "I can see you've got the Geermann craziness in there somewhere. Billy got it from Sallie and Sallie from her dad. Now it looks like you're pickin' it up from Billy. Only right for the next generation to carry it forward."

When the day arrived for our adventure in Big Bend, we packed up boy, instruments, tent, Porta Potti, red heelers with long leads and all the things needed to rough camp for four days. We decided that was all the break any of us wanted. While we'd show Noah the Chisos Basin and the canyons, we weren't going to camp in any of the campgrounds this time around. We warned Noah that he'd be communing with nature whenever the Porta Potti was needed.

He joked, "I bet I won't look as funny sittin' up there as either of you two old men."

The younger generation had finally made it official. We'd moved from "the boys" to "the old men" we knew in our hearts we were slowly becoming. To Noah, we'd already arrived!

Obviously, Billy was thinking much the same thing. He responded, "Gee, I might actually feel self-conscious sitting up on the throne this trip."

Well, maybe not this trip—not just yet. Privacy had never been much of a thing for us and modesty not much more. At home we were often traipsing around in our underwear, and Noah seemed only too happy to join us in our leisurely mode. We all communed with nature in the back of the pickup without any embarrassment. We took a little shovel along to bury anything the dogs deposited as their contribution to the fertilization of the park.

We left the dogs in the truck for brief hikes into the two canyons. We did take them on the trail down to the window in the Chisos Basin which didn't seem too risky. We'd seen a few others take their dogs on that particular trail. Once at the end, Billy persuaded Noah to join him in the large, stone bowl that has been washed out over centuries—by water coming down the canyon and through the window falling below for a very seasonal waterfall. The one thing he hadn't counted on was how slick the rock was. Once in, they couldn't get out.

I said, "It's a good thing we didn't all three get in there."

He replied, "We probably would have if one of us didn't have to hold onto the dogs."

I decided the best way to get them out was to lie on my belly, with one hand holding the dogs and the other hand stretched out to them so they could pull themselves out. At least that way I couldn't fall in and have all three of us trying to get out.

I put my plan into action. "All right—grab ahold, Noah."

He popped right out.

I instructed Noah, "Here, you hold the dogs in case I need both hands for the genius."

Billy took hold of my hand but his cowboy boots slipped back down in the hole.

I said, "You're gonna have to trust me to pull you more."

Second attempt he was out.

Billy was amused by their temporary predicament. "I don't guess I'll do that again. If Sallie was here, she'd be rolling on the ground laughing."

I added, "I'm pretty sure your mom and dad would be too."

Noah said, "Memo to Uncle Jaime—order video recorder for Noah's Christmas, so he can record Uncle Billy on next trip."

Billy responded, "Memo to self and Jaime—cancel all Noah's Christmas presents."

In the evening we sat with our instruments and sang cowboy songs to Noah and some of his grandpa's lyrics we'd set to music. We did "Tumbling Tumbleweeds" every night, so that he could begin to learn to sing along. By the third night we asked him to sing the first verse, which is also the last verse, by himself, which he did.

I said, "Grandpa, Grandma and Aunt Sallie would love to hear you sing that. They'll say, 'Oh, that boy sings like an angel.'"

He seemed as genuinely surprised as I had been when the Cardonas told me I could sing. "Do I? I just like to sing."

I confirmed, "That's the best reason to sing."

Billy added, "Never hold back your gifts."

We put the instruments down for the night and, as we sat there, I felt like we'd been a family our whole lives. I had often wondered about Noah's memories, of not only his mother's murder but all the years that preceded it. If he was troubled by these thoughts, he never let on. I wasn't sure that was a good thing. On this particular night, he was ready to talk.

His first question was to Billy. "Did you know my mother at all?"

Billy answered truthfully. "I was gone for twenty years. I never met her. She was at the ranch twice, but your grandpa and grandma never got to know her either. Do you miss her?"

Just as truthfully he answered, "I don't know. I don't think so, though I think I'm probably supposed to."

I asked, "Before the last boyfriend came along, did you feel close to her?"

"No," was all he said.

I thought, he's certainly got Billy and Sallie's inability to tell a lie.

"What about your dad?" Billy asked.

Noah asked, "Do you mean did I feel close to him?"

Billy asked it another way. "I guess I'm asking, did you then or do you now?"

"No and no."

I said, "Billy and I both spent a lot of years of our lives feeling very lonely. Did you feel lonely living with your mom?"

"All the time."

Billy asked, "Do you remember good times?"

"Not really."

Billy continued, "Jaime can tell you better than anyone I've ever known what it's like to grow up not feeling close to anyone around him. The good thing is, when the heart is open, love finds a way in."

I confirmed, "He's right about my life and right about love finding a way in. He has beautiful thoughts, don't you think?"

Noah said flatly, "I don't know about his beautiful thoughts, but I know I'm not lonely anymore."

Billy asked what we'd both wondered for months. "Do you have nightmares about that night?"

He replied, "I did, but only the first couple nights. I've never had any since the night I came to live with you and Jaime on the ranch."

I said, "Let's hope none of us ever have to experience the loneliness we once knew ever again."

Noah responded, "I know I won't as long as I'm with you."

Billy assured him, "We're not going anywhere and don't plan to let you go anywhere either."

Noah added, "Memo to self—unpack suitcase at ranch. Looks like I'm stayin."

Chapter Thirty-one

Elma had been praying for Noah and for us from that first day Noah arrived at the ranch. We had made a concerted effort to keep in touch with Lupe on how things were going. Elma was beside herself when she learned that she and Noah shared a birthday. On June 10, Noah would be 10 and she'd be ninety-three. We asked Lupe if Elma would be up for coming to the ranch for a birthday party—and no, she didn't need to bring her own cake!

Lupe exclaimed, "Oh, she'll be up for it! And I'll let you tell her you don't want one of her cakes. She's made her own birthday cake my whole life, and I see no sign of her stopping now, although I always take the pans out of the oven for her. I don't know who's going to do it when I'm gone and she's still living. She barely ages from one year to the next. Chuy and I feel five years older every year!"

When I told Betsy I'd invited Elma, Chuy and Lupe and planned to invite Ernesto and Rosalinda as well, she said, "Oh, please have it over here. Elma loves our little chapel, and I'd like to take her in there for a time to pray together like we did before."

"Sounds wonderful to me."

Then Betsy added, "In my fundamentalist days, I would have judged Elma harshly for her prayers to Mary. I viewed praying the Rosary more like witchcraft, but then I also thought all Catholics were going to hell because they weren't born-again like me. Now, I look at Elma, and I see a saint."

I added, "She's as close to one as I've ever known, though you and Sallie are gaining on her."

She was pleased with what came to her next, "I don't know about all that. Me, maybe—I'm not too sure about my sister."

I smiled, saying, "Well, Sallie and Billy are the kind of saints who keep the rest of us from falling into boredom."

Betsy laughed, "To quote Sis, 'Too true. Too true.'"

I updated everyone with the time and place. Their birthday fell on a Wednesday, and we didn't see any reason to move it to the weekend. Having it on Wednesday would allow Sara and Mateo to join us as well.

Billy asked in the presence of his mom and dad, "Should we invite John and James? And for sure Sallie should invite Norman."

I noted, "That's the first time I've heard you call him Norman and not Santa Claus."

Bill responded, "Norman would certainly understand being invited. I'm not sure John and James would, but you've talked to them more than we have. The only time we met them was at that one Quiet Day when they came to talk to Jean and Mary-Alice. We'll leave that to you and Jaime to decide."

"What do you think, Jaime?" Billy asked.

"We've not seen them in months—in fact not since they started working on opening their restaurant. I'm not going to call them, but if you want to, it's fine by me."

Bill replied, "Good plan, Jaime."

I said, "I wonder how their bistro is going."

Bill noted, "I can report that they continue to pay their mortgage on time. Beyond that I have no idea. Running a restaurant can be a hell of a rough ride."

Bill and Betsy were planning on having Brett's other three children out during the summer. When we told them about Noah's assessment of their relationship, or lack thereof over the years, Bill said, "We will not have them here for his birthday party though hopefully, they've grown up enough to behave a little better towards Noah."

Noah was ten going on sixteen. Between the circumstances of his life and the security he now felt, he seemed to be maturing incredibly quickly. Billy would contend that ranch life does that to one, and I could certainly see how that could be true. Whatever the combination of factors in Noah's life now, he was thriving.

We could see that he was going to favor his tall, lanky grandfather. He had Bill's fairer hair and narrower shoulders. He didn't get the "recessive gene" that only Billy seemed to possess. Billy thought, "Maybe he'll grow into it."

I said, "Maybe—though unlike his grandpa, Ernesto and me, at least he has enough of a hind end to hold his pants up."

His homeschooling was going well, though he much preferred to be outside or playing with the dogs. We helped Bill rework his office to be Noah's schoolroom as well as office. Noah would spend the mornings with Betsy as English instructor, followed by Sallie teaching him Spanish and Bill teaching history. Part of the afternoon he worked on his online academy's math and science courses and had the late afternoon to help us with chores.

We all mucked the horse stalls, though Billy would always remind Noah that he felt real bad not letting him muck all the stalls on his own. He hated denying him the pleasure which always made Noah laugh. It had the effect of making the tedium of the work more fun for all of us.

Thankfully, Noah volunteered to do a daily brushing of both dogs. He did it with great patience and pleasure. The dogs loved it too. Billy and I loved it most of all because our little short-haired heelers shed like crazy. With Noah's brushing, we could actually pet them without getting a handful of hair, and the "tumbleweed" of dog hair rolling down the hall with any little breeze through the house was cut down considerably.

The night before the party, I was lying on the couch with Kola at my feet. Billy was out on his chaise lounge with Koala lying on the patio next to him. Noah was in Sallie's old office, which is where we kept the computer and had a small desk set up for him to do his homework undisturbed. Something suddenly hit me—I suppose just because of Noah's party being so much on my mind.

The patio door was open. I called out loud enough for Billy to hear me.

"Billy, sing that chorus of the Noah song."

"Why?" he asked.

"Just sing it," I instructed him.

He asked, "Is Noah in there with you? He's supposed to be back studying."

"He's studying."

"Just checkin'," he replied. Then he did as ordered.

Noah found grace in the eyes of the lord.
Noah found grace in the eyes of the lord.
Noah found grace in the eyes of the lord.

And he landed high and dry.

"Sound familiar?" I asked.

He answered, "Of course, it sounds familiar. I've known it my whole life."

I asked, "And I guess your mom knows that song?"

Billy responded, "We *all* know that song. Raised heathen, you're the only one who doesn't."

As we carried on our louder-than-usual conversation between the living room and patio, I said, "I think it ought to sound familiar for another reason."

That motivated him to get up, and he peered at me through the screen door. "What the Sam Hill are you talkin' about?"

It was my turn to sing.

Oh, the rich don't go to jail.
No, the the rich don't go to jail.
No, the the rich don't go to jail.
They go to the country club.

"Holy shit! It's the same, except for that extra note in that last line on the word 'high.'"

I said, "I can't believe your mom or dad never realized it was the same. Your mom especially."

Billy replied, "She'll have a fit when she realizes we perverted the Noah song for 'Wall Street *Bandidos.*' That's hilarious!"

I noted, "I think we need to let that cowboy singer know he needs to take my name off as the one who wrote the tune."

"I was right there when you came up with it!"

I acknowledged, "I know, but someone else might not think it was that innocent. Just goes to show, you can claim something as original, but it doesn't mean someone else hasn't written down the same words or notes somewhere else along the line."

Billy headed to the kitchen. "I gotta call Dad. He'll be as surprised as I was that we knew that tune all along and never made the connection."

I didn't move from the couch but had a second dog looking at me and scratching at my arm demanding that my hand get to work petting her.

I heard faintly coming from the kitchen the Noah song. Then Billy muttered the same question and apparently got back the same answer as from our own exchange. Then I heard the singing of "our"song. Then I heard laughter.

A minute later he was back in the room and plopped in the wing chair. "Dad said the same thing I did, 'Holy shit.' Then he was off to play the same trick on Mom you pulled on me and I pulled on Dad. Dad said, 'I can't wait to hear your mother's reaction.' I said to Dad that I didn't think she'd say 'holy shit,' but she'd wonder how we could pervert that Sunday school song. Dad response was, 'It should be interesting.'"

A couple minutes later the phone rang. Billy answered. It was his mom. He was only on a minute with her and didn't say much. He was soon back to give his report of her reaction.

"She was laughing so hard I thought she was going to wet herself. She never did get a whole sentence out without breaking into more laughter."

I responded, "I'm glad she's amused by my inadvertent plagiarism. Here it was the very first tune I'd ever written, and I find out five years later I didn't write it. I'm crushed!"

Billy added, "Surely someone along the line told our cowboy singer that tune was set to other words."

I noted, "I suppose an audience is used to that and wouldn't generally know who wrote the tune originally."

"I suppose that's right," he acknowledged.

"My claimin' to writin' tunes is over. I don't know how you'd ever go about researching if a tune is already used, but I am sure it involves more trouble than I'd ever want to give it. Of course, neither Bill nor I ever tried to say anything we 'wrote' was copyrighted. At least I'm innocent in that regard."

Billy replied, "In the case of 'Bandidos,' you were innocent enough that's for sure. A heathen duplicating the Noah song—that is just too funny."

When we arrived to help get ready for the party the next day, Betsy was still tickled by my "misfortune," as she put it, for my song-writing career.

I told her, "Now, I wonder how many houses exist just like this one that I 'thought' was unique, or every other house I've drawn for Ernesto."

"Oh, Jaime, it wouldn't matter if there are others—though I doubt there are any exactly like this one. It's the love that's built into a home that makes it one."

"That is true enough," I confirmed.

She added, "And I'm pretty sure that is the only chapel of its kind. Simple as it is, it is very unique."

"For sure, I never thought any of this was my doing. I just let whatever was guiding my hand move across the page." Then I asked Betsy, "Is Brett going to make it to the party this evening? I never did hear a final word on that one way or the other."

Betsy said, "He'd better be rolling in here pretty soon. We wired the money to pay for the plane and the rental car. Bill told him, 'If you don't have money for meals on your trip, you'll have to fast.'"

"Tough love," I noted.

Besty replied, "That's what I said, and Sallie muttered back, 'Not tough enough.' The benefit of being an aunt and not a parent—you get to be tougher in theory and don't have to worry about the actual practice."

Brett did show up and was staying for three nights. To our surprise, Noah informed us, "I guess I'll camp out with Dad in the bunkhouse at least for a night or two. He might be feelin' kinda lonely otherwise."

I said, "And we all know that feeling, don't we? Noah, I think that's really nice of you to do that for your dad."

In his Sallie-Billy humor, he added, "I'll just have to make sure he knows the suitcase is unpacked at the ranch and not gettin' packed again anytime soon."

I added, "You know that will always be yours to decide one way or the other, but Billy and I would just as soon it stay unpacked for good."

He replied, "Uncle Billy told me if I got any ideas about packin' that suitcase, he'd give it to Goodwill."

I suggested, "You'd better check your closet again. Could be he already has."

Noah responded, "It was still there this morning. I guess he trusts me to not get any ideas of leavin'."

"Yes, I think he trusts you to stay. You've become his article of faith where hope is concerned."

Noah replied, "I'm not sure I know what that means, but if it means you two hoping I like ranch life more than city life, you'd have to drag me back to El Paso."

"I like the sound of that," I said.

Late afternoon on the day of the party, I called to Billy, "You about ready?"

I doubted he heard me. The shower was still running. "That boy takes the longest showers," I said to Noah. "We need to get you to your party. It's about time you meet Elma. We'll see if she thinks you're a nice boy like me and Billy."

Noah said, "If she's prayed for me the way you say she has, I'm pretty sure she'll find something nice to say about me."

"Of this I can assure you—when she says she's praying for someone, it's no nice sentiment offered to sound good. She's running her fingers over her rosary beads multiple times a day asking for divine intervention."

Billy emerged ready to go. I noted, "You shower forever, but you sure can dress fast once you're out."

We drove over and saw Jean and Mary-Alice's car, Sara and Mateo's car, Brett's rental and Ernesto and Rosalinda's truck. Just as we were getting out of our truck, Chuy, Lupe and Elma drove up. We waited to walk in with them and help carry what would, no doubt, be a large cake and an equally large platter of deviled eggs.

I opened the car door for Elma and helped her out. What a tiny little thing! She looked so fragile and yet is so much tougher than she looks. She smiled brightly and asked, "Oh, how are my two favorite boys?"

Billy answered, "We're doing great, Elma. How is our favorite *abuela*?"

She giggled and said, "Your *abuela* is ancient!"

She walked over to Noah, who at ten was as tall as ninety-three-year old Elma, and put her hand to his cheek. "Who might this be? Could it be the birthday boy?"

Noah replied, "Hi, Grandma Elma. I'm Noah. Happy birthday."

She looked at Lupe and smiled. "Oh, isn't he a nice boy?"

Chuy had the cake under control and Lupe the platter of eggs. Billy said, "Elma we feel bad you had to make your own birthday cake."

She laughed and said, "My daughters make my eggs these days, but I can't trust them to make a good cake. Lupe always helps me. She's a pretty good helper. The other girls just get in my way."

I added, "You and Lupe always did work in the kitchen together like it was a dance. Watching you decorate all those Easter eggs was a sight to behold."

"We're still doing them. You need to come over next Easter if I'm still here."

"We'll be there," I assured her.

When it came time to sing "Happy Birthday," Ernesto had been drafted to lead—not that it took any arm-twisting. He called the two honorees to come forward to where he was standing next to the cake. Rosalinda was lighting the four large numbers stuck into the top—a "1" and "0" and a "9" and "3." As Elma and Noah stood next to each other, Ernesto noticed as well their matched height and slim figures. He pronounced, "Look at these bookends. Something tells me a year from now one of them is going to start towering over the other one."

Elma put her arm around Noah's waist and he held her in return. Lupe snapped a couple pictures of them and Ernesto broke into song—first time through in English with Noah's name and again in Spanish with Elma's.

Elma said, "Noah you blow your candles and mine. I don't need to make a wish. You're here which means my prayers have already been answered."

Noah gave her a hug and blew out the four candles. Rosalinda started to cut the cake and handed the first pieces to Noah and Elma.

198

Elma took the piece from her, and said to Rosalinda, "He's such a nice boy!"

Chapter Thirty-two

The day following the party, Brett had a long heart-to-heart talk with his parents. This time he wasn't trying to wrangle cash out of them or coax them into selling the ranch for a get-rich scheme. He said what we all knew, but what needed to be said just the same.

He'd made a terrible mistake moving to Phoenix and losing the only wife he'd had who he actually knew he loved. He said he had reached out to Pamela, and she made it plain she was not going to get back together with him no matter what change of heart he may have had. He acknowledged as well how, in addition to being a failure as a husband, he had at best been a mediocre father—and when the big housing market was booming, he'd moved from mediocrity to being completely self-absorbed for which Noah had paid the biggest price.

He said how much it meant to him that Noah spent the night with him in the bunkhouse even though Brett knew that Noah would rather be home with Billy and me.

As Bill put it to us after Brett had gone, "For the first time, he seemed to be looking at the world from someone else's perspective."

Betsy added, "That's enough to give a mother and father hope."

Sallie asked, "What's he gonna do about Phoenix? There is certainly nothing or no one there for him. Is he going to move back to El Paso?"

Bill responded, "He told us he knows he needs to close the chapter on Phoenix, and the only reason he is still there is because he's just making enough to pay on his debts. He also knows he has to have something solid to go to before he moves. Of course, he is licensed to sell real estate in Texas, but that market is still pretty poor—though better in El Paso than most cities."

"He's just not sure about moving back to El Paso," Betsy said. "He said he'd rather move closer to us."

Billy noted, "That gives him a choice of Fort Davis, Alpine or Marfa. There's nothing else close."

Bill replied, "Alpine seems to be what's on his radar. Doing what, he hasn't worked out. I couldn't have recommended him to anyone six months ago or five years ago, but I think he's learned the most essential lesson a man needs to which is, greed and one's ego are a deadly combination on all kinds of different levels."

Betsy shared their thoughts on the possibility of moving nearby. "We were wondering if Annie at the real estate office in Fort Davis might consider opening an Alpine office and letting Brett run it."

Billy interjected, "I assume his mother and father would provide the start-up costs for him to be able to bring something to the table."

Bill said, "You assume correctly."

As I listened, I thought I should be amazed that they were saying all this in front of Noah—who sat quietly and just listened. I wasn't amazed, because I knew that in this family there was no pretense to pretend things were any other way with Brett, and Noah might as well hear the good with the bad.

Afterwards, I asked Noah if hearing all that bothered him.

He replied, "I know what my dad is like, and to hear he's changing and that Grandma and Grandpa are willing to help him with all he's done just makes me happy."

"They're pretty special, aren't they?" I asked.

"They're pretty special," he replied.

Bill and Betsy had not made any promises to Brett about the possibility of helping him get an office set up in Alpine. All Bill had done was assure Brett he'd "keep an eye out for any opportunities." Bill called Annie to set up a time for them to go into town to meet with her.

She asked, "You aren't putting the ranch up for sale, are you?"

Bill said, "Don't get dollar signs in your eyes. We do have a business proposition to discuss, but only one that could be classified as a long-term investment."

When they met, Bill laid it out straightforwardly enough. They weren't asking to buy into the business or loan Annie the money at a risk to herself. The money put in up front would be strictly for Brett to pay off them over time. Going in, Bill and Betsy would pay for a two-year lease on an office, pay for all the up-front costs and cover a base salary for Brett. He'd have two years to make the office pay for itself, or they would close it back down. Given his previous experience in El Paso, they believed he could make a go of it—even as they acknowledged the very different market between Alpine and El Paso.

Annie declared, "I think I'd be dumb not to jump on your offer!" Then she added, "The whole town pretty well knows Brett went down with the crash, but plenty of people out here lost investment money, too. Nobody worthwhile is going to hold that against him. And, of course, everybody knows the terrible thing Noah went through, and we're all pulling for him."

Betsy responded, "Noah is doing wonderfully, and he just loves living out on the ranch."

Annie said, "That is *so* good to hear. I know you're not here to pitch an idea without being serious about doing it. I'm all in whenever you're ready to get the ball rolling. Does Brett already know what you have in mind?"

"No," Bill answered. "We wanted to work with you first to see if it was going to come about, and we didn't want to get his hopes up if you weren't interested."

"Talk to him. If he's in, I'm in. I'll look for a suitable office in Alpine the minute you say 'go for it.'"

"Wonderful!" Betsy exclaimed.

Hearing of the latest developments, I said to Billy, "Looks like the Schlatters might end up with three of three to the good after all. It seems only right given the parents. I don't mind the Cruzes taking second place."

Billy added, "I just hope he doesn't get here, fall into his old bad habits and break their hearts again."

I noted, "That's always a possibility, but not one we have any right to project on him, given he does seem genuinely repentant."

"Yes, he does," Billy acknowledged, adding, "I'm not too keen on the possibility of Noah going to live with him in Alpine."

"We have to remember what Rosalinda told Ernesto back in the day about me working for him. *'Jaime's* on loan.' Noah's on loan to us. We'll be grateful for whatever that ends up being. It could be he stays out here and takes over the ranch. It could be he goes to town and sells real estate with his dad. And it could be he leaves for twenty years or forever."

Billy replied, "Dogs are a lot less worry!"

Chapter Thirty-three

We knew that Bill and Betsy had pitched their idea to Brett. That next Sunday morning in our chapel service, Betsy read the story of the prodigal son and afterwards commented on how the story points out that neither son is wholly deserving of the father's love, but they were loved just the same.

She concluded her reading saying, "The son who has been lost to us is coming home. When Billy was gone, it was I who was lost —not him. Jaime may know of an account in the Bible where there was a prodigal mother who drove her children away. If there isn't one, there should be."

She reached to take Billy's hand. "I drove you away, Billy." Then to all of us she said, "Now for the first time, we have a chance to be whole as a family. There is only one song to sing in this moment."

She didn't need to announce what that was. Billy and I started to sing "Blest Be the Tie That Binds."

On Monday morning, Bill called Annie to say, "If you haven't changed your mind, start looking for an office. I'll get you a check the minute you have something nailed down."

Annie replied, "I haven't changed my mind. I'll get right on it!"

Brett offered two weeks' notice and arrived back in Texas the same week his two kids from Odessa were coming to spend two weeks on the ranch. The son living in El Paso would overlap the other two by one week. That first week of August would be the first time in a while that all four of Brett's kids would be in one place— and the first time with a dad who, if given a chance, might bring them all closer together. Bill and Betsy drove up to Odessa to pick up Jaxon and Quinn. Jean made the run to El Paso when it was time to pick up Aiden.

I kidded Billy, since a while back he couldn't remember Pamela's name after chastising his mother for not calling her by name. I asked, "You do remember your niece's and nephews' names, don't you?"

He answered, "Names I know. I only know one birthday—June 10."

"I'm not sure how much credit you get for that. It's been recent enough you might forget before too much longer. Do you think the week all three are here that they would want to go riding out on the ranch?"

Billy responded, "I have no idea. Of course, Brett never took them, and they didn't stay around here long enough for any of us to get the chance to even offer. I don't feel like any of us even knows them."

"I think your mom and dad would say much the same thing, though they've made obvious efforts over the years."

Billy asked, "So do you think Dad has betrayed his own promise not to bail Brett out?"

I replied, "Given the terms, I'd say he's only reinforced his promise. Brett still has to pay his way over time, though I wouldn't be surprised if Brett holds it altogether that your dad will one day say, 'close enough' and let him off the hook for whatever might be remaining on his debt."

Billy noted, "Of course, that's Dad and Mom's to decide. I was just wondering."

I didn't have to ask if it would bother him if they did. Whatever problems he had towards Brett over the years, resenting any overture his parents made on Brett's behalf was never something he wanted to stew about.

Billy suggested the possibility of the ride to Jean and also suggested she, rather than he, might be the better one to take them on it. He even made a sound case to that end.

"Jean, you know we're a six-horse family. Unless we borrow some, there are only six who can go on the ride. If Brett goes, that leaves Quinn with all men. If Brett doesn't go, that leaves Jaime going along and the equation ends up the same. At least if Brett goes, Quinn would have you along, and if he doesn't then with you and Mary-Alice, it's 50/50."

She responded, "I guess I could do my auntie-duties for one afternoon of their time here. I don't even know them."

Billy added, "I assume you realize I don't know them any better than you do."

"I should have said, 'we,' I'll grant that. Count me in. We'll make it work in our schedule if you narrow it down to a day or two depending on the weather."

Billy said, "I know you know this, but this time of year you'll need to ride early to miss the afternoon lightning if it builds up."

"Sure," she replied. "Besides, unless they ride somewhere we don't know about, I doubt they are going to want to be in a saddle for more than a couple hours anyway."

Billy said, "They always told Noah he was a baby. He may just show them who the real babies are. He can ride all day."

Jean offered, "You've broken him in quick."

"He didn't need no breakin' in. Just a gentle hand to point him in the right direction."

She smiled, "It's nice of you to give Jaime the credit with his gentle hand."

Billy gave a fake chuckle, "Haha! But to give credit where credit is due, we're equal partners in tending to Noah just like we are in the rest of life."

Jean confessed, "Mary-Alice and I used to think we should try to give you two a run for your money, but she finally said, 'They get the odd-couple award for highest achievement.' I told her that was a good way to put it."

"We're here to both amuse and inspire."

She confirmed, "And you're masters of both."

Neither Billy nor I thought it would be too smart of Brett to spend the day riding when he ought to be in Alpine getting the office going. He could see the kids in the evening. He apparently thought so as well, so Jean and Mary-Alice performed their auntie-duties and took the four siblings, of a kind, on a ride to the outcropping and back.

We asked Noah how the ride went.

"I think Jean could tell the four of us know each other about as well as y'all know the other three. It was kinda weird the whole time. Nobody said much. I'm not even sure Jaxon and Quinn are any too eager to spend time together."

Billy asked, "Anybody call you a baby?"

He replied, "I guess my baby days are over."

I noted, "I'm not sure you were ever allowed to have any baby days. You were robbed of most of your childhood.

He replied, "But I'm doing all right now."

I repeated, "But you're doing all right now."

Brett stayed at the bunkhouse just long enough to find a place to rent in Alpine. He set up shop and got to work.

Bill cautioned, "I just hope it builds up slow and sure. I'm afraid if he gets a couple huge sales up front, it might tempt him to get cocky again."

Brett became a regular on Sundays for our chapel service and lunch. He hadn't brought up Noah moving with him into Alpine, and no one else in the family had asked him if he was thinking about it. He still had the look of the odd-man-out more than not, but all of us were warming to his more awakened self. We could even see him catch himself when he'd start to say something about work more in his old boastful fashion. He'd quickly retreat as though to say to his pride and ego, "You're not bringing me down again!"

Within a few months, Brett was back to making his own child support payments. Jaxon would soon turn eighteen and Quinn the year after that. He confided in me that he didn't see how he was going to be able to help them much with college, but kept that concern essentially to himself—taking one day at a time. He wasn't going to ask his folks to help.

He had joined the Lion's Club in Alpine and was doing volunteer work a few days a month as work allowed. He got comfortable enough riding that he would take Noah for rides on many Sunday afternoons. Sometimes Billy, Sallie and I would join them. Sometimes not.

On one ride when Sallie was along, Brett stopped up close to her horse where he could look at her straight on. "Aunt Sallie, I was indeed both jackass and dumbass. It wasn't until you stood in my face shaking your finger at me that I realized both were true. The only one being fooled was myself all those years."

Noah looked at me with a look of surprise. We'd never told him about Sallie's confrontation after Brett had referred to Billy as a fruitcake.

Sallie chuckled, "My sister says it's easier for an aunt to be tough in theory than a parent in practice."

He replied, "You put theory into practice that day, and it has left an indelible mark on the backside of my pride. At the time, I resented the *hell* out of it. Now, I'll never forget how much it redeemed me to have such truth spoken to me. When my world fell apart, I finally had a clue of what another kind of life—a simpler life —could look like. When I need a reminder, you're the one I picture in my mind."

Perhaps the real moment of truth came one Sunday at lunch when we were talking about young Chuy's work in El Salvador. Ever since we'd gotten connected to the Internet, Bill would correspond with Chuy with regularity. We knew through Jean how well his sister, Conchita, was doing with this end of the fair trade coffee. Chuy kept Bill abreast of the clinic, the fish farming and a new school they were building. Of course, Brett knew nothing of the financial support the family had provided.

On hearing the latest update of their efforts to finish the school, Brett said, "I can't afford a lot, but I would certainly be willing to send them what I can afford. It would be nice if we could put together a gift as a family and send some money down to them somehow. God's plans require our hands."

We all looked to Bill. He looked at Brett, "About that, Son...."

Epilogue

Now, nearly a decade has passed since the Cardonas came into my life in my new existence in the west Texas desert. Since then, after my immense gratitude for the redemption of my life, I found myself adopted into the Geermann-Schlatter family—a family still trying to recover itself from self-inflicted pain. My healing continued just as their own continued.

I reflect on the singular days that change everything. No one day stands out more so than the day of Noah's mother's murder—that day such a tragedy not only brought him to us, but ended his own life of loneliness and estrangement. Now, Noah has found his way from pain to a new life amongst the living, and is here to witness his own father's redemption. What it will mean for his half-siblings he cannot know, just as I could not know when I sent my four letters to my own family.

My redeemed sibling and her husband returned to us for a visit in late August. We again picked them up at the train and returned them two weeks later. As we now had Internet, Mark said perhaps they could have stayed longer. Both find the ranch and its isolation a balm from their urban lives. I wouldn't be surprised if they move here when each feels they could make it work somehow. It might only be when they can retire.

Noah, ten going on eleven or ten going on twenty (the latter seems more the case most days), informed his dad that he loved him, but not to expect him to live in Alpine. He said he believed he should make that choice himself, and until Billy and I said otherwise, or he changed his mind, he wanted to stay on the ranch and be a gen-u-ine cowboy. Alpine would just be a hindrance to that end, and it was not something his dad should take personally.

Fortunately, Brett assured him that he was there for whatever kind of father-son relationship was possible, but he knew that the ranch was important to Noah as was his time with all of us living there. He would do nothing to alter or interfere in anyway—a pledge, by all indications, that he will honor.

Reflecting on Brett's downfall, it occurred to me that not even a hint of "I told you so" ever rose up from anyone in the family as it would have with so many families. This is one of the many graces imbued in this family. Billy, who never held back on his disapproval of Brett, also never rubbed his brother's failures in his face. Bill, Betsy and Sallie, who certainly could have made hay of his misfortunes, as he had certainly tried to lure them into his greed-driven schemes, never talked about that day after Christmas again. It was forgiven and forgotten—well, filed away. As Billy and I had talked about those years ago, there is that place where wounds of the past reside as a kind of solace for us to understand how far we've come on the journey. This family would not yield a power to their old wounds, as so many do, to inflict their harm over and over—never letting go, never forgiving.

Billy and I finally had done the unthinkable. We told Brett when he came out to stay overnight that he could use the one remaining bedroom in our house. If he wanted to leave clothes there so that he didn't have to pack and unpack each time, he should think of it as *his* room. We even bought two more chaise lounges for the patio, so father and son could join Billy and me out under the stars. I know this pleased Noah. He'd no longer have to choose between his home and the bunkhouse.

On one fine Sunday afternoon, Bill, Brett, Noah, Billy, Sallie and I rode up to the far ridge where the Geermann matriarch and patriarch are buried. Sallie got off her horse long enough to stand in one particular spot.

"Here's where I want my hole dug when the time comes," she said, adding, "and over there about ten yards you can dig the hole for Nellie if I go before she does."

She gave her horse a couple slaps on the neck, and with her little chuckle said, "Jaime, I'd recommend borrowing Ernesto's backhoe, especially for Nellie's grave. Diggin' her hole could wear all of you out, and by the time you get 'er deep enough, you might not get back out."

Brett noted, "I have experience getting out of holes I've dug myself into, though it takes the love and support of others to do it."

Sallie responded, "Yes, you do, boy. A lesson well-learned, I might add."

Billy and I had noticed that the dogs had begun to abandon us soon after we'd fall asleep. When we'd look in on Noah in the morning, there would be Koala on the pillow next to him and Kola curled up by his feet.

Billy said, "I guess that's what we get for not brushing 'em."

"I guess, so," I confirmed.

Billy added, "He probably doesn't roll around as much either."

"Probably so," I agreed.

The dogs still haven't wholeheartedly accepted Brett into the pack. For Noah, there was no period of adjustment. From the first sniff—he was in. Perhaps they'd gotten the memo of the tragedy and loneliness of his life and decided together that,"wither he goest, we shall go."

Or maybe dogs just like small boys. Billy thought Momma Dog had probably told them, "Be nice to small boys. You never know what troubles they're facing."

I'm not one to argue with his or Aunt Sallie's recitation of animal kingdom communications. I had no evidence to the contrary and assumed he was right.

Sallie continues to see Norman once a month like clockwork. While he did get invited to Noah and Elma's party, and he did come, that remained his one invitation to the ranch thus far. Betsy was right. He does look like Santa Claus—so much so, that he spends most of December going around Alpine for one group or another or hired out to parties to be Santa.

Sallie set the ground rules. "I have made it clear to Norman, I enjoy his company, but I have no intention of becoming Mrs. Claus."

Billy and I were both pretty sure from what we observed at the party that Norman would like nothing more than to marry Sallie. Still, he seems to be willing to accept her terms if that's what it takes to stay connected in some way to her.

One Friday evening, we four men were lying out on the patio looking at the stars. It was December—really too cold to be sitting outside. We'd come prepared, knowing the night air would soon descend upon us in its cycle of warm to cold that defines the desert.

We each had on a coat, stocking hat, gloves and even a lap blanket. We had come out as the sun was setting on one of the shortest days of the year. It had been too lovely a day to stay cooped up inside, and we just weren't ready to yield to the cold night. The sky was cloudless. There was no moon out and so the Milky Way slowly illuminated as the night grew darker. It was now brilliant and seemed close enough to reach out and touch. Not a word was spoken between us. Silently, to myself, I said my little night prayer.

Now, I lay me down to sleep.
The night is dark. The sky, so deep.
Oh, gentle Spirit, bless this peace,
and in my death grant sweet release.

I was still holding on to the serenity that prayer always gives me when Billy asked, "We've been out here a long time. Are we too cold to be lying out here?"

I gave the other two a chance to answer but neither did.

I said, "I don't know. Are you too cold?"

Billy asked, "Noah, are you too cold?"

Noah replied, "I don't know. Dad, are you too cold?"

Brett said, "I'm not if Billy's not."

I noted, "I'm beginning to think this conversation is going to string on the way Billy and I did once about whether we had anything to argue about."

Noah asked, "Did you find something to argue about?"

Billy responded, "We sure tried."

I agreed, "We came up empty, though not for lack of effort."

Billy noted, "As I recall, we were so tired that night we couldn't have put much effort into it. That might have been the problem."

Then I said, "That's true. It could be we *thought* we made a good effort but just lacked the energy it required—though it seemed like we worked it pretty well at the time.

"But to the subject at hand, I could almost be too cold, but not if Noah's not too cold."

Noah had both dogs with him on his chaise. He said, "These dogs ain't too cold."

I replied, "It can't be too cold for them—best I can tell. They like the cold."

Billy said, "I feel bad I didn't ask the dogs if they were too cold."

"It ain't too late," Brett noted. "You could ask 'em now."

Noah instructed, "You should ask 'em each separate. You wouldn't want to assume one answers for the other."

Billy asked, "I guess you're right. Koala, you cold?"

He gave her a minute to think about it.

"Kola, what about you?" he asked.

Then he gave her a minute to think about it.

I inquired as to the human to animal conversation. "What'd they say?"

Noah replied, "I thought I heard 'em say they was in no hurry to go in. Did I get it right, Uncle Billy?"

Billy responded, "Boy, you got the gift."

Then Billy stated, very matter-of-factly, "If the dogs aren't too cold, I'm not either."

Brett in solidarity with his older brother stated, "If Billy's not too cold, then I'm not either."

I said, "I guess I'm the only one getting too cold then. My feet are freezing, as is my nose."

Noah joined me. "I was thinking maybe I was gettin' a little cold too."

I asked, "Noah, you think you and I should go in and leave these two geniuses to freeze?"

Noah replied, "I think it'd be better than freezin'."

I agreed, "That's what I was thinkin'."

Billy said, "Brett, I think these two are achin' to start an argument with us and put me in a disagreeable mood. I never worried about it too much with Jaime. He ain't too good at comin' up with arguments, but I fear since Noah's in the mix, he's smart enough to think of something we might have to argue about."

I asked, "Noah, you see your uncle trying to stir you up? He's a mess, ain't he?"

Noah answered, "Yeah, he's a mess, but, Uncle Jaime, he's your mess."

I corrected the boy. "Now, Noah, I don't think you've got that quite right. Things have changed. He's our mess together from here on."

Noah chuckled, "Too true. Too true."